NIGHT JOURNEY

NIGHT JOURNEY

Roderick Mackenzie

KARNAC

First published in 2013 by
Karnac Books Ltd
118 Finchley Road
London NW3 5HT

British Library Cataloguing in Publication Data

A C.I.P. for this book is available from the British Library

ISBN-13: 978-1-78049-086-1

Typeset by V Publishing Solutions Pvt Ltd., Chennai, India

www.karnacbooks.com

To my extremely precious and beloved wife Jo Anne Woolf.
You are truly the most wonderful happening in all my life

Truly it is in the darkness that one finds the light.

—Meister Eckhardt

CHAPTER ONE

*I*cannot seem to elude my deadly pursuer, even in the night darkness of the thick and tangled forest. Unfailingly he scents me out, and I am compelled to flee once again, ever deeper and further into the dense and dark wood. Eventually I come upon a wide river and wade through the water, but before I can make the far bank, I hear a branch snap nearby, and instinctively I lie down in the river. I am fortunate to be in a part of the water overhung and shaded by willow trees, because on this clear night the starry heavens emit such a radiant light, that the exposed water shines mercurial silver. Then I see him emerge from the forest, the eternal hunter, who never ceases to hound me. He is dragging something large, heavy, and sinister with frightening ease. He comes to the river's edge, and into the light of the stars but twenty feet from me, and I see that he holds the body of my stepfather by the neck with his left hand, and in his right hand is a rifle. My hunter pauses and sniffs the air for scent of me. I know he can smell me, he can smell my trembling fear. I know that he senses me, and I am concerned that he can hear my pounding heart. He stands quietly, patiently, sniffing, searching into the darkness, waiting for me to make a movement or a sound. My rifle is under the water in my left hand, my weak hand, and my right hand is pressed to the river bed to keep my nostrils just above the water. The tireless hunter is on the bank to my right. I raise my rifle very slowly above *the water, and swing it cautiously towards my tormentor. I know I will only get one shot. The barrel wavers in my nervous hand, he perceives the danger, I squeeze the trigger and know instantly that I have killed him. My daemonic pursuer falls forward into the water, and he and the corpse of Dugald float away. With huge relief I clamber from the water onto the far bank, and find myself on a track which runs alongside the winding river. I am still extremely wary of danger, and keeping my rifle at the ready, I walk cautiously and quietly, following the flow of the sparkling star-spangled river. I hear a noise, and wait at the ready with my finger tight on the trigger. Out of the dark woods strides a woman and a group of seven men. I know this woman. She is a familiar, and I understand that she and the men are to come with me. I caution them to keep quiet, to be vigilant, as there are many dangers to be faced. On and on we walk until eventually we come to a stretch of the river where the bank is clear of trees. I stop to admire the ever-flowing water, and my heart fills to bursting with a nostalgia from the future. I say to the night woman, "Do you think that in years to come we will remember this moment, this marvellous silver river?" She says, "Look at the stars," as she points to the sky. As I look up, the beauty of the heavens pierces my heart with a great force, and I am stunned by the grandeur and splendour of the Milky Way, how incredibly clear the stars are, how very many. She points to a section of the heavens and says, "Do you see those three stars, they are Hochma, Bimha, and Kether." I am amazed by this, and say, "I thought that was Orion's Belt." Then as I am staring at the sky, I perceive that some of the stars have become a deep blue. These blue stars are in patterns of even numbers, in twos, fours, or eights and I wonder what this mysterious phenomenon can mean. The men have become rowdy and talkative, and she says to me, "We had better be moving on." I am deeply reluctant to leave the magnificent sky, but I know that she is right. After a few hours of steady walking, we come to a fork in the path, and I become uncertain as to which way to go. While I am debating with myself, the men carry on walking, laughing and talking down the left path, and the noise of them gradually recedes. I decide to try the path to the right as it could prove to be a short cut. She and I wade across the river and find a path on the other side, but after a little while we come upon two houses, and the path seems to cross their rear gardens. I am worried that there might be dogs about who could give us away or some other danger. I consider the idea of returning to the river and taking the path to the left, and then the dream ends.*

It is the last day of January in the year 1978. I am nineteen years old, and I find myself in a military prison, sentenced to seven days on spare rations, in a punishment cell which is completely blacked out. As companions, I have time which is measured in heartbeats, and silence which listens quietly to my breathing. I have solitude, hunger, and perpetual darkness which wraps tightly around me. Some of the prisoners gave me a good beating a few days ago, as did the guards even more recently, so I am black and blue all over, and throbbing with pain. I also have anguish in my heart, for there is no escaping myself in this cloister of oblivion. Sealed up in a molten blackness, I stew in my own juices. I ferment and bubble, putrefy and rot in my own being. Sometimes I have visitors. There are many dreams and fantastically vivid flashbacks of the past which come to me here in the darkness, and they are my only source of light. I am beset by a gamut of remorse, nostalgia, guilt, and my fear. Waves of feelings and emotions sweep continually over me, they creep through my veins like tendrils, which seek to bind themselves around my heart and strangle me. I do not have emotions but rather it is emotions that have me. Though I try, I cannot stop my brain from thinking, endless thinking, which tangles me in a web. I stumble around in a maddening maze from which there is no exit. Many of my thoughts are not my own, and more often than not, it is my thinking that has me. As I cannot escape the darkness of this cell, I shall try to befriend it. "Hello darkness, I will try not to resist your heavy embrace, although I am so alone, so very lonely with you, and my fear of the world's ending."

I often have this suspicion that it is God who pursues me. This angry God hounds me, and never lets me rest long enough. Like Jonah I have fled from this terrible God, but now I have been cornered, and find myself swallowed up in your belly, lord darkness. Half of me will not believe in God, and the other half insists that God is and must be. I am divided against myself in an unending combat between doubt and certainty, and like Jacob I wrestle with an unnamed demon. My dear darkness, I have also been possessed by a conviction that humankind is headed for a great catastrophe in the not too distant future, and though I try to banish this fearful idea, I cannot shake it off. I know that in part, it is my irrational fear of Armageddon which has driven me to take this fanatical stance, which has led to my incarceration in this cell.

In large part it was my stepfather Dugald who bequeathed me the gift of fear, which has gripped me so relentlessly down my days. Standing at just under six foot and four inches tall in his socks, with coal black hair and piercing blue eyes, he beat me viciously and often from the age of three until I was nearly fifteen. It was fear that possessed him, my darkness. He was very young, and hopelessly inadequate to the task of parenting four children. I am the child of another man, and sometimes Paula loves me too much, which makes him madly jealous. He was always weighed down with the endless stresses and strains of a grinding poverty, which made him furious with the world. There are many extenuating circumstances for his brutality towards me, and I forgive him for being what he is, and what he did to me, my darkness. Although Paula, with her very short fuse, often instigated my hidings, she usually stepped in when she felt justice had been served, or when she perceived that Dugald had completely lost himself to his fury with life, and then she would shout something like "Dugald, you are a gorilla, an ape! You don't realise how big you are, and how small your fucking brain is! He is a child for God's sake!" If Dugald was not about Paula was not averse to dishing out some punches to the body, or a good slap or two across the face, but these were as nothing compared to Dugald's violent ministrations, my darkness. In spite of the reckless thrashings, I loved him faithfully, and love him still. As a family, we are closely bound together by our chaotic lifestyle and our exclusion from the mainstream. The truth is that his aggression towards me hides a timid man, one who lives in perpetual fear of a malign world, which he feels has dealt him a poor hand. I was almost perpetually fearful of his brutal injustice, but far more debilitating to me, my dark friend, was his own mortal terror of the world, which I seem to have absorbed into my very marrow.

When I was five years old and we lived on Bryanston Farm, Dugald kept my grandfather Jack's Luger next to his bed. One night during a tremendous storm, as the hail thundered down onto our corrugated iron roof, Dugald leapt from his bed shouting, "The rats are coming! The rats are coming," and he unloaded all the bullets into the ceiling. I heard the commotion, and ran to my parents' bedroom to find Dugald standing in his underpants looking bewildered and scared, as rain poured in through the holes he had made in the roof. In later years Mom would amuse her audiences with highly exaggerated versions of the story. The number of bullets grew from seven to fifteen, the rats became rhinos, he had peed in his underpants, he was sucking on Samantha's dummy which had been next to the bed. I understood from this incident that we were under constant threat of attack, and that the world is full of menace. I have been waiting for the rats ever since, my darkness.

There are boots clumping down the stairs, so I stand up and wait. The prison guards have come with my daily ration, my six slices of bread and two litres of water. My heart is beating fast, and cold sweat pops from under my arms and runs in icy rivulets down my sides. The door opens, blinding light explodes into my cell, and I must close my eyes to slits until they adjust to the glare. A prisoner hands me my rations and exchanges potties with me while the guards examine me intently for signs of frailty. With deep gratitude, I breathe in the fresh air that sweeps into my cell. The steel door is closed, bolted, and locked, leaving me sealed off from the world and the light for another twenty-four hours.

Dugald was particularly afraid of the police, in fact he was scared of all people in uniforms, and even nurses or members of the Salvation Army could set him atremble. I remember a number of times when we were pulled over by the traffic police for having a battered old car. Dugald would turn maggot white, and his hands would tremble as he handed over his driver's licence. His tremulous voice quavered and he was full of yes sir, no sir, three bags full sir. His fear was contagious, and I would cower on the back seat. He had a real dread of men in authority and I instinctively sensed from his fear that such people are a dangerous threat, my darkness.

His fear might even have had its upside. It gave him an acute nose for physical danger, and on more than one occasion it proved life-saving to us and others. When I was three years old, and Mom was pregnant with Stella, we went camping in the Pilanesberg hills. We were sitting on a blanket, eating beside the campfire, when Dugald sensed that something was badly amiss. Although he spoke very quietly to me, I immediately understood that we were in terrible danger, for he had the maggot look. He leaned towards me and said very quietly, "Go and get into the car, lock the back doors, and lie down on the floor." I obeyed without a word, and I was barely settled when Dugald and Paula made a dash for the car, leaving all our camping gear behind. As they were clambering into the car a group of men stormed from the bushes and attacked us. They tried to open the doors, and they bashed the car with clubs and sticks. According to Paula some of the men stood in front of the car and Dugald drove right over them. That was the way she related the event afterwards, but I wouldn't know, as I was lying on the floor terrified out of my wits.

Though he was never warm or loving towards me, I must acknowledge that there is also an admirable side to Dugald, my darkness. He is an absolute gentleman with women, and he has never raised a hand to Paula, who provokes him incessantly. He plays the clarinet and the mouth-organ exquisitely, and he is at peace when in the bush. Whenever we went camping in the wilds his better nature would emerge from beneath his usual morose disposition. He has excellent bushcraft skills and a strange affinity with nature. Buck graze peaceably near to him, and huge baboons will sit in close proximity to him as if he were one of their own. He picks up deadly poisonous snakes with his large bare hands, and they seem to relax in his loving embrace. I am grateful to him for giving me a part of my deep appreciation for nature.

It was from my mother Paula that I learned anarchy, literature, and defiance, my darkness. She is a born rebel and a persistent hellraiser, though some of her friends would generously call her a free spirit. When she was seventeen years old in 1957, she had an affair with a forty-four-year-old married man named Harry Paul Lesley Cluer, who was at that time the governor of Salisbury Prison in Rhodesia. Paula fell pregnant with me and about six months after I was born, Harry Paul's wife was discharged from the asylum, and he booted Mom and me out of his life. That's Paula's version of it. Anyway, she then went on a misadventure down the Congo river with some crocodile hunter dude, and that is when I contracted cowpox which badly damaged my right ear. When I was two years old, Paula made her way to Johannesburg in South Africa, where she met Dugald who was twenty-one years old, and although they were penniless, they married within three months. Within the space of five years these two hopeless alcoholics had produced three daughters.

All this fear and brutality, anarchy and obdurate rebellion, mixed with a million bottles of wine, and the bizarre twists and turns of fate, has shaped me and predisposed me to be the way I am. We certainly reap what our parents have sown, my darkness. In 1975 when I turned seventeen years old, I began to be slowly but surely possessed by the idea that the world is heading for a catastrophe. This affliction, probably born in part out of my inherited fear, has governed my choices, and has brought me to this. To a roasting confinement. Through my flame-tinted glasses I cannot help but foresee a devastating third world war looming, or a global ecological disaster, a revenge by Mother Nature for our desecration of her. There are movies like *Soylent Green*, which depict Apocalypse in our time, and many books of that genre, but millions of people read these books and see these movies without becoming afflicted with the idea that Armageddon is nigh. Why me, my darkness? Is it my fear? Or am I just a natural-born pessimist? Yes, I realise now, that I have another companion, my darkness. I have my past, my memories, and my short life. I lie with eyes open and it comes back to me.

South Africa is at war on three fronts at the moment, but media reports are heavily restricted and the public is kept largely ignorant as to the true extent of the conflagration. South Africa took possession of South West Africa from the Germans during the First World War, and we have come to consider this territory as a province, but the native people of that land are fighting a war of independence with the help of Angola, Fidel's Cuba, and to a smaller extent the Soviet Union. As this war has grown in intensity, the time white boys are conscripted has been extended from one year to two years, and recently there has been talk of it being made three years. Another front has been opened up by Samora Machel, the president of Mozambique, and a third front has arisen from within our own borders, as the disenfranchised people of South Africa rise up, and bombs are going off all over the country. Anxiety is in the air, and many people are afraid of where all this is going, but it seems to me that nobody else shares my belief that the entire planet faces extinction. Why am I distressed that the seas are being overfished, and the forests and jungles overharvested, or that the rivers are being destroyed with industrial effluent, or the fact that we have stored sufficient plutonium to keep the planet poisoned for ten thousand years? These things do not seem to alarm and frighten anybody but me.

Dear darkness, is my fatalistic state of mind born out of our anarchic family lifestyle, is that what predisposes me to the idea of Armageddon? I constantly seek a rational explanation for my irrational ideas, but I can never know if I am on the right track. There are many forks in the path and they all seem to end in uncertainty. From my earliest memories my family has been under constant threat of fragmentation, which I have perhaps translated to include the disintegration of the world. As it is, the family has finally dissolved, and everyone is the better for it. None of my school-mates entertained such morbid ideas of catastrophe, in spite of the fact that the government has declared a state of emergency due to the black uprising. Like young people everywhere my friends are interested in surfing and parties, and in their future careers. So I have felt very much alone with my dread of the looming Armageddon. I suppose it does not help my paranoia that I am fascinated by the First and Second World Wars, the Holocaust, the atom bomb, the gulags, and the Vietnam War with its agent orange. I am drawn to literature which confirms all my worst fears. Although my parents are completely irreligious, I have since the age of thirteen been plagued by metaphysical questions. I took to reading the New Testament of the Bible, the Koran, the Upanishads, the Bhagavad Gita, writings on Buddhism, and other religious works. I was drawn to religious writers like Lao Tzu, Herman Hesse, and Chaim Potok, and in my certain fear I began to pray to an unknown God. Dread has that kind of effect on some people, my darkness.

In '75 when I became ill with the idea of Armageddon, we were living in the coastal town of Muizenberg, and life had been unusually stable for us as a family for about two years, even though we were dirt poor and constantly living on the edge. Dugald had a reasonably well-paid job with a long-term contract, though he did have to live away from home for months on end, and Paula wrote to him almost every day.

CHAPTER TWO

27 Clevedon Road
Muizenberg
Cape Town
March 1976

Dearest one,

Fear, horror, dread—I have one rand left, and Behr is not at office or home—he was supposed to be back today. What am I to do? Stel and Rod are hitching into town, Stel has something badly wrong with her eyes and must go to Doc. I had the rand in my office drawer so could not give them train fare, and school starts tomorrow, they need pens, rulers, etc., and I definitely cannot ask the Germanics again. That's out.

Had a rather dismal weekend, lack of boodle. On Saturday morning we were so touched to receive your R2 for Rod's birthday, considering how very little you had yourself. I had to go to the post office to identify him (can you imagine, for R2?) and took the opportunity of popping into Tuzee's. Who did I run into but Harold Keehn. Shame. He told me they're living in Cinnabar and that he hates the place and can't wait to get out, and that

Gertie's mind has completely gone. She's bedridden and completely senile, and it takes strange forms with that religious mania in the background, shouting and singing hymns, oh dear. Weird things seem to happen in life.

Had a 50 cent line on Sat, was one out yet again (sigh) on Avon's Pride, if only I'd taken Kingsgarth in that race, he was coupled. Paid R700. So near and yet so far.

It's nearly twelve and still can't raise the Behr. Really life is just about too difficult. The kids starving, had to leave them without food again.

I work it out that you should be back this weekend, but you haven't mentioned anything, maybe they will make you wait another four weeks because of the week off? I don't think I can go on like this. It's too shocking, all sorts of awful bloody things keep happening and I don't know how to cope.

Tuesday

Thank God Behr back in office, had such a terrible time yesterday, no food, couldn't buy them school things and couldn't get Stel's prescription—she can't see at all, has some severe eye infection. But he's letting me have R70 at lunchtime and will wire you some. Behr says that Stannard have asked for urgent tender for 35 holes at Saldanha which we're almost sure to get and he's telexed Tom. All the old rubbish again, dances, parties, scenes, I can't stand it—just one more straw and I swear by the Almighty I'm getting some entertainment for myself. Life's too hard with no joy and that lot I can't take again, ever!

The Richards Bay contract is still slightly in the future but when it starts they have no objection to the family going up there. St. Croix is definitely going to take place as well, was announced today. That's all news, will express this, it's worth 20 cents that you should get it in three or four days. Lots of love, try to write more later, do love and miss you (but plenty of lover material around if I wanted it, which I might if I have any more Marys).

All love.

My dearest love,

Such a sweety letter from you, I keep thinking your drawing is an elephant, and the children say no, it's a fat swamp rat. But so respectable in his dungarees.

Have written Behr a short note, saying I couldn't make it financially beyond Friday, had severe crisis as usual, Lu had to have a prescription for a throat infection, and Stella had that conjunctivitis, also Rod has to have rugby boots, his second-hand ones have fallen to bits and important match on Saturday. If I get some money from him I'll express you fifteen on Fri. If I don't, I don't know what to do. Rod finally managed to fix the light after much goading, not a fuse, the wires had pulled loose from the central thing.

Last night there was the most terrible storm I've ever heard, thunder shattering. The ruddy White One got horribly upset and kept Sammy and me awake for hours, screeching, meowing and walking about on our faces. We bunged him in Rod's room in the end to get some sleep and Rod wanted to kill us this morning—too lazy to get out of bed to throw the Guru out and had to put up with the screeches. The children get most upset at the thought of leaving Muizy, all their pals, etc. Stellie is doing very well at school now and is taking a pride in herself for once. Took Laurie to have her ears examined, thought maybe that was why she is so dim, but doc says her hearing is absolutely perfect.

Darl,

Behr suggested making an offer re car; like paying one or two back instalments; but darling, don't you realise, they grab the instalment and STILL repossess the car, which they're legally entitled to do if you are more than three months in arrears. We're six months now. Have hidden it at Cinnabar and no further hassles—yet.

The Gold Cup was of course quite ridiculous. You're right, you've got to be in on the inner ring if you want to win. Yes we do owe your Mom a lot of money. The strange thing is that none of us miss her as a person, a sad indictment. I wonder why. Because we always used to get on so well. Francine, the maid has to have an operation and won't be back. We have a rather untrustworthy half day thing now called Vina, found by Stella as usual when the work really got her down. Not too wonderful but better than nought.

All love sweet one.

CHAPTER THREE

I can hear the guards coming with my six slices of bread. I wonder if they will beat me again? The door opens and the light blasts its way into my cell: the severity of it surprises me every time. They do not beat me, they lock the door and blackness envelopes me again. It is strange thing, my darkness, but the longer I sit with you, the clearer the past becomes, and I am often right in the scene again. What I thought was dead and gone, dances deep within like some eternal flame. As I began my last year of school in 1976, Paula was once again fired for being drunk at work. This time she was defeated and she threw in the towel, her fighting spirit had suddenly deserted her, and we moved out to a smallholding on the windswept Cape flats in a region called Philippi. Paula has always been possessed by a romantic longing to live on a farm, and twice before we had tried farming and failed, but Mom was not one to learn from her mistakes.

Philippi had once been an extensive expanse of huge rolling sand dunes, but vast swathes of these large dunes had been flattened to make way for vegetable and pig farms. The pig manure is used to enrich the ill-nourished sea sand, and the area is perpetually pervaded by a sickening odour which seeps into one's hair and clothes. The ramshackle farmhouse was surrounded by a small forest of wind-blasted eucalyptus trees, and beyond these lay acres of bone white sandy fields, studded with a smattering of greenery provided by the invasive Australian acacia. A mere twenty metres from the sorry-looking farmhouse stood a motley huddle of old pigsties that could house about sixty pigs, and next to this was a sagging barn and a small reservoir filled with deep green water. To any reasonable person it would have been painfully obvious that these meagre utilities were not sufficient to provide a living income for a family of six, but such practicalities are never evident to Paula, who is repeatedly blinded by a reckless optimism. About two miles from the smallholding was the large black township of Nyanga which was a seething cauldron of unrest and rebellion. Helicopters with large spotlights regularly hovered over the township, and we frequently heard gun battles raging.

Though I did not have a driving licence, I would drive myself and my three sisters to school in our old pale green double cab Volkswagen Kombi pick-up. Paula purchased a boar and five sows and naturally it fell to me to clean the sties. I found that pigs can be very agreeable creatures in small groups, and grew far too fond of them. I am silly for animals. Paula loved the idle life on the "pig farm" while it lasted, and in a way she deserved it, as she had slogged away without a holiday for about nine years solid. This was because she seldom stayed in a job long enough to qualify for annual leave. In some ways I have great admiration, mixed with disdain, for my alcoholic mother. No matter how appalling her Monday hangovers were, she had until then, somehow or other always found the will to go off to work she hated, and to bosses she loathed. On the smallholding, she tended the vegetable patch, and fed the pigs, which took up less than one hour of her day, so most of the time she just lolled about doing nothing much except reading, smoking, listening to the radio, cooking dinner, and drinking steadily from morn till night. She was on a blinding binge like I had never seen before, and her usual fighting spirit had completely vanished. Paula had been inculcated to some extent with a keep your chin up, put your best foot forward disposition which had stood her in good stead until then.

At that stage of events, Dugald still had a fairly good job as a drill master. He worked on a drilling rig some 200 kilometres away in Saldanha Bay, where a huge harbour was to be built to export steel and copper, so we seldom saw much of him. We were poor as usual but otherwise happy enough until halfway through the year when Dugald was laid off for reasons I never did find out. That was the real tipping point, the beginning of the end, my darkness. I had to once again acclimatise myself to his sullen nature, and I found it very difficult to relinquish being the man of the house. He looked for work in a desultory fashion and could find none. During that fateful month of June '76 the Soweto riots broke out. Hundreds of thousands of schoolchildren burnt their school books as they refused to study in the language of the oppressors any longer.

Dugald had received a fairly handsome severance package, and he and Paula would regularly go off to the Kenilworth racetrack to gamble and drink. In the usual course of things, they lost money hand over fist; within two months they had used up pretty much all their savings, and our financial situation became more dire than usual. Paula sold Dugald's clarinet and some other trinkets, and they went for a last fling to the racecourse with the usual lack of success. Things became critical, so one night I sat with Paula and Dugald and we had a grave indaba to discuss possible ways of making some money. I came up with the absurd notion that we could sell our pigs as an investment. The idea was that townsfolk could buy one or two of our sows and keep them on our farm while paying us money to keep the pigs clean, housed, and fed. We would ensure that the sows were impregnated, and the owner would make money from the litter when they were sold off as six-month-old porkers, guaranteeing them a tidy profit. Incredibly, two gullible families actually took up the offer. So we sold off our five sows, and received a monthly income to house and feed the pigs. This money was not sufficient to make ends meet, and our financial situation remained perilous especially with Paula and Dugald needing at least one bottle of brandy a day just to cope.

It is so silent here in my dungeon, so terribly quiet, yet there is no quietus in me. In your hold, dear silence, I can hear the past ever so clearly. I am full of noises and voices all clamouring to be heard. Dear darkness and silence, how you embrace me, you smother me so.

Paula's last job was with a building society called the Natal Building Society. She reckoned that it would be easy to rob the place as she knew the combination to the safe. So one Friday night Paula, Dugald, my youngest sister Samantha, and I went off under the cover of darkness, with a crowbar and a canvas bag to rob the building society. The whole event had a surreal atmosphere, and I had this peculiar notion that I was acting in some very low-grade movie, with the wrong cast, and my head felt as though it were being squeezed in a vice. The building society backed onto the car park of a small hotel, and there we parked and waited for a while until we were certain that no one was about. Paula and Samantha went around to the main road to stand in front of the N.B.S. so that they could warn me if anyone was coming, or to act as a decoy if someone did. A profusely sweating Dugald, in maggot mode, was to wait in the car as the getaway man. I slipped over the wall into a small courtyard at the back of the building society and tried to jemmy the door open with the crowbar, but I could gain no purchase as it was solid and snugly fitting. After nearly ten frantic minutes of fruitless effort, I was becoming desperate, so I stood as far from the door as possible, which was about ten feet, and then ran at the door, jumping into the air, and kicked it with both feet. Amazingly the door smashed open with a resounding crunch, and I fell to the ground hurting my shoulder. I waited for about a minute to see if the noise had attracted anybody's attention, but all seemed quiet so I entered the office. I could see Paula and Samantha walking up and down the pavement holding hands, and they looked horribly conspicuous, like walking neon lights. Firstly I tried the safe but the three numbers Paula had given me did not work. So in fearful desperation, I foolishly tried my luck with a few random numbers while looking out to the street every few seconds. Paula gave me a warning sign and I ducked behind the counter until some people had ambled past. Then I resumed my attempts on the safe but with no joy. Eventually I turned my attention to the drawers under the counter. They were locked so I applied the jemmy to one. It bust open and the alarm screamed into life, freezing the blood in my veins. The drawer only contained coins, and I hurriedly poured them into the bag and departed rapidly over the back wall and into the car. We met Paula and Samantha on the road, picked them up and made our getaway. Back home we counted the coins. A measly one hundred and twenty rand for my soul. Soon after that harrowing saga, I received my call-up papers to do military service. I had been summoned for the July 1977 intake, and the thought of it filled me with anxiety.

We are crammed into Granny's yellow Volkswagen Beetle. Mom, Dad, the girls and me. I am driving and Dugald, who is drunk, sits on Paula's lap. There is a police roadblock up ahead and I am very anxious about this, as I do not have a driver's licence. The scene changes: I am walking up a steep hill, pulling at a long rope. I am becoming exhausted so I stop to rest and, turning around, I see that I am pulling the Beetle. My family are all sitting in the car.

I came home to the "pig farm" from school one day and found Paula lying drunk in her bed. She had sold my radio, record player, flute, and guitar, which filled me with rage and guilt. Apart from booze she had at least bought some food supplies. There was still three months to go before my O level exams, and I was fearful of not being able to write them. Dugald had four cheques left in his chequebook but no money in the bank, but needs must. I impressed upon Paula that the mission had to be done sober, and succeeded in restraining her to just one stiff brandy and Coke. She donned her finest work clothes and still managed to look like a bag lady on a rainy day. We took the girls for cover and left a defeated Dugald skulking about at home.

We went to the OK Bazaars and bought as much food as we dared. If I remember correctly it was fifty rand's worth. The girls and I were also dressed in our finest, which is not saying much. We had come at four in the afternoon when the banks were closed, just in case the management decided to make a phone call to check our creditworthiness. We already had experience of that embarrassing scenario. At the till Paula laid on the false charm, telling the till lady that her hairdo looked absolutely smashing. Laurie was sent to change the cereal so that we were holding up the queue, and when she finally returned the cheque was presented, and the flustered till lady with hair like copper wire processed it without any questions. Naturally there was a false address on the back. The next day we were emboldened to hit two other supermarkets with the same strategy. It was a very risky business but somehow we managed to get away with it. With the last cheque we bought a few sacks of pig food as the unfortunate creatures had been living on unripe vegetables for a few days.

It did not take long for the legal process to kick in. About ten days after our fraudulent raid, a police car arrived at our secluded home with two burly officers, just as I was helping Chetty to deliver her five kittens. Dugald hid in a cupboard in the girls' room, while I, with blood on my hands, went out to face the law. I told the officers that Dugald was in Johannesburg to attend a job interview.

"Are you sure of that?" enquired the officer cynically.

"You are welcome to search the house, sir," I replied blandly.

They looked at one another and then stared at me in that searching manner our police have. "When do you expect your father to be back?"

"If he gets the job he won't be back, and if he does not, he should be back next week," I replied.

"We will be back next week. There is an arrest warrant for fraud. Do you understand?" asked the officer.

"Yes sir, I understand you very well, sir."

I was studying as hard as I could under the circumstances as I had been accepted by the University of Cape Town on condition my final grades were good. Then Olaf, our boar became very sick and collapsed in a pitiful heap. A Danish Blue, he had never managed to impregnate any of the sows, and we strongly suspected that this sweet natured and intelligent pig was gay. Paula had even used a bit of hosepipe to rub his testicles in the vain hope of sexing him up so that he would take an interest in the sows. The vet came out to the farm, and after a thorough examination he told us that Olaf had some sort of spinal infection that would ultimately prove fatal and he recommended that we put Olaf down. I told the vet that we would not give up so easily on the boar and requested him to give Olaf a painkiller to relieve his distress, and the good man obliged. He told us he would send his bill in the post and I knew it would never be paid. The painkiller worked wonders and to our enormous relief, Olaf was able to stand up and even walk about. We immediately loaded him onto the van, coursing with drugs, and I drove him to the Maitland abattoir. He was weighed and given the highest grading so we received a handsome cheque for two hundred and sixty rand. That would pay our rent and give us food for a month. We were all distressed about Olaf, but at least I knew then that I would be able to finish my O level exams.

A few days later Paula and I drove out to Fishoek to pay Granny Stella a visit. She had stopped giving my parents money by then, and to be fair Gran had given them money for fifteen years before finally developing the resolve to say no. We told her that Dugald had a very promising interview in the Northern Cape, and asked if he could use her old Volkswagen Beetle for three days. I think she was just so grateful not to be asked for money that she agreed. The next day Dugald and Samantha, who was ten years old, took Granny's car, most of what money we had, and they fled up the east coast. The idea was that as soon as I had completed my exams, we would follow in their fugitive footsteps. The police did come again, and this time they did search through the house and even the barn. I noticed that they did not look in the cupboard of the girls' room.

The Saturday after Dugald's departure, both the families who had bought pigs came out to visit. Paula told them that their pigs were pregnant, and that they could expect anything from twelve to sixteen piglets per sow in just seven months' time, which made them delirious with excitement. The one family brought some paw paws for their pig whom they had named Lacy and the other family had brought big bunches of carrots for their pigs. On the Monday after writing my history exam I loaded up three of the pigs and took them to market. Come Wednesday I wrote the final exam of my school career, and on the Thursday I took the remaining pigs to market. On the way home I noticed a Pontiac parked in a lay-by under the shade of some trees, and sitting in the driver's seat was a large black man wearing a Stetson. On impulse I swung the car around and pulled up next to the gentleman.

"Would you like to buy some furniture at a very good price?"

He scrutinised me for a good thirty seconds before replying. "Where is the furniture?"

"Five kilometres from here," I replied.

"I will follow you," he said.

This man of few words ambled into the house and we started our negotiations in the kitchen. Ten rand for the stove. Five rand for the fridge. Five rand for each of the cupboards. Twenty-five rand for all the beds and mattresses. So it went until he had bought pretty much everything we owned except for our clothing and a few pots and pans. I told him that we were due to leave the next morning, and wrote out a letter saying he had purchased the goods. He pulled a huge wodge of notes from his jacket pocket and peeled off three hundred and sixty rand, doffed his Stetson and departed without a word. Afterwards Paula told me that she was seriously tempted to put the cleaver through his head when she saw that bundle of money. How did that happen, my darkness? There he was, just sitting there with all that boodle.

The next morning I put Stella's goldfish into the green reservoir. We then put the double mattresses we had sold to Mr Stetson onto the back of the Volkswagen pick-up, and loaded the cutlery, bedding, and clothes on top of it. I tied a tarpaulin down over this jumble, and then I stuffed Chetty and her five kittens under the front seat. William, our other cat, and Punch, my spaniel went on the back seat with the girls, and we were almost done. Paula was so inebriated that I had to carry her out of the house and fasten her into the passenger seat. Drunken tears streamed down her face, melting her make-up. "That's it. That was my last chance to have a farm. I might as well commit bloody suicide," she wailed. I remember well that it was a gorgeous summer's day, my darkness, and thinking that my schoolmates were probably all frolicking on the beach.

I walk out of the house into the garden and it is night-time. I look up at the sky, which is brilliant with stars. I notice the Pleiades, also called the Seven Sisters. They are twinkling most vibrantly. Suddenly they begin to move in a circle and then they rush towards earth, and towards me at great speed. "Oh my

God, Armageddon has begun," I exclaim, and awake with my heart pounding.

It was a journey I shall never forget, my darkness, my vision pit: our world had fallen apart and we were fugitives running from the law. On that first day of travel up the east coast we had to stop time after time so that Paula with her combination of acute hangover and motion sickness could vomit, and then just outside the town of Caledon, as we were climbing a steep incline, the Volkswagen began to judder and splutter. I pulled onto the side of the road with my heart sinking into my boots, as this was the last thing we needed. I opened the cover and looked forlornly at the engine. Although Dugald is very good with car engines, I am hopeless. Time and again when he was doing repairs on one of our many third-hand cars he would invite me to come and watch him. "If you learn something then one day it will come in handy," he would say. I would always find some excuse to run away, as car engines bore me to death. Now I was deeply regretful for my short-sightedness, and looking around helplessly I wondered how many days we would be spending on the side of that road. Barely five minutes passed and a car stopped, a coloured man came over and asked what the problem was, and it turned out that he was a mechanic. He hauled out his tool kit and within fifteen minutes he had repaired the fractured fuel pipe. I tentatively offered him five rand for his help but he very kindly refused to take it. I suppose it was obvious to him that we were on the bones of our butt. I confess, my darkness, that I did wonder if the Big Man had noticed our plight and had arranged a little helping hand, so I offered up a most sincere thank you. I drove more slowly after that, and it took us about six hours to reach Mossel Bay, by which time Paula was in a dreadful state, convulsing about like a headless snake. I booked her into a bed and breakfast, and saw her to bed with lots of water, aspirin, and some fruit. Then after buying some food for me and the girls, we found a fairly isolated road, and parked up in a lay-by for the night. The police arrived at about one in the morning. Stella and Laurie were sharing the mattress in the back of the van, and I was sleeping on the back seat of the cab.

"You are not allowed to camp here. Why are you here?"

"Well sir, we were heading for Knysna, but my mother became unwell so we had to take her to a guest house. We did not have enough money for all of us," I explained.

They began to search the car, and were of course rather surprised to find the cat and five kittens under the seat, and a dog and cat on the back seat. They found my Bob Dylan, van Morrison, and Pink Floyd records, and decided I was a hippie with short hair, so they searched through my pockets, my socks and then they even rummaged through our bags of clothes, presumably looking for cannabis. Amazingly they did not ask for my non-existent driver's licence, which is what I was most dreading. I was speaking in my best Afrikaans and full of yes sirs.

"You must leave tomorrow morning. If we catch you camping around here you will be charged."

"Yes sir, I understand sir."

We picked up Paula the next morning, and I am ashamed to say, my darkness, that upon an impulse, I stole a Gideon Bible from her bedroom. She still had the shakes so we had to drop by the liquor store to buy a bottle of brandy, or hair of the dog as Paula calls it, before we hit the road. On the way to the town of George, Chetty became ill and retched up all over the car. We found a vet in George and I took Chetty and her kittens in, and I told the vet that we were destitute and could no longer look after the cat and her kittens. "Most people in your circumstances would have abandoned them on the side of the road. You did well to come here. I will find a home for her and the kittens. She probably has motion sickness," said the vet. I offered up another thank you to my divine pursuer. That night we drove up into the hills above the small town

25

of Wilderness, and made camp in the forest near the town of Wilderness Heights.

The next day, after buying Paula another bottle, we journeyed to the town of Knysna where we were meant to meet up with Dugald and Samantha. We spent a couple of fruitless hours driving around the town looking for them. The only thing we could do was find a place to camp near the town, so I drove us to a coastal village called Knoetzie. We bathed in the sea and spent the afternoon on the beach, and that night we snuck into the woods to make camp. We were sitting around our camp fire when William began to yowl. In the two years I had known William I had never seen him do that. He came and stood in front of me and meowed plaintively. I knew what he was saying, "I cannot bear the car any longer. I am going my own way." I knelt on the ground and kissed his head. "Go, my dear friend. Go and find a good family." Stella and Laurie were crying. He walked off into the night with his tail straight up in the air. He turned one last time, his large yellow eyes blazing, gave a final meow and walked off into the forest. I don't think I will ever love another cat like I did William, my darkness.

We went into Knysna for the next three days and still we could not find Dugald and Samantha. Finally I had a furious row with Paula. "We are using up our money. We can't hang around any longer or the police will find us. We have to move on!" I shouted. I placated her with a large bottle of brandy and we drove up to Storms River, where we found a hidey-hole in the forest near the Blue Lilly Hotel. There was some big do going on at the hotel that night, a party of sorts with a band playing and loads of people dancing. I went to investigate and found that there was a magnificent open air buffet, so I stole a roast chicken, some rolls, a bottle of wine and escaped back to our squalid little camp.

The next day we were driving to Port Elizabeth, and as we were passing through the salubrious town of Plettenberg Bay I spotted Granny's yellow Beetle in the parking bay of a large petrol station. Dugald and Samantha were sitting helplessly in the car as they had run out of fuel and money. He was as white as porcelain and I felt deep pity for him. Paula was delighted and hugely relieved to see him, but she immediately started shouting abuse. "You bloody nonk. You witless fucking ape. We agreed to meet in Knysna!" she said, flinging herself on him with joy and fury. His first words were, "Have you got any drink?" Paula handed him the bottle of Blue Lilly wine which he took with trembling hands. He was plainly on the brink of delirium tremens, and we had reached him just in time. Samantha had not eaten for two days and was absolutely famished.

That night we camped under a bridge and to my surprise we were not alone, as there was another white family with six children hiding out. All they had to eat were some fish they had caught in the river so we shared our food with them. The next day we arrived in the harbour city of Port Elizabeth, and there we had little option but to book into a camping site, which seriously eroded our limited funds. On the upside we were able to shower and wash all our dirty laundry. That evening the camping site manager came over, and made a colossal rumpus when he discovered that we only had my two-man tent, that the girls were sleeping on the mattress in the back of the van, and me on the back seat. Punch began to bark and this was the final straw for this petty tyrant, who then threatened to call the police. It took some doing to placate the man, but finally he very reluctantly let us stay on condition that we were gone by six-thirty in the morning.

We scoured the Port Elizabeth newspapers for jobs, and for some ridiculous reason Paula and Dugald were enticed by a job over 200 kilometres away in the Transkei. A large pig farm near the town of Ugie was looking for a live-in stock manager and a cook, and in their usual delusional manner my parents thought that they would fit the bill perfectly. Paula could cook very well but Dugald knew next to nothing about pigs. What the heck, as far as Paula was concerned we were veterans of the trade. After all, we had once had our own pig farm. Paula phoned from a coin box to make an appointment for the next day. On the way to Ugie, we stopped by in the small city of East London to do some shopping for groceries, and of course Paula frequented the liquor store, where she bought a bottle of wine, and swiped a half litre of gin. I implored them to abstain from alcohol until after the interview and to their credit they managed to keep their consumption down to a few swigs apiece. Finding the farm proved to be a tortuous ordeal as there was no signage, and we arrived embarrassingly late for the appointment. We must have made for a very dispiriting and sorry sight. The rusted green Kombi with its tatty tarpaulin cover looked like "White Trash Removals", and the twelve-year-old Beetle was smothered in thick red dust. The girls and Punch waited in the car, but I went with my parents on the walkabout because I at least knew something about pigs. I had given Dugald a crash course on what little I knew, but it was never going to be enough. The adults had eaten some XXX mints to mask the smell of alcohol, but the gin won the day. The farmer took us to a gigantic warehouse type of building which housed about two thousand pigs, where the noise combined with the overpowering stench was sheer torture. The interview was of course, a complete disaster. Paula flirted with the farmer which embarrassed him and me. Dugald could not find his tongue, and was his usual inarticulate, uncertain, dithering self. He could not remember what a porker was, and I knew within three minutes of meeting the baffled farmer that there was not a chance in hell of them obtaining the post.

We drove off the farm not even knowing where we were going to go next, and after a furious row between Dugald and Paula, we spent the night on the sand dunes near the small village of Kei River. The next day we ended up driving back to East London where we set up camp on the banks of the Buffalo river.

CHAPTER FOUR

*I*t is evening and I come home with a basket of vegetables—onions, potatoes, and squash. Each vegetable has a price tag on it. In the driveway is an emaciated cheetah who is chewing on the bare skeleton of a sheep. He sees me and slinks under a bush. I realise that I am gnawing on a rib bone, and I throw it to the cheetah. I go into the house where I hand the basket of vegetables to Paula, and she says that she will make a soup. Then suddenly I am in bed with Dugald and the girls. He spreads himself out, and knocks me out of the bed. I climb back in and shove him over. In the morning I go to the kitchen only to find that the soup has been neglected, and is boiling away. I run over and take the lid off the pot and add water to try to save it. Dugald is sitting at the kitchen table eating ice cream, and I become furious with him, but say nothing. I go outside into the back yard which has a cement floor, and high fences of chicken wire. There I see a large bitch with the body of a ridgeback, but its head is far too small, and it has teeth like a game fish. This bitch comes towards me, and I put my hand on top of its head to restrain the repulsive creature from coming any closer, as am dubious about its intentions. The dog then turns around, and to my horror I see that it has two dogs' heads attached to its hind quarters, one on each side of the tail. The one head has six eyes, and the other has four insect type eyes. I am appalled, and wonder why the owner of this hideous animal keeps it *alive. I hear a noise behind me, and turn to see a smaller black dog with legs which are way too short, and sticking out from his one side are another four mutant legs. It is a horrifyingly disgusting sight which makes me shudder to the core. I turn back to the three-headed dog, and again she comes towards me. I put my foot against her chest to keep her away, but she shoves forward so that her neck is against my hip, which is simply nightmarish. Suddenly her neck grows very long so that her face is level with mine and I am sick with fear. Then to my astonishment, white feathers sprout from the dog and she becomes a large white swan. The swan puts her long neck across my chest with her head on my shoulder and I feel greatly honoured. The swan then turns into a woman wearing an exquisite pearl necklace, and she tells me that she loves me.*

When I think of it now, my darkness, our family is a sort of monstrosity. We were always hemmed in by high poverty fences, and Mom and Dad are ridiculously irresponsible and puerile. Paula regards us as extensions of herself and mutant Dugald is most definitely stunted, both emotionally and mentally. We were always living off scraps like scavengers. I was telling you, my darkness, about that crazy journey up the east coast, and how we ended up on the Buffalo river, all the while expecting the pigs to arrest us at any time. I was reading my stolen Bible on a daily basis, starting with Genesis, and though I am pretty familiar with the New Testament, I had never read much of the Old Testament before. It mostly makes for fascinating reading, but this God of the Old Testament seems to me to be a dark character, slightly pathological at times, to say the least. Is that why I flee him? Some children call the prophet Elijah "Baldy", and this God of the Hebrews sends out a she bear which mauls forty-two of them to death. I reckon that's a bit harsh myself. I think sending them to bed without supper might be more appropriate. A punishment more suited to the crime, don't you think. I am intrigued by the way God changes his mind when Lot argues with him. I had been under the misapprehension that his judgment is infallible. Clearly not; perhaps he learns something in dialogue with humankind. This self-confessed jealous God has a penchant for smiting cities, and vanquishing armies; he sends his chosen people into exile more than once and makes one of his prophets marry a harlot. This is a God quick to blazing anger and slow to mercy, contrary to the claims of some of his prophets, for as it is said, actions speak louder than words. He destroys Sodom and Gomorrah for not having twenty righteous men apiece. Is there any city in the whole world that has ever had so many righteous? Righteousness is an ideal, not an actual state of things, surely. I am most interested in the accounts of those people who have direct dealings with the Divine, such as the voice from the burning bush, and the appearance of angels bearing messages. Jacob's dream of a stairway connecting the earthly sphere to the heavenly realm fascinates me. When he told that dream to his people, no one scoffed and said, "It's only a dream, old chap." Instead they thought it merited being preserved in the scriptures. I wonder at this grim God of the Old Testament who appears as fire, who comes as a pillar of cloud, and who speaks through a donkey. I pray, but to what kind of God, certainly a silent one, a galactic void.

We celebrated Christmas next to the lazy Buffalo river, and that was also where we saw in the new year of 1977. Again we scoured the papers for jobs, and Paula even went for a few interviews. The trouble was that she could give no fixed address, and no telephone number, for invariably they would say, "We have a few more interviews to give and we will phone you if you are selected for the post." The money situation was becoming more critical and we were once again staring destitution right in its hideous face.

One night I was looking for something in the back of the van, and I came across Paula's crystal ball and tarot cards. She once had quite a reputation for her psychic abilities, and had made a tidy little income on the side from telling fortunes. I too had learned how to read palms, technically anyway. Paula had taught me a fair bit, and I had studied some palmistry books. I used to practise on the girls at school who never tired of having their palms read, and became reasonably good in the art of bullshit. Then two events happened which put me off the whole occult thing.

The first happened when I was sixteen. Two men arrived one evening for a reading. The situation was unusual for two reasons. One, most of Paula's clients were women, and the few men who did come tended to be friends or acquaintances. Second, the vast majority of clients came alone or at least they had their fortune told in private. These two men who were in their early thirties wanted to be told their fortune together. Whenever Paula received a client, I would bring in tea after half an hour, as this routine would enable Paula to bring the session to a close. So when half an hour had elapsed, I duly brought a tray of tea to the lounge, and knocked on the door. It was eerily quiet, which made the hair stand up on the back of my neck. I opened the door tentatively and looked in, and there was Paula lying on the floor unconscious. The crystal ball was rolling across the carpet, which looked most sinister to me. One of the men was slumped in the corner of the room with his head between his knees, and the other I could not see. Later I found him curled up behind the couch in a foetal position. I dropped the tray on the floor and rushed in. Paula was groaning, and I lifted her head into my lap. I tried to make her drink some water, but she just kept moaning, and so I poured some of it over her face. She gradually revived, but remained in a stunned daze, so I helped her to her room and put her on the bed, before turning my attention to the men. They were both deathly pale and inchoate with terror, and together they stumbled out of the house never to be seen again. All Paula could remember of the event was that they were sitting around the crystal ball chatting, when suddenly the ball lit up like a lamp. It then lifted into the air, hovered about their heads, and the last thing she could remember was a sort of flash like lightning.

She did not use the crystal ball ever again, and I became wary of the whole thing. I knew that Paula had the gift, but the ability for prediction used to come upon her out of the blue, and happen to her spontaneously. I always knew when Mom was in genuine psychic mode, as it gave me the creeps. Something about her voice changed, and so did the look in her eyes. She could not induce the gift or bring it out to command, for it would come involuntarily and even unbidden, so invariably when she told fortunes she had to busk it and tell people what they wanted to hear. It is best that way because usually when a psychic does have a flash, it is generally about something horrible. Just look at Nostradamus. Even Jesus and all the prophets tended in the main to prophesy disastrous events, and one thing is certain: there will always be disasters.

Then about six months later, while I was at a friend's house, he mentioned to his mother that I could tell fortunes, which embarrassed me enormously. Well, immediately his mother and her friend wanted me to look at their palms. I had my routine. I would start by saying, well, this is your life line and as you can see it is long and unbroken. Then, this is your head line and it goes completely across your palm which indicates a good mind and little chance of insanity. This is your heart line which denotes that you are a caring and sensitive person, and here is the mount of the moon which indicates passion and loyalty, and this is the mount of Jupiter which shows that you are creative, and here is the bracelet of health which tells me you will enjoy good health, and so on. This I would do so that I sounded knowledgeable, like someone who actually knew what they were doing, and then I would just talk crap of course. I would always tell them that they would travel widely and make a fortune. But on that particular day a strange sensation came over me from out of nowhere. My eyes felt hot like

33

little coals, I could hear a high-pitched ringing tone in my ears, and when I spoke my own voice sounded strange to me as if it were coming from far away, and a whole lot of stuff just poured out of me. Afterwards I could not even recall anything I had told them but the women were immensely impressed, and made me promise to come back the following week, saying that they would have a number of their other friends around. I left the house feeling most peculiar, slightly out of body, and not a little flattered by the gushing of the two women.

It was night-time as I walked home, and at one stage I happened to look up at a street light and it instantly popped and went out. This did not unduly unsettle me, but then a few blocks later I looked up at another lamp, and it too popped and went out, and then I did start to wonder what was going on. By the time I reached home I had popped about ten street lights, and I could not shake off the feeling that this was more than a coincidence. I told Paula about the events of the evening and she said, "I always knew you had the gift."

Sometime during that night, I awoke very suddenly and completely. The full moon was high in the sky and shining straight into my room and onto me. I stared at the moon for a while trying to work out what was wrong, and then I realised with a start that my curtain was missing which perplexed me greatly. Then to my horror I noticed that it was pressed up against the ceiling. I could scarcely believe my eyes. I glanced to my side, and it was then that I realised with considerable alarm that I was levitating above my bed. Suddenly there was a roaring sound in my ears and at the same time I felt a powerful force pulling me upwards. I knew this force, or being, wanted to take me into the sky, into the cosmos, and I resisted with all my might, and screamed very loudly. In an instant, the roaring and the force stopped, and I fell to my bed. The curtain fluttered down like a bat's wing and blocked out the moonlight. Scalded with terror I ran to Paula's bedroom and was amazed to find her fast asleep, as I thought that my scream of horror would have aroused the entire neighbourhood. I woke Paula up and told her what had happened. She offered me a dram of brandy to steady my nerves, and I decided there and then to have nothing more to do with fortune-telling.

I now also understand, my darkness, that the God of the Old Testament looks very unfavourably upon the occult arts and he severely punished King Saul for visiting a fortune-teller. But what is a prophet if not a fortune-teller? I hesitated for some while and then I decided that if God doesn't help, then one must help oneself. So I took the crystal ball and the cards to the campfire. "What do you say, Mom? We could set up a stall near the fun fair and make some dough." With the last of our money we hired a four-berth caravan for a week, and took it to the fair. We put up a rather rustic banner made on a somewhat faded sheet and Paula put on even more make-up than usual. Paula could not bring herself to use the crystal ball, but she told fortunes by palm and tarot card. I would do palms occasionally, and felt like the terrible fraud I was. By the end of the week we had made enough money to hire the caravan for another week, but after that the school holidays ended, the fair packed up, the holidaymakers returned home, and our source of income rapidly dried up. We decided then that we had no choice but to head for Johannesburg, the city we had fled nine years before.

That's what? One year and one month ago, my darkness, but so much has happened since.

CHAPTER FIVE

The prison guards have come with my daily ration, my six slices of bread and two litres of water. They examine me intently, with cold eyes, no doubt trying to ascertain whether I am becoming unhinged or not. I can feel my foetid cell exhaling, and a fresh draft of delicious air comes sweeping in. I am grateful to have a clean chamber pot, for a while. All too soon they lock the door, and cut off the exhilarating light of day.

We arrived in the Golden City, and spent two days in a guesthouse, and then we stayed a couple of nights with one of Paula's old journalist friends, after which we spent a few days camping in some scrubland near the airport with aeroplanes roaring low over us every few minutes, nearly driving me bonkers. Paula tracked down an old friend called Steve Marasvich who had come to South Africa from Yugoslavia as a young man, and Paula and Dugald had been kind to him. He had lived with us in Honey Street for a few months, and Paula had helped him to find his first job. Although he had not heard from us for over twelve years, he obviously felt some obligation to help. The girls and I moved into his garage and Paula and Dugald took up the spare room in his house. Steve had done quite well for himself financially; he had married a South African and they had produced two daughters. However, it was quite obvious to me that it put a huge strain on him to accommodate us, especially as his wife could not bear Paula, who after a glass or two could not refrain from telling Steve how good looking he had become. Steve put me to work selling plastic pepper spray guns door to door. I am a hopeless salesperson and cannot sell bread to a starving man, but I went out every day and tramped up and down the suburban roads. Many households had real guns, others were sceptical of the pepper gun's efficacy, while others simply could not afford it. With my apologetic approach I enjoyed very limited success for the first two weeks, but then I had a bit of luck. I came to a house where a young nurse opened the door. She worked night shifts, and had to walk home at six in the morning while it was still dark. She had been mugged twice, and immediately bought a pepper gun for herself, and one for a friend of hers. Inspired by this, I went to the hospital the next evening and presented myself to nurses arriving for night duty, and over the next few days I sold about forty pepper guns. Then Dugald managed to land a four month work contract in the Northern Transvaal and went off in Granny's Beetle. A week later Paula also procured a job in a plant nursery, and so we moved into a dilapidated unfurnished house in Northwood, and the girls were finally able to return to school some six weeks late. We never saw Steve and his family again, and probably never will.

I bought a cheap shiny suit, and went for a job interview in the city at the newly completed Carlton Centre, which stands fifty stories tall, and is reputedly the tallest building in Africa. I arrived early, and was dismayed to see the large number of interviewees vying for the job, and immediately lost all hope of landing it. I was eventually ushered into a plush office where the first question my potential boss asked me was what subjects I had done at school. When I mentioned that I had done typing he was naturally very surprised, as it is a subject traditionally taken only by girls. "You can type?" He took me through to his secretary's office, made her vacate her seat and began dictating to me while I typed. He then took me back to his office and offered me the job there and then. It was a shipping company called Safmarine, which had just acquired a computer, and this is apparently a very big deal. My boss tells me that there are only 50,000 computers on the entire planet, and there are apparently only about twenty computers in the whole of Africa. He took me to see the computer which was housed in a specially built room and I was duly impressed. It was the size of a six-berth caravan, and there were masked engineers in white dust suits working on it. For a while we watched proceedings from behind a glass wall, then he took me to another room where the computer screen was housed, and he showed me what the job entailed. On the screen was a map of the world and there were flashing red dots to indicate where all the containers were at any one time. Simply put, my job was to track all the containers as they travelled around the globe. I hated the job and the working environment, and realised fairly quickly that I was not cut out to be a suit in a skyscraper. As I left the building after the interview, I miraculously bumped into two girls from my class, and that was how I found out that I had passed my O levels with distinctions.

My boss had failed to ask me during the interview about my military service, which was rather remiss of him as I was due for my call-up in the coming July. I only worked at Safmarine for four months until the end of May and then I hitchhiked back to Cape Town and went to stay with Granny Stella for the month of June. I would go running every morning and swim for hours at a time, as I wanted to be as fit as possible when I began my military service. I also went camping for four days in Sandy Bay and only saw one lone beachcomber the whole time I was there. A few days later I said goodbye to Gran and went to the Castle in Cape Town to sign in. We were marched to the station and boarded a train for Kimberley where I began my basic training in the infantry division.

Hunger, silence, darkness, pain, time, and memories, you are my constant companions, my fellows, my familiars. I did not want to go to the army, my darkness. I am no patriot. I have never been part of a tribe. I hate the idea of war, for it is invariably such a travesty, even though I know full well that life is by necessity a constant battle. Without battle there is no evolution, and I tend to believe that evolution has a goal. It seems as if we cannot evolve without an arms race. Even nature herself is a ceaseless play of continuous battle.

Like every white boy in the country I had been thoroughly indoctrinated to believe that the South African army was the most formidable in Africa, and on a par with the best in the world. Yet chaos reigned from the outset. The military had run out of uniforms for people my size, so I was issued kit two sizes too large. We often sat around for ages, bored witless while waiting for things to happen. We would all run off at the double for our medical examinations, and then spend two days lounging about, waiting to be seen. Then we would charge off somewhere to be issued with rifles only to be held up for six hours because the key to the armoury could not be found. Hurry and wait was the order of the day. We would go off to the shooting range, and then find that the ammunition or targets had not been brought along, hang around listlessly, and finally get to shoot for five minutes. Accidents and sickness abounded. A chap in my unit jumped off the back of a truck holding the barrel of his rifle in one hand and put his right eye out as he landed. Another fellow lost four fingers when the tail gate of a truck swung down on his hand. Another fit-looking boy died while we were doing a routine full pack run, and three or four lads died of meningitis within the first three weeks of training. We took part in a large three day mock battle which involved tanks and artillery from other divisions. Most of the time my unit and I had absolutely no idea where we were or what we were meant to be doing. Our rifles were clogged with mud, our food supplies were contaminated with dust and water. We had insufficient bedding, and froze during the night as fires were forbidden, and our compasses all gave different readings. Apparently about seven soldiers died during the exercise, and scores were injured. It was ineptitude on a grand scale. There were the usual tensions between the Afrikaans soldiers and the minority of English-speaking soldiers, and fights were frequent and violent.

It was obligatory to attend church on Sundays which was a problem for me. As my family have never belonged to a religious group, I was at a loss as to what to do. Added to which I have inherited a deep dislike for traditional Christian institutions. As I have never been subjected to a religious indoctrination, I like to think that I read the Bible without the blinkers of inherited beliefs, and it seems to me that the traditional churches of today have strayed far from the divine source. They tend to suffer from the delusion that the only source of metaphysical truth is the Bible, and that they are the only rightful conduit to the Divine.

I remember that on the first Sunday of my military training I attended an Anglican service. I was disgusted by the priest's outfit: he was kitted out with effete robes embroidered with gold and crimson. I loathed the ornate arched hat, straight out of the thirteenth century, as I feel that this is tradition taken to ridiculous extremes. I suppose that if a person is accustomed to such a sight from birth, it does not seem odd, nor can one then see the sterility that such an antiquated tradition denotes. Like the outfits, the theology dispensed to the masses has remained antiquated and undeveloped, something embalmed, and it is not fitting any more for the contemporary educated congregation. I was angry that the Bible was nowhere to be seen, and that the entire service was delivered by rote from some little book called the liturgy. Religion by rote is a religion for dumb sheep, and the time for being sheep has long past. The priest spoke in that customary sanctimonious tone that rises and falls monotonously with a false virtuousness. I know that I am emotional about these petty things which seem not to offend anyone else. It must be the Antichrist in me, this deep abhorrence I have of virtuousness, which I inherited from Paula.

The next week I attended the Catholic service which was much the same except that the priest wore an even more outrageous frock, which to my mind could only have been designed by a homosexual man. Heterosexual men generally lack the ability to make something so pretty, and yet this patently gay institution, with its beautiful stained glass windows and pretty choir boys, has the audacity to condemn homosexuals to eternal damnation and never-ending hellfire. Again the Bible was disappointingly absent from proceedings.

I attended the Dutch Reformed service the following week, for I know from experience that at the very least, the sermon is likely to be based on a scriptural reading. Being naïve in such matters I was stunned when the reverend came dressed in a military uniform. For some reason this outraged me far more than the ostentatious medieval garb of the Catholics and Anglicans. The priest held a sickle in one hand and a Bible in the other. He ranted and raved, frothing at the mouth in evangelical fashion. His sermon was all about how the sickle of communism wanted to tear the Bible in half, and tear us all from the true God. According to this man of God the communists were indoctrinating the black people with the ridiculous notion that they could rule themselves. The Bible was not opened or read from but at least it was there. After that I took my chances and slipped off behind the mine dumps with a good book on Sunday mornings.

My sleeping pattern is all over the shop, my darkness. I was awake for about seven hours before they finally bought me my bread and water. Thinking and remembering, loneliness, fear, and uncertainty make me lethargic in this airless cell. I fall asleep and when I awake, I do not know for how long I have been in the arms of my soul. I am now about the hungriest I have ever been in my life, and I am visited by tormenting visions of food.

"My God, where are you, do you know I am here? Do you know every hair on my head? Do you know that I no longer run from you, but seek you? Please help me to endure, my Father."

After three months in the army we completed the first phase of our basic training, and were given a seventy-two hour pass. I took the train from Kimberley to Jo'burg and arrived in Northwood on a Saturday morning. Paula was working at the garden centre so I came home to find Stella, Laurie, and Samantha sitting about in the bedraggled garden reading and sunbathing. We still had no furniture, nor had we managed to acquire a fridge, and we were cooking our meals on a slow hot plate. The only furniture in the house were the mattresses we slept on, the bedding we had brought from the Cape, and some cutlery. I felt sorry for my sisters in their tatty clothing, and gave them some of my army pay to buy clothes. Paula came home very excited. Her boss whose name was Leo wanted to retire and sell his garden centre. He had offered Paula the chance to buy the concern, on condition that she paid the asking price in instalments over a two year period. I smelt a dirty rat coming, and tried to pour some cold water on the whole idea, but Paula would not be dissuaded by my defeatist attitude as she called it.

That night, my darkness, there was a knock at the door and there stood an attractive young married couple with Bibles in hand. Tony and Bridgette are Jehovah's Witnesses, a sect I had heard of but had not met before. I invited them in, and they sat on my mattress whilst I sat on a wooden box. They were obviously shocked by the poverty of our circumstances, but they were very pleased to find a listening ear. Tony noticed the stolen Gideon Bible on the floor next to my bed with my packet of cigarettes on top of it. "I see you read the Bible," he said. After some discussion, I asked him what he thought the world was coming to, and he directed me to Matthew chapter twenty-four. Here Jesus gives his sermon on the last days, and the signs that will mark the end of time and the coming of

God's judgment. I must confess that the hair stood up on my neck. I had finally found fellow believers in the coming catastrophe, my darkness. I asked what their views were on military service, and was again astounded to find that they refused to do it, and were incarcerated for their neutral stance. I accepted the invitation to attend one of their meetings, and the following day I went in my shiny suit to the Sunday service. I forget what the service was about but two things struck me very forcibly. For one thing the Bible was very much in use. Every member of the congregation, even the children had a Bible, and it was constantly referred to.

Although I think and feel that there is much that is wise in the Bible, I also have many quarrels with the Holy Book. There is much that I simply cannot agree with, my darkness, things I feel have become outdated. I even have difficulties with some of the Ten Commandments as given to Moses. I have trouble with "Honour thy mother and thy father", for what if they are not worthy of honour? I even have a problem with "Thou must not steal" which on the face of it seems reasonable enough, but what if you are desperate, what if your children are starving to death? I think it is more of a sin to let the children starve.

I digress. The second thing that made a huge impression on me was that there was no priest. The man who gave the service was just a brother among brothers and sisters. This struck a chord with me as I have a natural aversion to the idea that a certain class of people have the inside track to the Almighty. Those would be shepherds of the flock. That night after the service I took the train back to Kimberley with many questions on my mind. A month later Paula signed a deal with Leo, and became the de facto proprietor of Leo's nursery. Dugald's contract came to an end, and he joined Paula in running the garden centre.

CHAPTER SIX

There is a fierce battle. The sky is catastrophe red. I am wounded and the medics put me in an ambulance. Next to me is a wounded black man, and though we were formerly enemies, we hold hands.

Four weeks into the second phase of our basic training things took a very unexpected turn. It was a Saturday morning and most of us were washing our uniforms or writing letters when the siren sounded. There was some mayhem as we scrambled to assemble, and our lieutenant was apoplectic with rage at the length of time it took us to do so. Some goons had even forgotten to bring their rifles. We were loaded onto some trucks, and taken to the airfield where to our shock we found ourselves being herded onto some helicopters. We had no idea what the hell was going on, and some of the troops were sick with fear. The noise in the helicopter was deafening. After about half an hour we landed on a road leading into a large black township.

We heard the protesters long before we saw them. Thousands of singing and chanting black people came like a swollen river down the road towards us. At the front of this human tide were pall bearers carrying the coffin of a fallen comrade, draped in the ANC colours. We young white boys were arranged into three rows. The front row lay on the road, the second row knelt, and the back row stood. Our lieutenant had a loud hailer, he told us to prepare and we removed our safety catches. The helicopters took off leaving us to our fate. I felt sick and afraid, and my hands were sweating profusely. As the masses drew closer the lieutenant began shouting through his loud hailer, warning them to stop, but his voice was completely drowned out by the loud singing. The lieutenant was clearly out of his depth, as were we all. We had not been trained for such an occasion, and it later emerged that we were not even meant to be there. Apparently we were merely there to back up the police, a sort of show of force, but the crowd had taken an unexpected route, and suddenly they were descending upon a group of eighteen-year-old boys who could not even shoot. We had been more or less mentally prepared to face the communist FAPLA terrorists in Angola, and the SWAPO terrorists of South West Africa, but we had not as yet been programmed to face down the unarmed singing citizens of South Africa. The lieutenant ordered us to fire over the heads of the crowd. I disobeyed that command, but most did not. The problem it seemed to me was that if you shot over the heads of those at the front of the crowd, the bullets would still descend into the masses further back, and I believe that is exactly what happened. Mass panic ensued and many people were trampled underfoot as the crowd broke in every direction. The coffin was abandoned, and the defiant singing was replaced by panic–stricken screaming. Moments later some police cars arrived, and there was a heated altercation between the police officer and our lieutenant. Ambulances arrived, and then the press appeared, and they were promptly surrounded by the police and forcibly shuffled away. The helicopters returned, we were hastily boarded, and back in camp in time for lunch. The next day I went into town and looked through all the newspapers, but there was not a single word about the incident.

Something snapped in me that day, something died, my darkness, and I felt a traitor to my own soul. Six weeks after returning to Kimberley from our first pass, we completed the second phase of our training and my unit was dispatched to the Mozambique border. We had only been to the shooting range about six times during our training, and now we were off to the front. Most of us were thrilled about our posting because we knew that the real action was on the Angolan border, where boys were dying on a daily basis. The camp was on the highest hill in the area with sweeping views over lush Mozambique. It was very basic with only a few temporary buildings, and we the soldiers were billeted in tents. Game abounded, and we spent the first few days putting up elephant fences. Occasionally we did a reconnaissance into Mozambique. Near one village we found a large plantation of cannabis, and the guys took about half a ton of the stuff back to camp, where drugs were already rife, and large numbers of troops were perpetually stoned out of their tiny skulls. The usual chaos and disorder prevailed. One idiot shot himself in the foot, and another was partially blinded by a spitting cobra. A pressure cooker blew up in the field kitchen, and badly maimed some of the cooks. A number of troops stepped into poachers' traps, and during the eight weeks I was there we never saw a single sign of the enemy.

Then the most bizarre thing happened to me, my dark companion. I was sitting with a bunch of mates on some large rocks overlooking the base, and in the distance we could see a vehicle approaching at considerable speed along the red dirt road. As it drew closer we could identify that it was an ambulance, and we were wondering what was up. It came into the camp at high speed, and we watched as the medics had some discussion with the captain. The captain went to his office and broadcast a message on the loudspeakers. "Will private 7747847B report to the commanding officer." I was astounded as the realisation dawned on me that it was me who was being summoned.

I jogged on down to the captain who told me I was to go with the ambulance without delay. I said to him there must be some mistake. He became angry and told me not to argue as it was an order. I was not even allowed to fetch my toothbrush or any of my kit. The medics stood back as if I were a black mamba, and slammed the doors on me without any explanation. The next thing I knew we were racing away from the camp at high speed.

I had no idea what was going on, or where we were going to, and started to become rather anxious. As it turned out we were going to the military hospital in Pretoria, which was a four hour journey at a consistently high speed. I was met by two doctors who were dressed in white protective suits and face masks, and taken hastily into an isolation unit with one glass wall, and that's when I started to have a mild panic attack. I asked the doctor what was wrong, and he told me that I would know soon enough. A blood sample was taken, and I was told to undress and lie in the bed. Dinner was passed to me through a hatch, and there I spent the night wondering what I was dying from. The next morning breakfast was again passed through the hatch. A couple of doctors deep in discussion stood on the other side of the glass wall obviously talking about me. About two hours later a doctor came into the isolation unit without protective gear. "I don't know how this happened, we must apologise. We thought you had cholera, but it turns out that what you have is an unusually high amount of cholera antibodies. You must have been exposed to cholera at some time in your life. The antibodies look very similar to the virus." He was actually blushing with embarrassment.

That was not the end of this fateful saga, my darkness. Firstly there was no transport to take me back to my base camp. The doctors did not know what to do with me, so I had to spend two nights in a hospital bed in a ward full of soldiers with horrific injuries. It was then that I first became truly aware of the actual extent of the war on the Angolan border, and the dreadful toll it was taking. Later I found that there were another five wards packed with mangled soldiers. I spent my time reading and playing cards with some of the lads.

The next day I was picked up by a driver who took me to the military headquarters in Pretoria, and there I stood outside a door for nearly two hours before a captain eventually came out to speak to me. He was irritable, as if I had caused the problem.

"Where is your kit?" he barked.

"It is at my base camp, captain."

"Why did you not bring it with you?"

"I was being taken to hospital, sir."

He stormed off, and again I waited for nearly an hour. Finally a corporal came along and took me to a huge metal barracks, lined with about 200 beds, and he told me that I was to stay there alone.

"Corporal, I do not have any spare clothing. No toothbrush, no shaving kit. No spare underpants."

"You will have to speak to the major about that." The corporal then took me to some offices, and again I was kept waiting for ages. I had not had lunch and was absolutely ravenous by that time. Finally I was ushered into an office, and met the major, who turned out to be a large fierce-faced woman who looked a bit like Stalin. I had to tell her how it came about that I was separated from my unit, and had become her problem, which vexed her enormously.

"What is your name?" she asked after some discussion.

"Mackenzie."

"Why have you got an English name?"

"I am English, major."

"You speak Afrikaans very well. I'm not sure what to do with you around here," she said, waving her hand towards the office full of women typing frantically.

"I can type, major." That raised her one bushy eyebrow, and she looked immensely relieved. That is how I came to be a typist in the military headquarters. The lady major was less pleased with me when I lumbered her with my problem of having no spare clothing, and no sanitary ware. Furthermore there was the difficulty of where I would eat and how I would receive my salary. Exasperated by all these complications she wrote out a seven day pass for me, and told me to report to her the following week. The next morning I hitched into Johannesburg and went to Leo's garden centre.

> *It is night time and I am running down a long dirt road. I am carrying Paula in my arms, and I feel very lonely. Paula says, "I love you, Rod." I say, "I love you too, Mom." I think to myself, who will carry me when I grow old? Up ahead is a small village, faintly illuminated by a few street lamps. I see a tall man crossing the road a few hundred metres away. Suddenly he turns towards us. He has a pistol and he fires off three shots at us. I swerve to the right and run across a field as fast as I can. Paula is becoming heavy, and I am growing tired and fearful.*

"Rod, my darling! It's so good to see you. I see the army has not managed to make you stand straight." Paula hugged me, and I could smell the alcohol on her breath. Dugald was sitting in the office, a sort of garden shed, eating a sausage roll over a magazine. I took a walk around the nursery, and was dismayed to see how little there was in stock. Waves of despair swept over me when I noticed that some of the plants were wilting for lack of water. A customer came in and looked rather bewildered to find new proprietors and no doubt by the forlorn state of the nursery. She wanted a rubber tree, but we had none in stock. "Do you have any roses?" she asked hopefully, peering about. "So sorry, we just sold the last lot, but we have some very nice hibiscus," said Paula weaving rather unsteadily towards her.

I brought Paula up to date on the events in my life and then turned the conversation to the state of the business. A customer ambled in who wanted some lawn fertiliser. We had none in stock but Paula, unabashed, tried to persuade him that shrub fertiliser is just as good for lawns, but he remained unconvinced. At thirty-six years of age, Paula with her blowsy hat, food stains on her bright pink shirt, her mane of tawny blonde hair in a tangle, has lost her edge, and the charm of youth that once spun male heads.

An hour later a man wandered into the garden centre and asked Dugald if we did garden clean-ups. Dugald was stammering some sort of apology when I interrupted, and told the gentleman that we would be very happy to give him a quote. I followed him in the Volkswagen to his garden. He had recently bought the house with a massively overgrown garden which he now wanted cut back. He also wanted some areas planted up, and an irrigation system installed. I took him a quote the very next morning, praying all the way that he would accept it, which he did. We found three hired hands to help us, and with them Dugald and I spent the next four days working in the garden, and to my unbounded joy the man paid us in hard cash. It was more money than the nursery had taken in eight weeks of trading. We drove directly to the plant wholesalers, and bought some new stock, so the nursery looked vaguely respectable. At home we still did not have a fridge or any furniture, and the girls were still badly in need of some new school uniforms. They were doing their homework on the floor.

Back in Pretoria the situation was odd to say the least. I could not for the life of me understand why the army could not get its act together, and take me back to my camp, or send my kit to me, so I harassed Major Stalin who was beginning to regard me as part of the furniture. Still the sole occupant of a huge barracks, I ate in the office staff canteen with about 200 women and four flat-footed men. I spent the days typing documents when they were presented to me, but on some days there was nothing for me to do, and I just sat at my desk reading or ran little errands. I was allowed to go home every weekend as the office canteen was not open. Most soldiers would consider that as a wonderful boon, but I felt like I had fallen through a crack in the system. Sometimes on my weekends off, I would go to the Kingdom Hall, or Tony and Bridgette would come around to discuss the Bible. Then another problem arose. A unit arrived and moved into the barracks which had been my residence, and my bed was needed. The captain of the unit had a heated conflagration with my lady major, the upshot of which was that I was booted out, and I was compelled to spend the night in a room reserved for officers. This caused a huge rumpus, and my major had to give me yet another seven day pass to give her time to sort out the unholy mess.

I came back home two weeks before our most dismal Christmas ever, and things had gone from bad to worse. We were late with our payment to Leo and he was becoming increasingly belligerent. The fertiliser company had sent yet another letter of demand for payment, and would not provide us with any more stock until the bill had been settled in full. There were two or three other wholesalers also screaming blue murder for the money we owed them. On top of this the stock situation in the nursery had once again fallen from dismal to pathetic. Back home the electricity had been cut off, we were lighting the house with candles, and cooking our meals on the barbeque. The rent was overdue and Stella broke down crying because she did not have any sanitary towels. We boiled water in pots and washed ourselves with a facecloth, and the only money we had was my monthly pay from the army which amounted to the grand total of 120 rand.

I found Paula lying stark naked and comatose in the garden and covered her with a blanket. She had responded to the crises with another blinder. Under these bleak circumstances I returned to my base where the situation was still chaotic, and promptly received another seven day pass. Two days after the new year that saw us into 1978, a customer came into the nursery who wanted some trees cut down, and I hired some chainsaws and spent three days cutting them down. I am ashamed to say that we illegally tipped the wood on the banks of the Jukskei river. The next day the sheriff of the court arrived to serve a summons on Paula, who had provided false information to the fertiliser company in order to obtain credit.

We had another one of our emergency indabas and decided that there was only one course of action, so the very next day, I took the four single mattresses, the lawnmower, the hired chainsaws, and sold them all to a second hand furniture store. We put the sagging double mattress on the back of the Volkswagen along with our clothes and cutlery, and headed back to Cape Town, the city we had fled just thirteen months before. Dugald and Paula travelled in the Beetle, the girls, Punch, and myself in the Volkswagen van. In the Orange Free State the van broke down and Dugald had to drive over 100 kilometres to buy a spare part. I think it was a carburettor, whatever that is, and it cost a small fortune. Then the following day while traversing the Great Karroo, a tyre burst and as we had no spare Dugald was once again required to drive a long distance to buy one, and we ended up spending that night in a lay-by near the oasis town of Colesberg. On the ninth of January, we finally arrived at Granny Stella's two bedroom flat almost destitute. Paula and Dugald slept in the spare room while the girls and I took up residence in the tiny lounge.

A few days later Paula and I went off in our finery to Wynberg Girls High School and met with the headmistress. She offered us tea, and we told her the state of our affairs. She is a prim spinster of the academic ilk, with a crisp mind, and I did not hold out much hope, but to my amazement she sprang into action. She made use of some kind of grant, and declared that the girls were to be in the care of the state. She provided them with uniforms and school books, and made them permanent boarders. So the girls were back at school two days later. I have forgotten the name of that venerable headmistress, but she is certainly one of the finest ladies I have ever met.

Two days later on the eighteenth of January, I went to the tidal pools in Kalk Bay for a swim, and when I come out of the water, I lit up a cigarette. A woman of about forty was sitting nearby and she said to me, "Why do you smoke. Don't you know that you are ruining your body?" I looked at her and said, "Are you a Jehovah's Witness?" She was very surprised by the question and replied, "Yes I am. How did you know?" "I know some Witnesses in Jo'burg and I have been to a few meetings," I said. I dressed and we talked for over an hour about the Bible. She told me about her nephew who was in a military prison as a conscientious objector. That conversation finally decided me, and I knew then that I would never return to the army. That, my darkness, is how I came to be in you.

That very evening there was a knock at the door. I answered to find myself looking at two military policemen. I fetched my toothbrush and razor and said goodbye to Paula, Dugald, Punch, and Granny Stella. I was duly handcuffed, and taken to the detention barracks in Wynberg just three kilometres from the girls' boarding school. My food was brought to my cell by a prisoner, and I asked him why he had a blue overall while all the other prisoners had brown ones, and he told me that he was a conscientious objector. Two days later I was taken by two military police to Cape Town station where we boarded a train for the thousand mile journey to the capital city of Pretoria. As I was handcuffed, the civilians stared at me in curiosity, probably wondering what heinous crime I had committed. Most of the time I was confined to the compartment with my one arm handcuffed to a handle, while my guards hung out in the train's bar. The scenery was stupendous, and I stared at it for hours, knowing that it could be a long while before I saw such vistas again. The goons left my charge sheet lying about in the compartment, and I was seriously tempted to throw it out of the window, but with some considerable effort I managed to restrain myself.

CHAPTER SEVEN

The next evening we arrived in Pretoria, and I was taken to the detention barracks where the fun really began in earnest. The officials took my watch and my civilian clothing, and issued me with a brown prison overall and military boots. I told them I wanted the blue overall of a conscientious objector. They told me that I was not an objector, and then they gathered about me and gave me a couple of hefty punches. At that point, a lieutenant came into the charge office and remonstrated with me for a while, and I told him I that I refused to continue with my military service which made him terribly excitable. I was then forcibly manhandled into the army overall, and frogmarched to a cell where I was locked up, and I then realised that in all the excitement my prison boots had been left behind. The next morning we were unlocked and after emptying our potties in an open drain and brushing our teeth, we were assembled in a large courtyard facing the raised administration block which is fronted with a long *stoep*. I had left my brown military overall in my cell, and stood barefoot in my underpants much to the amusement of my fellow prisoners. On the balcony of the administration block, an assemblage of military police of various ranks gathered to do the roll-call, and as I was in the back row I was not noticed at first. After the head count has been completed a strange ritual began. A large trolley was wheeled out which holds the prisoners' cigarettes, each packet with a prisoner's name on it, and one by one the smokers were called up to receive a cigarette which was lit by a guard. That mission accomplished, another trolley loaded with medicines was wheeled out, and the same procedure began all over again, with a surprising number of prisoners seeming to need medication of some description. It was during this procedure that someone on the stoep noticed me and pointed me out to Sergeant Major Liebenberg who was in charge that morning. He has a very short temper does the sergeant major and when he saw me his face turned varicose purple with outrage. He came storming down the stairs, across the quadrangle, and standing with his face but two inches from my own he bellowed, "Where is your overall prisoner!?"

"I asked for the overall of a conscientious objector and was not given one, sergeant major." He grabbed me by the scruff of the neck and propelled me to the balcony, all the while shouting obscenities and threats. He ordered one of the guards to fetch my overall from my cell, and then roared at me to stand to attention. I refused and stood with my legs apart and my hands held together in front of me. It has always been a strange thing with me, the more someone tries to bully me the more obdurate I tend to become. He then punched me to my left cheekbone which sent me sprawling to the balcony. I stood up a little giddy and I could actually feel my cheekbone swelling. The guard had by this time returned with my overall, and the sergeant major shoved it at me and commanded me to put it on. "I refuse, sergeant major." Some of the guards closed in on me, and lifting me into the air they battled to put me into the overall which I resisted by wriggling about, and for my pains I receive some solid punches and kicks. Finally they managed to put the overall on me, and one Corporal Steyn began yelling at me to stand to attention. I ignored his command and he kicked my ankle with his military boot. The pain was simply shocking, and I fell down in agony, clutching at my leg. Steyn is a big man and he yanked me to my feet with ease. I stood with my head bowed, but kept my legs apart with my hands held together in front of me. Liebenberg then had his mouth four inches from my ear, and he was shouting so furiously that his wife would have been very worried for his heart if she had been witness to his rage. Fortunately for me he did not know that he was roaring into my deaf ear, but spit was flying from his mouth and splattering the side of my face. He was warning me of the dire consequences of my belligerence, no doubt intensely aware that more than 300 prisoners were watching this unthinkable insubordination. After venting his spleen for a while he had a chat with another sergeant major who was present. This other NCO, who has chalk white hair and walks with a cane, did not seem to give a damn about me, in fact he even looked mildly bemused, and together they decided to resume with the dispensing of medicine and then deal with me away from prying eyes. I waited for about two minutes, and then a rush of hot blood surged through me, and I pulled my overall off before anyone could react. Some of the guards stormed at me, punching and kicking, and I covered my face with my hands. Liebenberg shouted at them and they all stood back. The major had arrived, and the red-faced guards and the sergeant majors all snapped to attention to salute him. The major is morbidly obese, weighing in at about 300 pounds plus, his uniform looks fit to burst, and the buttons of his outfit take tremendous strain. In a very soft voice the major asked Liebenberg what in the name of God was going on. Liebenberg was still caught up in his fury, but now coupled with his embarrassment, he struggled to speak coherently, stuttering and spluttering about my gross insubordination. The prisoners were having a very entertaining morning, and I noticed some smiles in the ranks. I could not hear what the major said to Liebenberg, but shortly after their discussion I was escorted back to my cell and the army overall was thrown in behind me. I went down on my knees and prayed fervently to the great silence.

In the cell was a thin foam mattress with one worn grey blanket, a water bottle, and a white enamel potty. I was not brought any breakfast but later I was given lunch and then dinner. The next morning we were again assembled in the courtyard, and once again I had come to proceedings in my black underpants. Liebenberg noticed me and came storming with eyes bulging like a toad. Veins protruded from his forehead and grabbing me by the neck once again, he hurled me to the ground. Then he again took me by the neck, and shoved me up onto the balcony, shouting diabolical threats. On that morning there was a lieutenant present at the roll-call, the same one who was present when I first arrived, and he seemed to take my rebellion very personally. He stood in front of me and loudly commanded me to stand to attention, but I just looked at his feet and shook my head in the negative. He grabbed my jaw forcing my face up so that he could look into my eyes. He knew that he was staring at implacable defiance, his face turned wattle red with outrage, and he let rip with a torrent of threats spiced with a choice array of expletives. "You will regret this day prisoner, you will shit bricks. You will piss barbed wire, you mother fucker. You arsehole. You dip shit. Do you think you can fuck with us? You are nothing but a Kaffir turd, a cunt face. Do you hear me prisoner?" He grabbed the hair on my chest and ripped out a handful, and then wiped his hand clean on me. Sergeant Major Liebenberg then stepped forward and beckoned to the lieutenant, taking him aside for a discussion. The roll-call, cigarette and medicine ritual proceeded, and I was left standing, and there I stood until the prisoners who are called punished ones had finished their breakfast.

The prisoners were broken into groups, and most of them were taken to the parade ground to do intensive physical exercises. On the edge of this parade ground, which is about the size of a rugby field, stands one lone acacia tree. I was escorted to this solitary tree, and seated on a chair in the shade; as it was late January, the day was brutally hot and made more acute by the glare that shone off the forty foot high corrugated iron walls, which are bedecked with barbed wire. The prisoners always endure gruelling drills from breakfast until tea at eleven, then from tea until lunch and from after lunch until shower time. On this day however the intensity of the exercises was considerably ramped up. The telephone poles were brought out, and four men were assigned to each pole. The punished ones had to lift the poles, run with the poles above their heads, run with the poles between their legs, run with the poles on their shoulders, but at no stage were these heavy poles to touch the ground. Corporal Steyn and Corporal Youngblood took turns choreographing the punishment exercises. From time to time Steyn would point to me on my chair and shout, "You must thank prisoner Mackenzie. You must thank him for giving you the poles! Are you comfortable prisoner? Is it nice in the shade?!" After tea the tortuous poles were resumed, and these exceptionally fit prisoners were worked until they were absolutely exhausted. Steyn and Youngblood bellowed and roared, they threatened and raged, much like ministers of the Dutch Reformed Church. After lunch a new torture was devised for the punished ones. The prisoners were made to lie down on the hard clay ground, littered with stones, and ordered to roll repeatedly from one end of the field to the other and back again. "Are you comfortable prisoner? Mackenzie says you must roll again. Roll! The prisoner says you must roll again!" Some prisoners were vomiting, and others were obliged to roll through the discharged lunch. Blood began to seep through their overalls, on their elbows and knees, where the skin was wearing away. It is impressive how much punishment the human body can tolerate but at the end of the day these fit young men were tottering on their feet.

After the evening roll-call we were returned to the cell block. The guards who usually supervised the shower before locking us up quietly absented themselves, and that's when some of the prisoners attacked me. After being punched and kicked for a minute or two a prisoner who obviously had some sort of authority called off the assault and he was obeyed. I had blood pouring from my nose, and my lips were split. One eye was so swollen that I could not see out of it, and each breath I took was absolutely excruciating, my rib cage feeling like it had a blade stuck in it. One prisoner kindly helped me to my cell where I collapsed in severe agony and that night I could hardly sleep.

> *I am on Muizenberg beach looking out to sea. Storm clouds are gathering and then I see a tsunami approaching. It races towards me growing higher and higher as it comes. The wind is now raging and the tsunami turns a sinister green colour, rooting me to the spot. There is no way I can escape. I am very afraid and then I look down and notice with surprise that sitting next to me is a golden Labrador, who is faithful to the end.*

The next morning after our ablutions and cleaning our cells, we stood beside our doors waiting to be summoned to breakfast, but on that morning there was to be an inspection of the cells. The grim lieutenant came with some guards, and looked into every cell before asking each prisoner if they had any complaints. My turn came and I was standing in my underpants in my objector's stance. The lieutenant studied me closely for a good while before speaking.

"What happened to you, prisoner?"

"I slipped in the shower, lieutenant."

"You must take more care when you are showering, prisoner."

"Yes, lieutenant." He then instructed one of the guards to take me to the sickbay.

The military doctor did not ask me how I came by my injuries. "Your nose is fractured. You have two fractured fingers, and two fractured ribs. You have a sprained ankle. I will book you off physical exercise for a week but you can only stay in the sickbay for three days. That's the regulations." He gave me a painkiller, and I gratefully climbed into a proper bed with sheets. There was a Bible to read, and a fellow prisoner for company though I could not speak much because of the ribs. I thanked God for the chance to wash my underpants.

When my time in the sickbay came to an end it was the weekend, and I was confined to my cell, where I could not gain access to my painkillers. The powers that be probably deliberately forgot to provide them to me. On the Monday morning, the whole saga began all over again. Once again I sat on a chair under the tree, and yet again the prisoners were put through a hellish day. "Mackenzie says you must do it again! The punished one says you are arseholes! Do it again, the prisoner wants you to do it again!" During lunch there was much muttering, and those near to me made it very clear that they were going to deal with me more thoroughly this time around. That evening the guards once again absented themselves during shower time, and I expected a dreadful beating. I was trembling with fear, wishing I could take a wee before they gave me my hiding. The block leader whose name was Van Zyl called for attention, and delivered a short speech. Though very muscular, he was surprisingly small for a block leader, who as a rule tend to be big chaps. "We will not do the work of the military police. Why should we break this man for them? If any one of you even touch this man you will have me to deal with." Some of the more psychopathic prisoners were bitterly disappointed by the decree, but there was no dissent, and I was overwhelmed with relief and gratefulness. When the guards came to lock us up they were tremendously surprised to find me standing. My relief was a little premature as it happened.

I am in a room that is ill lit. I am sitting in a chair but I am also standing in the corner of the room watching myself in the chair. Then Dugald comes into the room and begins to punch the me in the chair. It is a vicious barrage of blows. Blood pours from my nose like a rope and blood dribbles from my ears and mouth.

The me in the chair just sits impassively. The me in the corner is becoming more and more agitated and anxious. I shout to the me in the chair. "Do something! Do something, for God's sake do something!" Then the me in the chair stands up and punches Dugald in the face. He falls down on the floor, and I awake.

The next morning I was left in my cell for the roll-call, but Corporal Steyn and his sidekick Corporal Youngblood came to pay me a visit. Steyn is an impressive figure of a man who stands at least six foot and four inches tall. He is the Aryan ideal, with blue eyes and blonde hair, and could be considered as good-looking in a Germanic way. Youngblood by contrast is a runt with the face of a flea-ridden ferret; his close-set beady black eyes and his elastic band lips are his best features. This incongruous couple share an avid devotion to the apartheid regime. Like many white South Africans, they fear being swamped and swept away by the Nubian hordes, and fear can make one fanatical, I know. They came into the cell, and closed the door behind them. I had been using my overall as a pillow, and Steyn commanded me to pick it up and put it on. "Sorry, corporal, I can't do that." He smiled slowly, revealing a fabulous set of dentures; the ferret developed a nervous tick, and his head began to bob like a randy pigeon. "Are you a nigger lover, prisoner. Are you a communist?" I will spare the details except to say they gave me a bloody good beating. Most of the punches were directed to my solar plexus which does not bruise easily. I did not offer any resistance except to instinctively try to cover my stomach and my broken ribs. "We will be back, prisoner." This was no idle threat for they did come back, the next day, and the next.

Then came a weekend of respite during which I was kept in solitary confinement. Come Monday morning I was expecting Steyn and Youngblood, but two other guards came to collect me, and I was taken for a cold water shower, where I had to shave with soap and a blunt razor. In my wet underpants

I was taken to the major's office, and there I waited for twenty minutes on the stoep before being ushered in. The major was sitting at his desk, with the national flag on the wall behind him, alongside a large photo of General Magnus Malan, and perched on a stand next to the major was a large fan blasting air from close quarters in the direction of his head. Even so the major was sweating like a sumo wrestler in the tropics, and with a very large hanky he repeatedly mopped his face and neck. The grim-faced lieutenant, also present, commanded me to stand to attention and when I failed to respond he advanced on me to administer his concept of justice, but was stopped in mid stride by a soft word from the major, which caused him to flush with outrage. The incensed lieutenant could not seem to unclench his right fist, and he stared at me with murderous menace. The major sat reading through a file, which I presumed was mine, and I could not help but notice with some astonishment how thick it was. After a while he looked up at me with his small watery blue eyes and smiled almost sweetly, and I was reminded of Olaf.

"Mackie. What happened to you?" he said, referring to my still black eye, my swollen nose, split lips, and the bandages on my fingers.

"I was assaulted, major."

"Who assaulted you, Mackie?"

"Two of your corporals, major."

"You liar! You fucking liar!" shrieked the lieutenant, springing forward.

"That's enough, lieutenant," said the major gently.

Once again he took out a large handkerchief and mopped his wet face, then his neck, and then his face again. The sweat was popping from his skin before he had even put away his handkerchief. My own cold sweat was trickling down from my armpits.

"Was it Steyn and Youngblood?"

"I would rather not say, major."

"So you do not want to lay charges?"

I looked at the lieutenant briefly, his eyes were boring into me with fury. "Only if it happens again, major."

"Listen, Mackie. I am prepared to make a deal with you. I will let you work in the kitchen, or if you want you can do cleaning duties, but you must put on the prison uniform."

"I will wear the prison uniform of the conscientious objectors, major."

"But Mackie, you are not a Jehovah."

"I have been to their meetings, major."

"Ja, but you are not one, and you could end up in civilian prison for many years." I remained silent. "Well, you leave me no option, Mackie. I am going to sentence you to seven days in the punishment cell on spare rations. Do you understand?"

"Yes, major."

CHAPTER EIGHT

That is how I came to be locked away in this dark punishment cell on spare rations, and I wonder, my darkness, what it will take for the powers that be to relent, and let me wear the uniform of the conscientious objectors? The cell has no light bulb and the window is snugly boarded over, so that it is pitch dark and very stuffy in here. In this black cell I have already learned a good deal about myself, and I am starting to perceive what happens to the human mind when it is subjected to sensory deprivation, my darkness. I have entered some sort of underworld. I think it was Dante who wrote of the netherworld, "Abandon hope, all ye who enter here!" I have never had much hope so there is not much to abandon. You can sing or you can pray. You can try to imagine the future or think about the past. You can entertain yourself with fantasies or you can sleep, if sleep will come. You can muse or meditate. You cannot do much in the way of exercises for broken ribs and lack of air and food. You can eat when you have food, and you can scream your crazy head off. It is not healthy for the young to be overly introspective, but under such circumstances one is compelled to look inwards. "Introspection is a morbid occupation," Paula said to me disdainfully on more than one occasion. I have little else to do but to try to recall from memory as much as I can about my life. I sit and think about every tiny detail, the good and bad, the trivial and the fantastic.

It has come as something of a shock to me to find that within a few days I have pretty much dredged up everything I can recall of my entire life from the age of two. It seems I have depleted the memory bank of my life's narrative. Surely not. Is the mind such a sieve? I try to remember the lyrics of songs, and find I know less than I had imagined. I search for all the poems I have read, and the movies I have seen. I try to remember all the books I have read, and I am disconcerted to find that I cannot even recall how some of my favourite books ended. I rack my brain for scriptures. In short I have tried to recall everything I ever learned, only to find that within five days I have exhausted the cupboard. There is so much less in me than I had thought or imagined, and I feel like an empty vessel. I recall my grandfather Jack once saying that the worst kind of poverty is poverty of mind. After five days in the punishment cell I have discovered that I am somewhat poverty-stricken. Now I have found that when you dredge up memories, when you hover over them, touch them, and taste them, you bring up with them more, so much more. Fondled memories bring with them emotions that have lain dormant and sleeping, and I have perhaps unwittingly unleashed a volcano within myself. Up gushes a rage that has been slumbering: it comes like some fiery dragon; up comes guilt, sorrow, and frustration like a frenzied tsunami. My body is wracked with love and hate, longing and despair, agony and ecstasy, all of which has me writhing about on the floor like a lunatic at times. I convulse and thrash like an earthworm sprinkled with salt, the sweat pouring from me, and at times a roar irrupts from my breast, to discharge the unnameable feelings I cannot bear. I have taken my finger from the hole in the dam, the dam has burst, sweeping me along in a torrent of flashbacks which I cannot stop. Memories now come that I did not want to remember. Emotions I never knew existed surge through me. I laugh hysterically, I cry bitterly,

I shout in rage, I swear at God, and then I beg God to forgive me. I pray fervently and pleadingly. I make promises and I bargain with the unknown. Even during my sleep the lava flows, the dreams come crackling and hot. I have dreams while awake and sometimes I am awake in my dreams. I do not know what time of day or night it is, and I am so desperately lonely. I am drowning in the blackness.

Each morning the cell door is unlocked and there are two guards with a prisoner. The prisoner hands me six slices of bread, a water bottle, and a potty. I give the prisoner my empty water bottle and my potty with "sweets". The door is then locked for another twenty-four hours. Today is day eight and I expect to be released. They have brought me a proper breakfast. Porridge, a boiled egg, two slices of bread and, my darkness, I must tell you that never in my brief life has food tasted so good. They bring me lunch, and I ask the guards why I am not being let out as I have done my seven days in the punishment cell. The guard calls me a couple of choice names and locks me in, and now they have brought my dinner.

I have been in here for three days on full rations and finally the guards have arrived after a proper breakfast, and they take me to the showers where I shave my ten days of beard and wash my rancid body. How beautiful the concrete prison looks, it is a thing of wonder. How marvelous the blue sky, it makes my heart leap. I hear a bird singing somewhere and am enthralled by its mystical tunefulness. The cold shower feels glorious, heavenly, and I drink till I am bloated. In my wet underpants I am led to the major's office. This time Sergeant Major Liebenberg and his bad mood is present as a witness. The major mops his sweaty head and stares at me for a long time with his piggy eyes. The fan is on full blast, flapping weighted down papers on the desk, and Liebenberg is slapping his baton against his leg. The major is kindly, and again offers me a place in the kitchen if I will only wear the military overall. Like Pontius Pilate, his hands are tied by the law. He can't allow me to be a conscientious objector as I have already done nearly six months of military service. This for some reason disqualifies me. He tells me once again, that one has to be a fully fledged member of a recognised religion like the Jehovah's Witnesses to qualify as an objector. I respectfully decline the offer of kitchen work and am sentenced to another seven days on spare rations in the punishment cell. Some prisoners on their all-fours are polishing the balcony, and they stare at me as I am led away to my cell and my hell. The door is locked and bolted, the dense eternal blackness envelops me, I fall to my knees and pray as I have never prayed before. I beg, implore, and beseech for strength, endurance, and courage. Oh my God, I am imprisoned by my apocalyptic self.

I do not want to think of the past any more, but it comes streaming of its own volition. Images of the past come like waves and wash over me, and I am drowning in my own dark self. I try to ward them off by singing but each song brings the past alive. Each song signals a period in my life and people in my life. It takes energy to sing, but in the breathless cell I feel weak and listless. I try praying, but images intrude, they irrupt and distract me. I try to remember what I have read in the Bible. Did Paul not say in the book of Corinthians, "You shall not be tested beyond what you can bear." Or did he say tempted? Maybe it means the same thing. Perhaps I am being tempted and tested and I do not know how much I can bear. Perhaps I can bear the unbearable. Or perhaps God has overlooked me, forgotten me, and I will be taken beyond what I can bear. I try to imagine a happy future, the things I would love to do when I get out of prison, but instead I find myself thinking of things that I enjoyed in the past, and not happiness but a painful nostalgia comes over me. I feel guilty for not fully appreciating those good times. Guilt and even anguish assail me for not realising how important those rare happy occasions were, how valuable, how fleeting. Even with open eyes I see images of the past, so clear and vivid, so remarkably real. It is astounding what the mind can offer up in a prolonged darkness and a steady silence. The dream world is becoming as real to me as the physical one; it is simply another realm now, another dimension. I try to recall the happy times but it is the difficult and traumatic events that insist on being seen and heard, and I am helpless against the onslaught. I lie on the mat quivering and endure the lashing as best I can. I let go and allow the images to come, and come they do.

I am two and a half again, and I wake up in hospital with my very own shocking red blood all over my pillow. I cough and fiery life blood comes out of my mouth. My hair is matted with blood, my lips crusted with blood. "Am I dying, Mom?" Paula is hysterical, shouting at doctors and nurses who are trying to calm her down. I think they are attacking her and start to cry. I have had my tonsils removed to alleviate the earache. Later I eat red jelly. Earache, terrible, agonising, excruciating earache. It is a horrific kind of pain that fills the head, consumes the body, and overwhelms the mind. Paula heats some sort of oil and pours it in my ear, ostensibly to soothe the pain but the pain is now searing beyond unbearable. My broken ribs pale by comparison. I am simply pain manifest.

I am five and back in hospital for a mastoid operation. The operation deafened my right ear completely though I did not know that at the time. It is the injections that want to be remembered, and with such a remarkable clarity. I did not know that the mind could remember so much detail, and retain such forgotten feelings. For five days after the operation I am given an injection three times a day. It takes three nurses to hold me down and one to inject me. I am already screaming hysterically as they surround the bed. The very sight of the glass syringe with its huge needle absolutely terrifies me, but I cannot take my eyes off it. With cotton wool the nurse rubs a cold liquid on my thigh where the injection is about to happen. I would come to loathe the smell of that antiseptic forever. The nurse cruelly holds the syringe up and flicks it, the nurse holding my head is berating me. "Stop being such a cry baby. The other boys don't make such a fuss!" The needle is jabbed into my rigid muscle, my body thrashes, and I emit a jet of wee that sprays onto the one nurse and she jumps back releasing my left leg which I now use to try and kick the nurse who is injecting me.

The cell door is unlocked; my heart pounds with fear, as air and light come flooding in; my six slices of bread have arrived. To my surprise Steyn and Youngblood are there, and I expect the worst. I am scared but this fear is nothing even remotely as terrible as the injection fear. That was fear raw and unrestrained, a primal thing. How did I forget such sheer terror? The fear I have now is mild by comparison, it makes me almost disdainful. It turns out that they are just curious to see me, to assess my state of mind. "How are you doing, Kaffirboetie?" enquires Steyn, with his large smile. I imagine that he could be a charming person to have a drink with. Youngblood's head bobs, his thin lips part to reveal little yellow teeth, and his rat eyes search for weakness. I am hugely relieved when they lock the door without administering a beating. The bread smells so good, it tastes absolutely wonderful: I never knew that plain bread was so delicious. I have learnt not to eat all six slices at once as it gives me heartburn.

> *I am walking in a desert of blinding white sand. The sun is tremendously hot in the huge sky, pale blue with brightness. I am walking in a very wide valley with a far range of rocky hills on either side of me. Many miles up ahead the two ranges converge on the horizon but somehow I know that there is a gorge between them, and I know this is the gateway, the exit. I look down at the ground and notice with surprise that I am walking on a multitude of skeletons.*

What is this desert of the dead with hundreds of millions of skeletons bedded down? Countless bones. Am I that barren and dead wasteland? Is my soul a barren wilderness? I am certainly in a wilderness, lost and alone. Why am I walking through the land of the dead? "Though I walk through the valley of deep shadow I fear nothing bad," sings David's psalm. Are those the bones of our ancestors? All those who have lived and died since the beginning of human time. I have perhaps walked over them oblivious, ungrateful. Not any longer. I can hear the scrunch of my footsteps on the bones of those who have laid the ground of this world I walk through. There is an exit up ahead and even though it is far off it gives me hope to know it is there. Will I make it to the exit, my darkness? What of the scorching, blinding sun, is that the world of reason and rationalism, which scorches everything with its light? For no apparent reason I am back at the hospital and it makes my body fearful; I remember the smell of the place and my legs tremble. Dugald takes me in and there is Paula lying in a bed. She is there to have a baby. We bring Mom some Black Magic chocolates and I put my hand on her big tummy and feel the baby kicking. I am so hoping it will be a brother.

> *There is an aeroplane about to take off and then I notice that tied to the back of the plane on a long rope is a tricycle, and on the tricycle is a small boy. The plane takes off and I watch with trepidation. The little boy clings on to the handles with all his might. I think to myself, "That pilot is crazy. How does he expect the child to hold on. Then the pilot does loop the loops and he flies over some power lines and dips the tail of the plane so that the rope is severed and the boy and the tricycle fall to the forest below. I am tremendously shocked by this.*

It is my third birthday, my darkness. Here I come down the stairs holding the banister tightly, and there in the lounge is a glorious red and white tricycle and it turns out that it is for me. A thrill of huge excitement surges through my little body, and since then no other acquisition has given me the same intensity of unspeakable delight. I am electrified by this gift and cannot believe that I could be so lucky. Mom is delighted by my ecstatic response. I ride my new tricycle all day long, and never for one moment do I become bored. Dugald tells me to come for my lunch, but I want to eat on my beloved, and he becomes tremendously angry. After some fuss Paula intervenes and I am allowed to eat sitting on my tricycle much to Dugald's annoyance. That evening we are going out somewhere and I want to bring my tricycle. Dugald says no, it must stay at home. I sit on my tricycle and will not let go. Dugald forcibly dislodges me.

I am seething with rage and fury and scream till I turn blue in the lips, then Dugald, now enraged with frustration, picks me up and holds my head under the kitchen tap and pours cold water over me. Paula is screaming at Dugald and they argue aggressively. Paula wins and I get to bring my tricycle which I insist in sitting on. Furious, Dugald is shouting at me and whacks me twice across the head as he places me and my tricycle on the back seat of the car, but I will not let go of my life's joy. Paula is shouting again, Dugald relents and so we drive off with me sitting on my true love. Still they argue and bicker. Dugald snaps, he stops the car and takes me and my tricycle out of the car and puts us on the pavement. He climbs back in the car and drives off with Paula screaming at him. A woman walking by sees me, and takes me to her house where I am permitted to stay on my tricycle. Dugald was obviously obliged to come back within two minutes, but I was not to be found. Now he has to go from house to house until he knocks on the door of my hostess, who gives him a vicious dressing down. I am still on my tricycle as the irate Dugald carries me back to the car.

It is my fourth birthday. I am taken as usual to my crèche which is on the roof of an eight storey building in Hillbrow, but this time Mom brings a cake for me to share with my crèche mates. On my rest blanket is a picture of a teapot with a rhyme, "I'm a little teapot, short and stout … Tip me up and pour me out". At lunch time the supervisor brings out the birthday cake; she places it on the floor and we all gather around. It is an exquisite chocolate locomotive with a driver waving from the window. The supervisor slashes off the nose of the train, and hands the slice to another boy. I am enraged that she did not give me the first slice, and because she mutilated the train, so I dive forward shrieking and grab the slice from the boy. She scolds me and puts me in the crying room, and I am so incensed by the injustice of it all that I scream my head off. Two supervisors come into the room and force me to drink something like cough mixture which makes me drowsy and I fall asleep. I can feel that rage now, so very keenly. I would dearly like to give that bitch of a supervisor a hard slap across the face.

CHAPTER NINE

In 1961 when I was four years old we moved to Honey Street in Hillbrow. It is the first house I can remember in some detail. I can see the L-shaped stoep with its red polished floor as if I saw it yesterday. How I cycled up and down that balcony. Paula was twenty-two and Dugald twenty-three years of age, and loads of friends came and went. Some of the men had long hair and wore beards, some had musical instruments and they would jam with Dad who plays the clarinet and harmonica. It was a sort of open house and on most mornings I found someone sleeping on the couch, and more than once even in the bath. Stella was about one and a bit and Paula was pregnant with Laurie. It snowed in Johannesburg that winter, a rare occurrence in that part of the world, and I remember urinating in the snow and turning it yellow. Paula would sometimes read me a story when I went to bed, and strangely enough she taught me how to pray. "Gentle Jesus meek and mild, look upon this little child, please God look after Mommy and Daddy, Roddy and Stella, and please look after all the creatures great and small. Amen."

I kept up this ritual with only minor alterations until I turned eleven. It is odd now to think that Paula who declares herself to be an atheist taught me to pray. She never did that with the girls. Honey Street holds some of my happiest memories. I first met Jack while there when he came and lived with us for about three months. Paula had not seen her father for something like five years, and I had not even been conscious of his existence. I was delighted to discover my grandfather and we got on extremely well.

I had a little girlfriend who lived in the house next door. I probably would not have remembered her but for one event. My little girlfriend and I had somehow or other consented to undressing, and I was lying on top of her naked body in the driveway when Dugald looked out the kitchen door and spotted us. He was morally outraged and bellowing like a wounded ox. He ran over, picked me up by my arm, and spanked my naked bottom furiously. "You dirty boy. You disgust me!" Paula emerged to see what the commotion was and there was an almighty row. For all Paula's wantonness, Dugald is prudish, priggish, and moralistic, as any devout Presbyterian can be. What we did was innocent; there was simply a desire for closeness. I remember that while I was lying on top of her I felt happy, and I wonder if she can recall that incident.

Hillbrow has a Catholic cathedral and one morning Paula and I were walking past it, and upon some sudden impulse she decided to go in and pray. We were probably in dire straits financially. Paula sat in a pew with me sitting next to her, and then she actually kneeled and said a prayer. I was tremendously impressed by the huge stained glass windows which were predominantly yellow. To my knowledge Paula never saw the inside of another church from that day forth.

One evening Paula and Jack had a monumental row. Jack packed his suitcase and I did not see him again for nearly two years. Laurie was born six weeks premature, probably because of Paula's excessive use of tobacco and alcohol, and she came home from the hospital without her baby. I wonder if that is why she never bonded with poor Laurie. Time is surely one of the strangest of all phenomena. It flies by when you are having fun, and it drags and stretches when you are suffering. Young people spend most of the time wishing their lives away, waiting for the next holiday, the next party, the next weekend. Certainly that has been true of me.

In the darkness with no morning and evening, time becomes stranger still, and it seems to play tricks. I go to sleep and when I awake I expect to receive my bread within the hour. Many hours pass, with much thinking and praying, remembering and waiting, and finally I fall asleep again. I awake, starving, ravenous, mad with hunger. I see food clearly. I can damn well smell it. Roast chicken and potatoes with gravy and green peas, and it is torture. Finally the door opens. The guards step back in disgust as the bottled up stench of my potty and unwashed body exhales from my hermetically sealed cell. Eating a diet of bread alone makes the "sweets" stink like death itself.

I am startled from my sleep by the door being unbolted. What, is it bread time? Or are they pissing with me? They were here only a few hours ago. I don't even need to change my potty. I speak to the prisoner as he hands me my water and bread. "What day is it?" "It's Sunday." "No fucking talking, do you hear!" shouts the guard with severe acne.

Now time is all but standing still; each second falls like the stroke of a whip. My body clock has gone for a complete loop, I have left the orientation of the time zone. I wonder if any of my schoolmates ever think of me. I doubt it. When you are nineteen you are always thinking about tomorrow, next week, and next year. You think about those you are going to meet, and only very occasionally and fleetingly do you think of those you have met. Why not? Life is so full and busy, so very hectic, so much to be done: everything exciting lies in the future. Here I am though, engaged in this unnatural business of wondering what my friends are up to. Remembering things we did together, conversations we had, the arguments, the laughs. The adventures and misadventures. I miss them all more than I could ever have imagined, or is it just desperate loneliness? In a silent black hole it seems that time can even flow backwards. The past is now so much more alive than the future.

Monday comes and I expect to be seeing the major again. They bring me a full breakfast consisting of two boiled eggs, two slices of bread, and porridge. A feast fit for royalty. Then joy of joys comes a full lunch, to be followed by a whole dinner. The next day is thankfully the same. It's only on Wednesday that I am taken for a shower and shave, by which time I stink like a hyena's den. My mattress and blanket are rank, for they reek with the foul odour of my fearful sweat. In the mirror I look pale and gaunt, and my eyes look slightly crazed. I am kept waiting outside the office for nearly two hours. I don't mind, for I am so enjoying the intoxicating air, the abundant light, and all of the magical sights and sounds. A little white cloud bobs merrily across the bluest of serene blue skies. Prisoners are marched by, and each face is a fascinating story. I notice a little weed with tiny delicate pink flowers heroically growing from a crack in the cement. Finally I am admitted into the major's office. He is sweating like a baker, and the fan is swirling on the double. The major is in a hurry today, probably because it is nearly lunchtime. He makes the kitchen offer again and when I politely decline he does not bother to sweet-talk me, but hastily sentences me to another seven days in the punishment cell on spare rations.

I am five years old again. I am walking through a garden centre. The plants are in clay pots, wooden boxes, and even in tin cans. The cow manure is in hessian sacks, there are geraniums with lilac, white, and purple flowers and I think to myself, "How different it is in the future." I come to a table where some children my age are sitting and I say to them, "Hello I am from the future," and I show them a picture of a computer. Nearby are some men standing around a radio listening to a boxing fight. I see Steve Marosvich as a young man and I recognise the other men too. "I know who is going to win that fight," I say.

"Who?" asks the one man. "Jack Dempsey," I reply and they all laugh. Then I walk along and come to a hexagonal swimming pool and there are some women with their children swimming about. I sit next to one woman on the side of the pool and we hang our legs in the water and I say to her, "Is this a jacuzzi?" She laughs and says, "What is a jacuzzi?" I walk along and here is Dugald sitting at a table under a tree. I sit in the chair next to him but he ignores me. He is eating scones and cream and they have his full attention. I walk down a slope and go into the house through the back door. I enter a lounge where there are a number of children and two women, but the first thing that grabs my attention is an armchair. It is covered in a green paisley pattern and the material is fastened with large brass tacks. I am astounded that I can see this chair so clearly in every detail down to its paws. I had utterly and completely forgotten that we ever had such a chair. Then my attention is drawn to the two women who are seated side by side on a couch. I know that one is my mother and that the other is my Granny though I am not sure which is which. Their faces are made of mud and they look very similar. After looking at them for a while I decide that the less ugly one on the left is probably Mom. I then walk into the centre of the lounge and most of the children stand around me in a circle. I begin to dance and sing. "Let's twist again like we did last summer, let's twist again like we did last year." The children all dance in synch with me. Then I see a girl with ginger hair sitting on a cabinet. I go and stand on the chair next to the cabinet so that my face is level with hers. I say "Hello Queenie, it's good to see you again." I kiss her pale white forehead gently and wake up.

My darkness, I thought the mind was a sieve but I was wrong. Now I find that the mind remembers far more than most people would believe possible. I realise that I am the same person now as I was when I was five. My essence is exactly the same. I did not become a loner out of choice or by disposition. My family's itinerant lifestyle and our perpetual poverty largely cut me off from any consistent socialising. I imagine that exceptionally few young humans willfully choose the loner's road. The masses huddle together in cities and towns where the lights never go out. We are social animals and the vast majority of people dread being alone for prolonged periods, and as a species we tend to suffer from an almost universal fear of the dark. Darkness is perceived as dangerous, for what we cannot see we fear. My darkness, you release the haunting ghosts of my mind, and I cannot escape them. On the upside, our poverty led to an adventurous and unconventional lifestyle. When one of my friends told me that he had lived in the same house for all of his seventeen years of life, I was horrified. It sounded so utterly dull.

It is often glibly stated that silence is golden. Yet the truth is that the majority of humans detest silence, many are even terrified of prolonged silence. This is why incarcerating a human alone in a dark, silent place is considered a severe form of punishment. Add to this little concoction the deprivation of food, and one has a recipe that has been found to have remarkable efficacy as a modifier of behaviour and attitude. This form of punishment has proved over and again to produce servility and compliance in the internee. I am starting to waver under the strength of darkness, the power of silence, the frailty of aloneness, the lashes of time, and the pangs of hunger. I am so lonely, feeling so fragile, and self-pity, that most loathsome of emotions, has come to drown me. My brain is no longer under my direction, if it ever was. I cannot control or repress the images that come to me. I can't direct my thinking for more than two minutes at a time, and I feel a bit crazy now and then. I have known hunger often in my brief life but never ever a maddening hunger like this. Images of food are more frequent, the tables groaning under the weight of glorious food and at times I even try to grab it. The more hungry I become, the grander the feasts that appear. Such images probably propelled our cave-dwelling ancestors to heroic efforts. Killing mammoths with little stone-headed spears, facing down the ferocious sabre-toothed tigers, trekking across vast deserts. My dear body, I would kill a lion with my bare hands if I could. Please stop sending me visions and smells of food, so that my saliva runs and my stomach howls.

I'm also desperately uncertain as to whether God is with me or not. Why should God be concerned with this insignificant speck of very dubious character. I am a scintilla that is almost completely invisible in the grand scheme of things. In fact I am not really sure about this being called "I" any more. I took it for granted that I knew who I was, it seemed self-evident. Now I am uncertain, confused, and disoriented because the I seems to have become we. We have fallen into dissociated parts and we fight one another. Thoughts come into my mind I feel sure I did not generate, but I am also not sure. Voices speak words that are not of my making. All my certainties are going or gone, dissolving into chaos. Are there independent thoughts produced by the brain or some part of the brain? Thoughts of the body or perhaps the central nervous system? It seems to me that before there was only one voice in my head and that was my own. Now there are other voices and they say things I could never have thought, they are a conflicting cacophony and sometimes they even speak with different accents. Images I do not want come and though I try to resist them, ultimately I must submit and endure them. My God! My Father! I am sinking and fragmenting. Sometimes I do think of something funny, or something funny thinks in me, and I laugh out loud, but then immediately worry that I am losing my mind. In these narrow walls my laughter sounds like a manic cackle and it makes my skin crawl, my darkness. It sends a shiver down the spine. Perhaps silence is a prerequisite if we are to allow the still quiet golden voice to come through. I wait and listen, I look for the shimmer in the blackness.

The door is unbolted and unlocked. My daily bread has arrived. Hallelujah! There is a new guard who I have not seen before, and he is adorned with a pug nose which looks like a sawn-off shotgun. At first I think he is smiling but it turns out to be a fixed sneer, his top lip curling back like a growling dog. Acne Head is with him and they make for a pretty pair. The prisoner takes my potty and empty water bottle, but the new guard does not lock up, he wants to talk. I am surprised when he speaks to me in English because he looks like an Afrikaner. "Why do you want to be an objector, hey? Are you scared of fighting on the border?"

"I am searching for the Kingdom," I reply.

"But you are not a Jehovah's Witness, you were in the army!" he shouts accusingly.

"I have been to some meetings with the Witnesses," I reply.

"I was a Witness. My family are Witnesses, but I decided to fight for my country," he shouts righteously, now red in the face. Acne Head is becoming very uncomfortable because talking with the punished prisoners is not permitted.

"As Jesus says, when salt loses its saltiness it becomes worthless and must be thrown outside," I reply.

"Don't you fucking talk scriptures to me, you hear? I know the Bible better than you."

"Yes guard." Pug Nose slams the door closed and I am left thinking. On reflection I regret my quotation of Jesus's words about salt. I find somewhere in me a respect for Pug Nose, for he was indoctrinated as a Jehovah's Witness, yet for whatever reason, he has ventured to find his own mind. We share something in common, him and I.

"Darkness my old friend, have you come to talk with me again?"

Well, we moved from Honey Street to a flat in Park Town North and there we had a black maid who looked after Stella, Laurie, and myself during the day while Paula and Dugald were at work. I think she was an agreeable soul for I would completely have forgotten her, but for one incident. We were in the communal garden that fronted the flats one sunny day, and she was playing with me on the lawn. Suddenly she had a terrible fright, and falling to her knees she began crawling along the lawn towards the hedge, where she cowered in terror. Her large chocolate brown eyes were rolling in fear. "What's wrong?" I asked. "Shoo," she said with her finger on her lips, a look of abject fear on her face. "It is the police," she whispered. Her panic was so palpable and so apparent that I too was gripped with fear, and I huddled up next to her. I did not know then that black people had to have a special permit to work in white residential areas. Those who were found without them were dealt with harshly. The illegals who did not have the required permits were much cheaper to hire than those with permits, so whenever we did have a maid it was usually of the fearful variety.

In that same flat I had a tricycle accident. I rode into a large iron ashtray attached to a heavy metal stand, and gashed my forehead on the rim. God knows where my parents acquired this contraption as I have never again seen another ashtray like it. Looking back I suspect that it was home-made. I was rushed to the emergency ward of Johannesburg General and was given a local injection and five stitches. The doctor praised me for not shedding a single tear during the procedure, and I was extremely proud of myself. Paula fell pregnant with Samantha, and this time she did cut down radically on the vices, and we moved to Bryanston Farm. I wonder if a life without accidents, without beatings and operations, one without fear and rage, terror and fright, is a forgotten life. Some of my friends seem to have no memories of their lives before the age of seven.

I am walking through an ancient forest and I am struck by how huge the trees are. Eventually I come to a beautiful open dell where the sun pours down like honey. This little vale is bedecked with green grasses interspersed with joyous wild flowers.

I stare entranced at this peaceful and pretty place for a while, but suddenly I notice that on the far side of the dell something or someone is moving between the trees. I catch only fleeting glimpses of this shadowy creature and with my heart anxiously pounding, I wonder if it is man or beast. Then I catch another brief glance of the creature and it looks like a large man with a ram's head, and I freeze in terror. I furtively sneak behind some trees and climb a steep bank to make my getaway. After a while I emerge from the forest into bright sunlight feeling greatly relieved. I stop to take a pee on the dry ground and I start to wet next to a meadow flower, a sort of buttercup, with the intention of giving it some water, and then to my surprise a jet of water spurts from two small ant holes in the ground and showers all over me. The water sprays over my face and chest and I wake up startled.

Where from this strange primordial forest so heavy with ancientness? Who is this beast man? I have escaped him for now but will he not surely hunt me down? I had the feeling that he was looking for me. Drawing ever closer. I am deeply honoured that mother earth should baptise me when I poured my urine on her parched surface. I cannot shake off the tremble and shudder of the beast man though.

In this dark place, cut off, blinded, silent, the real world seems increasingly unreal, a phantasmagoria. Now my inner world of dreams is becoming the more real world, a sort of parallel universe. Without the distractions of "normal" life my dreams live on vividly long after I wake up. Sometimes when I am thinking about a dream I go right back into it, and the drama continues while I am presumably awake. Some of my dreams leave a strange atmosphere which pervades the cell, the characters and mood lingering on. Sometimes I realise I am in a dream, and then I take especial notice of my surroundings, and it always amazes me how fantastically detailed the psychic world is. In one terrifying dream I even thought to myself,

I wish this was a dream so that I could awake from it. In some cases I have woken up after a dream, or at least thought I had, only to wake up yet again. Those dreams are always tremendously impressive. I often wonder who the dream sender is? They are certainly not of my making, they come from a source of nature, they are the language of nature. They seem to be from a non rational dimension. Some perhaps come from the soul, and she speaks in symbols and metaphor, and with emotions and images. Many dreams are bizarre to the rational mind, their language is strange and fantastically effective. The Bible is loaded with dreams and dream interpreters. Yet Christianity and her shepherds set no store by these treasures from the deep. The Divine often communicated with the prophets, mystics, and saints in dreams, which makes sense to me. Somehow one can deal with the uncanny far more readily in a dream than in waking life. In a dream one seldom questions how it is that one is flying without wings, breathing under water, talking with a swan, for one is sort of anaesthetised to what we call reality. The Talmud says dreams are letters from God. Yet it is fair to say that most people nowadays leave these letters unread; they stick them in the bottom drawer. When Jacob dreamed of the stairway to heaven his compatriots did not doubt that he had been granted a glimpse of the divine realm. Today anyone making such a claim is ridiculed or given shock treatment. Real and unreal, do I know any more? All certainties are melting. Why have I chosen this path? Or has this path chosen me? Is Armageddon really coming? I am not so certain any more. Faith is not really something you can choose or discard.

It is something that happens to you and like love it is a wound. It comes like a thief in the night, and it can part of its own volition. It seems to me that we are afflicted with faith, or we are not, and the cause for either state is never rational though we tend to give rational explanations for our faith or our lack of it. I am afflicted with a "faith" that Armageddon is coming in the not too distant future, even though I did not choose to believe this. My rational brain baulks at such an absurd idea. Yet from another side of me, from a side I cannot shake off, I have this conviction that the riders have already come. That pale horse of famine is with us as a quarter of the world goes to bed hungry each night. The red horse of war rages everywhere. The black horse of pestilence and death is rampant. They come charging because humankind is largely severed from the sacred and the profane ground of being. Most of those who claim to believe in the myth which they have inherited from their forbears live now off a diet of dust. They believe in a redeemer but do not feel redeemed. They believe in grace but never receive it.

Severed from our natural heritage, by our rational mindedness, we live perilously close to self-destruction. Now we wait only for the gentle Jesus, the rider on the white horse to come charging with his satanic sword of light held high. That will be an almighty bloodbath. Humankind will pay a terrible price for losing contact with the divine ground of all myth. I can see the cities falling, the fat cats plummeting. Those sanctimonious shepherds of Christendom, and other religions, huddling in their confessional, as their cathedrals of hypocrisy crash down on their self-righteous skulls. Earthquakes, tsunamis, hailstorms, and floods will devour the masses, who have raped the earth. Nations turn their deadly weapons of light on one another as political and religious ideologies clash. Political ideologies have replaced religion, and they too demand exclusive devotion. I long for the coming of this righteous war and I pray for it. I can see Liebenberg shitting in his pants. Bring it on gentle Jesus, bring it on!

I am lying on a couch lost in deep contemplation, in a basement room which is dimly lit. I look up and notice a large python come into the room through a dark hole, and it glides along against the far wall. It is a pale snake, about six metres long. I sit up and say, "And where are you going?" The python then

*turns and comes directly towards me. I become anxious and
wary as she slides past me, and just as her head comes level
with me the snake rears up with her dreadful fanged mouth
wide open to bite me. I grab the python with both hands tightly
around the neck.*

I am in mortal danger. My dark contemplations have unleashed
the sleeping and hidden forces of my mind, which at bottom
touches on that other realm, and now those forces have come
sliding into the darkly day of perception. The pale python of
the depths, this goddess of the underworld, threatens to swallow me up. I am indeed swallowed up by the darkness of this
cell, and I am caught in the darkness of my soul and mind,
but I cannot allow myself be devoured by this python. I must
resist being swallowed up in my own self, and I must get a
grip. I have stopped doing what little exercises I used to do.
I feel weaker with each passing day, and I am losing far too
much weight. I'm weary of singing the same old songs. I am
exhausted from praying to the galactic void. Darkness, you
have come as a python to devour me, but I will resist you.

I must not be consumed by the psychic realm which is also
a real world.

CHAPTER TEN

Another seven days of spare rations are up. When my breakfast is brought to me I am suddenly overcome by emotion; the smell and taste of the oat porridge, buttered bread, and boiled eggs bring tears of gratitude welling up. I eat the eggshells with my bread. I was expecting the guards to take me for a shower, and then to a trial but many hours drag by and finally my lunch is brought to me. Chicken, beans, pumpkin, and mashed potato. I eat all the chicken bones and they give me heartburn. The afternoon slowly trickles by like cold bitumen, and still they do not fetch me. The next day I am surprised when after breakfast Steyn and Youngblood unlock the door. I assume that they have come to collect me for my shower, so I step forward towards the door but suddenly Youngblood punches me with a straight right to the chest which has me reeling backwards. They both rush into the cell and begin giving me a barrage of punches. All of a sudden Steyn exclaims, "Jesus Christ! Jesus fucking Christ!" and gagging, he runs from the cell. The runt rapidly follows him. The rotten stench of me and my putrid cell has taken them completely by surprise, and has totally defeated them. Steyn and Youngblood stand in the passage, gasping for breath; they are both a bit green in complexion and for a while they curse me with strangled voices. "You stink worse than a Kaffir! You filthy pig, you disgusting dirty fucking pig! We are not finished with you, prisoner! When you have been scrubbed we will come and deal with you, you arse wipe!" They lock me up with my appalling pain.

This morning Acne Head accompanies my breakfast and with him is a new guard whose mouth hangs open like a filter feeder, revealing long rusty teeth. I decide that this creature is desperately thick, probably inbred, and name him Cadbury.

"I have run out of toilet paper, and I want to see the major," I say to Acne, who has puss oozing from every pore of his tortured face.

He instructs the prisoner to fetch a loo roll. "The major is sick," says Cadbury, who looks very anxious as if he suspects that I might make a mad charge at them. I notice that his baton is at the ready.

"I want a shower, I haven't had a shower for ten days," I say to Acne.

"There are no instructions to give you a shower," he says, before returning me to the darkness, where the image of the unfortunate duo of Cadbury and Acne stays clear in my mind for many hours.

1962 A.D.

I have many vivid memories of Bryanston Farm, after all it was but fifteen years ago. These snapshots and sequences are mostly in a jumble with no linear time sequence. Even so it's all too easy to go back there, to that solitary house, and be the younger me again. The rooms of the farmhouse were huge, compared to our former homes and the ones to come. There were wooden floors throughout the house, except for the kitchen which was tiled with cement blocks which were polished a deep red. I was fascinated by the large coal stove which was kept burning pretty much day and night. With the farm came Jenny and Smuts, two huge blonde Great Danes who had a propensity to howl at the full moon. I have never since come across any other dogs who do that. I was also fixated by the old piano which stood in the living room and I would spend hours making music with two fingers. Then there was John, the houseboy as he was called, though he was a man. John was born in Rhodesia like me, and he was for a brief time to become like a father to me. He cleaned the house, made the beds, polished the floors, looked after us children, fed the chickens, and tended the vegetable patch. He milked the cows, made cream and butter, cooked our meals, bathed us children, tended our wounds, and I ran after him like a puppy. Built like a brick shithouse, I remember him as a gentle, hard-working man with a radiant smile. Not long after moving to the farm I turned five and shortly thereafter I began to attend primary school. I was unfortunate in that my first ever teacher took a strong dislike to me. I was repeatedly forced to lie over her ample lap to receive two stokes from her wooden ruler for having dirty nails, or no plaster on my festering farm sores, and other misdemeanours I cannot even recall. The hidings were not painful but they would leave me smarting with humiliation. Looking back, I realise now how completely inept I was socially, as the only children I ever interacted with were Laurie and Stella who were two and three years old.

Paula and Dugald would drop me off at the bus stop in the morning on their way to work, and when I came home John would be at the bus stop to pick me up and walk me the two kilometres back to the farm, carrying my suitcase and holding my hand. We use to talk, but I cannot remember what about. I loved watching the cows being milked, and I was absolutely mesmerised by the sight of the chickens being slaughtered, how they flapped about without their heads, as blood jetted from their necks. I formed a close bond with Smuts, especially after the farmer next door shot Jenny for trespassing. I received my first really serious beating from Dugald for hitting Stella.

In the years to come I would have many more beatings on Stella's account.

Out of the blue, Anthony came to stay for a few weeks. I had never met my wild uncle before though I had overheard something of his notorious reputation. Three years younger than Paula, he was just twenty-one years old when I first met him, and I loved him on sight. He arrived in his camouflaged army uniform, with a rifle slung over his shoulder. He had roughish good looks, and struck me as a sort of male version of Paula. I loved his big army boots, his hunting knife, and his loud booming laughter. I did not know at that time that he was a mercenary in the Congo, committing unspeakable atrocities for money. He would come and visit every few months for the next two years, and I grew to adore him in part because he spoilt me, but more so because he showed me a lot of affectionate attention. Much to Paula's consternation he bought me a pellet gun and taught me to shoot. He also gave me lessons in boxing, and he would seat me on his knee and tell me the most outrageous stories. Like Jack he found much of what I said highly amusing and I delighted in making him laugh. He is also an alcoholic but of the binge variety. He can go for days or even weeks without a drink, but when he does indulge, he will drink to fantastic excess. Then he flips from wild hilarity to violent rage and back again, and his eyes roll about in his head like a madman. When he and Paula became drunk together, the situation would inevitably degenerate to sordid depths, they would become embroiled in the most ghastly rows, and Anthony would depart under an acrimonious cloud.

Samantha was born while we lived there and once again I was very disappointed to find that I still had no brother. I was essentially alone much of the time, especially at the weekends and during school holidays. There was a drive-in cinema not far from the farm, and we would go there every second Friday. I was hidden under a blanket on the floor behind the driver's seat so that my parents did not have to pay for me, and the girls being under five years old were allowed in for free. One afternoon after school I was hunting for slow-worms, and for some reason I jumped over a bush and landed with my bare foot on a broken bottle which sliced a deep gash in it. I lost an astonishing amount of blood and poor John did not know what to do except to bandage my foot with a sheet. That night when my parents came home, they took me to the hospital where the doctor put seven stitches in my foot, and gave me an anti-tetanus injection. I did a poo in my pants on the long bus trip from school; the kids rapidly located the source of the smell and jeered at me. I emerged from the bus weeping, and John carried me home and washed me. I can still feel that complete humiliation now. Stella and Laurie caught the mumps and in an effort to infect me, Mom made me sleep in the same bed as them, but with no success. Laurie and Stella both peed in their bed, and I woke up wet and stinking of urine. They both wet their beds until they were nearly nine years old, and I can only suppose that this was because they were more or less in a constant state of high anxiety.

Paula bought some Pekin ducks as there was a small river at the bottom of the farm, and when they were fattened up she sold them in Chinatown during the Chinese new year and actually made a good profit. Flushed with this minor success, she increased the flock greatly and hired Daniel, a tall black man who had no tongue, to look after them. The ducks followed this mute obediently from the pens down to the river, had a good swim and happily followed him back up the hill. Not long before the next Chinese new year Daniel and 300 ducks simply vanished. Paula said that he probably walked into a waiting lorry, the ducks loyally followed him, and that was that. For years after that Paula would tell her friends that it was the Chinese mafia who had stolen the ducks.

Paula decided to grow cut flowers for market and it looked like it might be a great success. Up came acres of bonny flowers, and just before we were due to begin harvesting, a devastating hailstorm arrived which flattened the lot in one hour. That was the selfsame storm when Dugald shot the roof to bits. It was the end of the cut flower venture, and our savings. The earache returned with a vengeance and I underwent the first of four ear operations, in the by now familiar Johannesburg General Hospital, where I received my three nightmarish injections a day, and I ended up missing the last six weeks of the school year.

Dugald expanded the chicken runs using an assorted range of second-hand building materials, even old tables and cupboards. He repaired the antiquated heating system which delivered hot water through pipes into the chicken runs, and all our spare money was poured into breeding more chickens. He regularly brought home boxes of golden pullets, and these lived in the kitchen near the coal stove until they were big enough to go into the coops. Sometimes in the morning there would be one or two pullets lying with their feet in the air, and I would give them a solemn burial, and commit them to gentle Jesus. On one such occasion as I was giving a sermon for the deceased, Paula said in her strange prophetic voice that I would become a priest. One night we came home from the drive-in to absolute pandemonium. John and his two girlfriends were in a high state of agitation, and Smuts was barking frantically. It transpired that the pipes had burst in the chicken runs, and most of the chickens had been steamed alive. "We just can't win," said Paula.

One of our cows, named Mary, had a male calf, and when it was about seven months old Paula decided that we must slaughter this poor creature. As the condemned bullock was tethered to a tree stump, Paula told me to go indoors but I so wanted to see the execution that I begged her to be allowed to stay, and for once Dugald took my side. John came to the proceedings with a large axe, and it being a Saturday afternoon he was probably mildly inebriated on milk beer. My parents were definitely a bit worse for wear. John seemed to be very hesitant about the proposed methodology of the execution, and suggested that it would be better to sever the jugular vein with a knife. Dugald however was insistent that the axe was the best tool for the job, and he showed John the exact location on the neck where the blade should strike. I can see it all so very clearly like it happened yesterday. John raised the axe high above his head, the bullock's eyes rolled in terror, the axe came down opening a gash on its well-muscled shoulder and the helpless beast bellowed mournfully. The second stroke also missed the mark, struck the shoulder blade and thick blood began to pour out of the wounds, but the sturdy creature remained standing. Paula began shouting at John to do the job properly in the name of Christ Almighty. Again he brought the axe down with all his might, and again the blade was wayward and once again it found the shoulder area rather than the neck. The mournful bellowing then became more insistent, even desperate, and I began to weep for the blighted creature. John's girlfriends who had come with buckets to carry away their share of meat also began to shout and scream, while Dugald was barking instructions frantically. The air was absolutely alive with madness. Poor beleaguered John then began chopping at the neck as if it were a log. Emitting a vulgar stream of expletives, Paula dashed to John and grabbed the axe from him. "You foolish bloody wog! You simple, stupid Kaffir, can you not fucking well do anything right?" Dugald ran to the house and a few eternities later he came charging back with the Luger which Jack had brought back from the war. The forlorn bullock was by then bleeding profusely from his numerous wounds, and his large eyes looked desperately sad to me. Dugald fired a shot into his forehead, and the bullock went down on its knees, but with a Herculean effort it struggled valiantly back to its feet. Dugald fired off a few more shots into the forehead of the beast, and finally the poor creature found peace. It was a truly gruesome spectacle; it was sad, and yet it was also utterly compelling.

I thought a lot about death after that and for a while I felt guilty about eating meat.

Jack came to visit us at the farm with his new wife who is called Noreen Royce, and after a few whiskies he sat down at the piano and played some exquisite classical music. I remember saying to him, "You never told me you could play the piano, Jack!" and he replied, "That is because you never asked me."

Soon after that I went to stay with Jack and Noreen in their sumptuous city apartment which is bedecked with Persian rugs and bejewelled with fabulous antiques, tall grandfather clocks which chime on the hour, and large polished tables with ornate legs. The walls were furnished with tapestries and many large oil paintings, and there were numerous silver objects on the mantelpieces. Their apartment was on the eighth floor and it overlooked the beautiful Joubert Park, and just standing on the balcony and watching the frenetic city from those dizzy heights was endlessly thrilling to a rustic farm boy like me. I went to stay with them at least once every two months and Jack and I would always go to the barber for a haircut. We sat side by side, me on a plank straddling the arms of the chair, and after being groomed we would go to the vast Johannesburg city library and change our books. As a six year old this grand old library with more than a million books simply boggled my miniscule mind, and it ranked alongside Johannesburg Zoo as one of the seven wonders of my world.

On the way home we would drop into the butcher, and buy a specially prepared joint for our Sunday roast. Every time I visited Jack during the next three years, we would follow this same comfortable routine. The dining table would always be set with flowers and gleaming silver cutlery, and I was trained to use the utensils in the correct order and manner. Jack insisted that I eat my green peas with the fork the correct way up, and I was taught to stand up for women on the bus, and how to shake hands when being introduced to people.

Apart from the discipline of school these visits to Jack were pretty much my only civilising influences. Noreen is a genteel and otherworldly type, with hair that is white, and she dresses like those female movie stars from the 1930s. She speaks in a low throaty voice with a plummy, upper class English accent, and she smokes her twenty cigarettes a day in an ivory and gold cigarette holder. She makes liberal use of a perfume which smells like jasmine blossoms and wears quirky hats long out of vogue. She always wears pearl necklaces along with dazzling brooches and earrings, and she used to talk to me as if I were an adult and assumed that I understood the meaning of words like "prerequisite".

I was nearly six when I shot Stella in her right shoulder with my pellet gun. I honestly thought that my gun was unloaded, and I can only surmise that I did it subconsciously. For this moment of stupidity, I received a particularly brutal beating with a cattle whip, and my beloved gun was bent in half. Even so, it was one of the few hidings which I felt was deserved as I had been intentionally scaring my sister. Shortly after the shooting, we moved to the Ship House.

The guards have come to take me for a shower and shave, and I am so grateful as it is eleven days since I last walked in the fresh air of day. Cadbury orders me to march, and gives me a punch to the kidney when I do not comply, but Acne Head calls him off. I have this feeling that Acne feels a certain sympathy for me. The fresh air is like champagne, I gulp it gratefully and it makes me feel high as a cloud. The prison seems very noisy, as my ear has become unaccustomed to sound, and is somewhat overwhelmed by the influx of information. I cannot deny that I am feeling a little stir crazy. I have to restrain myself from whooping. In the shower I notice that my once black armpit hair has turned ginger from being coated in salt and folic acid for days on end. When your world is shrunk to a needle point then small things assume great importance.

Looking in the mirror is to look at a stranger. "Who the hell are you?" we both seem to think. I have these scary moments when my reflection seems to genuinely be another person. My world is definitely becoming more surreal, or is it that my eyes are being affected by the perpetual darkness? For a few bizarre moments I thought that Acne Head was made from plastic. The major seems more gargantuan than ever; he has large blue pouches under his little eyes, coupled with a dangerous purple tinge to his lips, and his sweat continues to flow relentlessly from his face and neck. He has barely put the huge handkerchief away than it is out again to do another mop-up job. He has my file in front of him and he studies it for a while before looking up and speaking to me . "Your mother has been making enquiries about you, my boy. I have written her a letter explaining why your writing privileges have been suspended. However, I am going to allow you to write a short letter to her so that she knows you are well." Lieutenant Grim steps forward and puts a pen and writing pad on the table, and gestures to me to begin writing.

Dear Mom,

> I have declared myself to be a conscientious objector. The powers that be are most disaffected by my decision, and have sentenced me to a stint in solitary confinement. Apparently my writing privileges are suspended, and I will write again when they are restored. You need not worry, as I am well. Please give all my love to the girls and Gran.

The lieutenant steps forward, and taking the letter he reads it before translating it into Afrikaans for the major. The major tells him that the letter is acceptable, but the lieutenant who censors the prisoners' letters is seriously unhappy, and vehemently remonstrates about the phrase "the powers that be" but to no avail. "Look how thin you are becoming, young man," says the major to me, and it seems like his eyes are genuinely brimming with pity. Perhaps for a 300 pound man to see my scrawny body is a positively distressing sight. Maybe his very worst nightmare is the thought of being deprived of food, the very punishment he is obliged to inflict on me. "I am worried about you, young man. Very worried. If you just put on the overall I will let you work in the garden, or you can work in the kitchen."

Before I can give my routine reply there is suddenly one hell of a commotion outside, with much screaming and shouting and running boots. The lieutenant is out the door in a flash, the major heaves himself from his chair, and lumbers after him, leaving me standing. Someone's boots bang across the corrugated roof above the office, and the pursuers pound after him with much shouting. I am desperately keen to look at my file lying on the table, but I know that if I am caught there could be serious consequences. I step forward and turn the file to face me and open it on page one, and to my complete astonishment, I find myself looking at a photo of the five-year-old me, complete with a smile. It is a school photo, taken during my first year in an educational institution, when we lived on Bryanston Farm. I turn some pages, and am again amazed to see yet another school photo of me taken when I was in standard three, along with the results of an IQ test, and my school report from the end of that year. There is even a health report from a school medical we had to endure when I was in year nine. I remember that medical well. We had to stand in a line to be examined by large matronly woman dressed for authority in a white overcoat. After the blood pressure test, we had our temperature and pulse taken, then our hearts were listened to, and our naked bodies were perused from top to bottom. Then the matron took our testicles in a firm grip, and made us cough a few times. I asked Paula about that, but she could give no plausible explanation for that embarrassing procedure. Then come the results of my year nine IQ test, and the headmaster's assessment of my character, which at a quick glance seems reasonably favourable. My IQ score has dropped a few points with the passage of time. Then there is a photo of me taken during my last school year, taken only what, eighteen months ago, but that face looking back at me seems to me like someone I knew in a past life or from a dream. "Is that me?" My final results for my O levels are even in the file. Good Lord, the apartheid regime has a dossier on every white boy in the country. Noises coming, I put the file back and retreat to my position, standing like an innocent statue. False alarm, but I dare not look at the file again. The major finally returns with huge rings of sweat under the armpits of his taut jacket and he takes a while to recover his breath under the blasting fan, while mopping away at his saturated head. The lieutenant returns a few minutes later, and for a while they discuss the attempted escape before resuming the trial. It sounds like the captured escapee has wounded some of the guards. I am sentenced to another seven days in solitary confinement on spare rations.

I thank God that I am not a black person, or I would probably have long since perished in some fiendish fashion. Still, I am increasingly concerned about losing my mind, and some of my crazier thoughts make me anxious. I think there are toxins in my body that are affecting my brain function, as I am probably living off my own muscle tissue. Yet I still have space to be afraid for humankind, all those billions who are out there running about oblivious to my existence. Do they not see that humankind is rushing towards disaster on a colossal scale? It seems to me that the world has become largely soulless, obsessively materialistic, shallow, and degenerate. We are rushing headlong like a freight train towards self-destruction. However, I am caught in the dark tangled forest of myself. Why am I afflicted with this notion of the end? There have always been those people who proclaimed the end of time. Were all of them deluded? Why am I so afflicted with this delusion? I must remember the blue stars, and she who walks with me by the silvery river of life. Time is creation and destruction. Perhaps there needs to be a destruction.

I wake up, and to my surprise I find that I am in a cave, lying on a sandy floor. The cave is perfectly egg-shaped and it seems to be made of sparkling granite. There is a man with me, a comrade, and I assume that he is holding a small candle. I notice that the small round entrance to the cave is blocked with a ball-shaped stone. My companion puts out his hand, and holds the light before my face, drawing my attention to it. I see that he is not holding a candle, but rather a small round flame which is dancing magically on the palm of his hand. As I watch this mysterious little flame it becomes brighter and brighter, till it shines with a brilliant phosphorescent white, which is so intense I have to look away. I am concerned lest "they"—the people outside the cave—might see this light and find us.

Then I really awake and though I am back in my cell, I find myself in a state of ecstatic bliss. My tortuous hunger has magically vanished, the pains of my body have ceased, and I feel lighter than a moonbeam. My mind is very clear and sharp, yet I do not have to think. I lie unthinking for a long time, and I submit my being to the clear holy ecstasy. There is truly a divine light in the human breast, and I feel utterly blessed to have experienced it. It is grace and redemption, it is undeserved kindness. This small flame was all the time buried in me, this slumbering God in my own being, and I have stumbled upon it in the deepest darkness, in the bowels of the earth, in the deeps of my dark self. Small and fragile though it appears at first, the flame of life has immense power, and the more you look into it the greater it becomes, till it is beyond bearing, and then it explodes like the cosmic birth of a dark star within.

What is more precious than this eternal divine light that resides in us? Has life any meaning without you, wondrous light? I do not think so, for you, dear light that lies in the

101

darkness, are life itself. The light and the dark belong to one another, they are meaningless without each other. Thank you, my dark egg of nature, for birthing the divine light. Oh sacred light, you desire to become conscious in me!

I hear a commotion and quickly put on my underpants which I do not wear for hygienic reasons. I put my ear to the door, and try to hear what is going on. Someone else has been sentenced to the punishment cells, probably the guy who tried to escape, and he is being locked in the cell next door to me. He seems to be kicking up a tremendous fuss, and it sounds like they are forcibly manhandling him to his doom. Finally I hear his door being locked, and the guards retreat with much muttering and cursing. My fellow inmate has found his chamber pot, and begins to smash at his metal-clad door with it, while roaring an impressive array of obscenities. I expect him to relent after a few minutes, but he keeps up the tirade for hour after hour. At times it sounds like he is kicking at the walls. Finally he stops and I am not sure, but I think I can hear him weeping. A few hours later he starts up his banging and shouting with a renewed urgency; he is smashing his chamber pot with great force against the walls and I wonder if the bloke suffers from claustrophobia. It certainly sounds like it.

This morning when they unlocked his cell he tried to make a dash for it, charging at his guards and making it halfway up the stairs before they catch him. By the sounds of it, he puts up a tremendous fight, whistles are blown, reinforcements arrive, and eventually after what sounds like a considerable battle, they manage to subdue and incarcerate him. He goes absolutely bananas for the next few hours, and though I find the racket extremely irritating, I am also seriously concerned about the poor chap's state of mind. His chamber pot must be trashed by now, beaten to a lump for it has long since lost its ringing tones, and it sounds like he is bashing his door with a stone. I marvel at his endurance, for he keeps up the shouting and banging for many hours at a time. Eventually he stops and all becomes eerily quite, the hair stands up on my neck, and my skin goes all chilly goose bumps. I shout to him but he does not respond.

This morning when they brought our rations he is found dead. Lots of people have been coming and going, and much serious murmuring and discussion is happening out there. I am caught by surprise when suddenly and unexpectedly my door is unlocked, and here is my friend Steyn. He beckons me to the door, and I approach slowly while my eyes accustom to the light. Lying on a stretcher is the dead prisoner. His green eyes are still wide open, fixed with an unholy terror, and only God knows what he saw in the dark. There is a patch of skin missing from his forehead, and I wonder if he charged the wall with his head. The young man has been bleeding from the ears, the eyes, and his nose. The medics pull a cover over his stricken face and carry him away. Steyn smiles at me with a broad delighted grin. "Not long until they come to take you away, prisoner," and he shoves me in the chest, and I back into my cell. He takes something from his pocket, and throws it on the floor. "This is for you." I fumble in the darkness to find that he has thoughtfully given me a razor blade.

I am in a serious state of shock and find that I am shaking all over. I have seen dead people before, in car accidents, and a drowned person hauled from the sea, but this is different somehow. His dead face and his eternal stare is very clearly imprinted on my mind's eye, and I cannot erase it. Surely there will be an inquiry, and I wonder if I will be called as a witness. I have as yet had no inclination to suicide, but I am increasingly worried that the urge or desire might come and overwhelm me. Suicide might have its time and place, but right now, I so want to live. Now the guards come every few hours to open my door to check that I am alive. It seems I am on suicide watch, but at least my cell is receiving a bit more fresh air.

CHAPTER ELEVEN

ven though we only lived at the Ship House for about six months, there are many memories of that place which still haunt me. They have come visiting, my darkness, they have come to life again, and make me a child of six years old once more. We actually lived in the ex-caretaker's dilapidated house, situated about 200 metres from the Ship House itself, which had once served as a clubhouse for the wealthy. It was a very large building built to look like a ship, with porthole windows, a funnel, and even an anchor. Large cracks had developed in the poorly engineered prow of this concrete ship, the building was declared dangerous, and the club was abandoned and boarded up. The extensive gardens had once been professionally landscaped, but these had been allowed to relapse into an overgrown wilderness, and the tennis courts were in a terrible state of disrepair. I loved the place instantly as any small boy would as there was so much exploring to do, and so many hidey-holes. It was the perfect place to be a small Tarzan.

The Jukskei river ran close to the house, and it was lined with a forest of mature willow trees along our stretch of water. I found a way into the Ship via a broken porthole, and with the penlight torch Jack had given me, I regularly explored the abandoned building. The furniture was covered with large dust sheets and the gloomy interior had a spooky feel that sometimes made my skin crawl, but my curiosity was always slightly more powerful than my fear of bumping into a ghost. I can smell the neglected wood of the Ship House even now. There was a large hall with a sprung wooden floor, which had in better times been used for ballroom dancing, and I set up my secret world in there. I was now at Lyndhurst primary school with a nice teacher, and I only remember getting into trouble once. During a singing lesson I whispered to the pretty girl next to me that I would like to make babies with her when we were grown up. She was very distressed by this suggestion and began to sob. Asked by the teacher what the matter was, she wailed, "He says he wants to make babies with me." The teacher was understandably shocked by my proposition and she promptly banished me in shame to stand in the corner.

I wonder what in hell I was thinking when I said that, my darkness, I don't think I knew then how babies were made. I did ask Paula how babies were made when I was about five years old and I remember her telling me that Dugald had planted a seed in her. I recall being content with the explanation as I had planted corn and sunflowers and had watched them grow to four times my height. One weekend while I was hunting for tadpoles I fell into the river, and sank like a stone, as I had never been allowed to swim because of my ear problems. I was strangely calm as I sank down to the river bed; I could see the sun shining on the surface of the water and was even struck by the beauty of it. Fortunately for me Anthony was sitting on the patio drinking a beer, so he dived in and pulled me out. I was banned from going near the river from that time on, which meant I went there more than ever. I remember that afterwards Paula said to me in her prophetic voice, "You need not fear water or drowning, for your death will be that of a martyr."

It was on the banks of that river that I had my first divine experience. I remember that it was a gorgeous sunny day, and I was sitting under a large willow, lost in some reverie of hazy wonder. It must have been spring for there were carpets of wild flowers and clouds of butterflies flouncing about. The willows hung like huge spring green curtains and swayed in the gentle breeze. The bright yellow weaver birds were busy weaving their marvellous nests on the ends of the pendulous branches which overhung the sun-sparkling water. All of a sudden, I became aware of how tremendously beautiful it all was, and I was struck by a deep and stunning sense of unspeakable wonder. A peace and tranquillity overcame me such as I had never known, and I wondered if an angel was present, or gentle Jesus himself. I looked about expectantly but saw nothing uncanny except for the unspeakable beauty of the natural world. I did however feel certain that the trees and the river knew I was there, just as I knew that they were there. Butterflies landed on me and languidly cleaned their gorgeous wings, and I felt honoured. It was suddenly the most enchanted garden, and it was the most holy two hours of my six years of life. Thereafter, I would often go to that same spot on the river bank and wait for that wondrous experience to reoccur, but it did not happen again. The butterflies would not land on me again, even though I sat as still as a stone and willed them to. I told Paula about the experience some years later and she said, "You were such a lonely boy, my darling."

Not long after the holy presence, I experienced the profane. Memories of my parents are few and fleeting from that period except for two occasions. Paula and Dugald threw a party which was attended by many friends and friends of friends. A makeshift bed was made for me in my parents' bedroom in case my bed should be needed by someone who became excessive, and during that night I was constantly woken up by the raucous racket of the loud music and the rowdy intoxicated adults. At some point during the night most of the revellers took their leave, and Dugald drove some of them home. He had scarcely departed when Paula and some man came into the room, stripped off their clothes and bounced about together on the marital bed. Paula had probably forgotten about me. Some light came in through the partially open bedroom door, and I could see the two of them bouncing up and down on the bed, him on top of Mom, and they made some strange noises. It was all over in about three minutes and when they stood to put on their clothes, I pretended to be asleep. I did not understand what they were up to, but I did know that whatever they had done, it was wrong, very wrong. It became my terrible secret until I confronted Paula with it when I was about sixteen. That was the first and last time I ever saw her blush.

As usual I would take the school bus home, and then walk about a kilometre down a dirt road to the Ship House, and one day when I returned home there was a car waiting in the driveway. A man and a woman emerged from the vehicle, asked me my name, which they wrote down, and then somehow or other they persuaded John to stand next to me while they took a photograph. I pretty much forgot about the incident until the next day when Dugald and Paula returned home in a terrible fury. It transpired that the visitors were journalists from the *Rand Daily Mail* and the photo they had taken had appeared in the newspaper. I was in my school uniform and John was holding a handful of marog, a sort of wild spinach which grows in damp shady spots along the river bank. The article explained that there was almost no food in the house, and it described the children as malnourished and wearing threadbare clothing. It went on to claim that the houseboy was feeding the children on Kaffir spinach. To my terrible distress, Dugald punched John about, as if it were all his fault. The following day the social services arrived, and explained to my parents that they were seeking a court injunction to have us children taken into care. I was sent to stay with Jack's brother and his family in their posh Houghton mansion and there I met my wealthy cousins for the first and last time. When I came home two weeks later we had moved to Siesta Guest Farm, and I found myself yet again in another school.

CHAPTER TWELVE

*My family have a little garden centre near Hout Bay harbour.
I am standing with the girls waiting impatiently for Paula, who
is trying to convince a couple to buy a rather forlorn-looking little tree. She is wearing a tatty brown coat and is mildly pissed,
her thick mane of blonde hair is tangled and matted. The black
labourers are waiting for me to drive them back to the township
but I cannot do so until Paula is finished. Stella hands me a letter in a blue envelope which I put in my pocket. Then suddenly
I look to my left and I see a young man riding on a black horse
and a white horse. He has a foot on each saddle. For some reason
I am alarmed by this attempted escape, and run in front of the
charging horses, and hold up my hands to try to stop them.
The horses split apart and the rider stays with the white horse
which comes to a halt, but the black horse veers off to the left and
runs up the side of a very high wire fence. I am worried for this
black horse as I am sure it will be hurt. The black horse somehow makes it to the top of the fence, but to my consternation he
plunges down the other side and out of sight.*

I wake from the dream but I cannot open my eyes. A very
strange sensation comes over me, there is a weird high
pitched ringing in my ears, and I am convinced that something terribly evil is in the cell with me. I break out in a cold

sweat as a terror of the uncanny seizes me. I struggle to open my eyes, but realise with horror that my body simply will not respond. The evil being grabs me around my throat and begins to strangle me, while I am desperately struggling to breathe. I try to pray. "Please God, help me, in the name of Jesus please help me!" Suddenly the being lets me go, my eyes open to the darkness, and I gasp for breath. What the hell was that?! Was it the Devil or an evil demon, was it the beast man, or was it my crazed mind? I have experienced terror often in my short life but never like that. That was absolute evil, sufficiently harrowing to shatter the mind. Is that the black horse I rejected? I rejected the darkness that belongs to the light. Now it has come, and I must accept it if I would heal myself.

Satan plays an important role in the Biblical narrative. He is there at the beginning of humankind's awakening, as the serpent who opens the eyes of Adam and Eve to the knowledge of good and bad, and this birth of consciousness makes them aware of their nakedness. They became self-conscious and thus discriminating, and they could now call things and deeds good or evil. They could now say this is light and this is dark. Consciousness was born and with it suffering. No longer could homo sapiens live in Edenic bliss. Satan is there in the book of Job talking with God in a heavenly council, arguing before the myriad angels, that Job, the only righteous man on the face of the earth, should be tested and severely at that. Here Satan is still in the company of God who actually agrees to Satan's diabolical proposition with only one caveat, that the life of Job must be spared. On that occasion God and Satan worked together, as did the black horse and the white of my being once ride together. When the divine light manifested from the darkness of Jesus he saw Satanael cast down from heaven, where he had dwelled since time began. The black horse had fallen and became the responsibility of humankind. It was we poor mortals who now copped the blame for the darkness. We were suddenly to blame for the existence of evil. While the Dark

Lord is restricted to the earth, God in his heavens remains split, he is Christian, all good, all merciful, all light, all white, all male. Split in twain. There is no darkness in the Christian myth it seems, except in man. Satan plays a leading role in the last book of Revelations, rousing the Antichrist to battle. After the heavenly army's victory, Satan is ostensibly imprisoned for a thousand years. Yet Satan is not destroyed or extinguished. What is a thousand years in the scheme of things? A mere jot. It seems that the universe cannot be freed of evil. We live now in the time of the Antichrist. It is now time to restore the darkness to its origins, to its rightful place in heaven. The Antichrist has arisen. It has come as rationalism, and a host of other isms. It has come as communism, materialism, and realism. It has come in the form of science and reason. Science has become our new myth, and so-called realism claims the sole devotion of billions. I remember a book by Hermann Hesse, where he writes about the god Abraxas who is both good and evil, and so transcends good and evil. Satan is part of God, and thus can never be destroyed. Can the light exist without the darkness? Do they not belong to one another in holy matrimony. Christ needs to be united with his dark brother, the dark horse, and then can there can be a synthesis between the sacred and the profane. The Christ and the Antichrist. Between sense and non-sense. The rational and the non-rational. Science and religion. I am sinful and good. I carry good and bad in my heart, and I must wonder if the evil part of me can be rooted out? God cannot be rid of Satan after all. Am I being attacked by the darkness, the evil I have longed to root out and reject? Does the beast man in me seek acceptance? My desire to be pure, sinless, good, and righteous has caused me to split myself in half, to reject the black horse. Did Jesus not say be as sly as a serpent and innocent as a dove. What a paradox, for that is akin to saying be evil when necessary, and good when necessary. Did Jesus not become darkly enraged with the money-lenders at the temple and throw their tables over, and make

111

a whip to flay them? Did Jesus not curse a fruitless fig tree with dark venom so that it withered? Did not Jesus parley with Satan his dark brother even if he did say, "Get thee behind me." Jesus was wrong, for his dark brother is most dangerous when he is behind us, where he is forgotten, to our peril. Did not Jesus descend into Satan's hellish domain for three days and three nights, was he not crucified between thieves, to give us a balanced image? Did God not allow Satan to murder Job's family, destroy his flocks and his crops and inflict Job himself with agonising boils. Questions, I am drowning in questions, my darkness. I am thinking the unthinkable or is it thinking in me?

The door is unlocked so I slip on my underpants and stand up rather unsteadily. They have come to check that I am alive. There is a new guard with Cadbury who I have not seen before, and like a snake he appears to have no lips. I come to the doorway to present myself and Snake Lips punches me on the arm. Before I know what I am doing I have grabbed him by his jacket, and I have pulled him into the cell, where I ram him up against the wall very hard and his cap falls off. I wrench his baton from him and say, "Don't you touch me you fuck face or I will kill you, do you understand!" Cadbury is blowing his whistle loudly, while fumbling to un-holster his pistol. I throw Snake Lips out of my cell and his baton and hat after him. More guards arrive to find Snake Lips in the crouch position threatening me with his drawn pistol which is aimed directly at my chest. In the meantime Cadbury stands like a pillar of salt, with his mouth hanging open like a cave. The corporal shouts at Snake Lips to put his pistol away twice before he finally responds. I am standing in my doorway incandescent with rage even though I am expecting an awful beating, but to my surprise the corporal just locks me up.

I have lost track of time completely. I am lost in my past, I am trapped in the present. I am not sure if I am on day six or day seven of this bout in solitary, so I am very surprised when a proper breakfast arrives. When the guards depart I unexpectedly break down crying. I have never been so grateful for anything in my entire nineteen years of life as I am for this humble breakfast. They have come to take me for a shower and a shave but instead of taking me to trial they return me to the cell.

The guards have come for me again and they escort me to the sickbay. A doctor examines me, my blood pressure is taken, and I am weighed. I have lost twenty pounds from a lean body. After my medical, I am ushered into another room and told to sit down in a chair. After a while a woman in military uniform comes in, so I stand up. She is young to be a captain, and she flushes when she sees that I am in my underpants. Someone ought to have briefed her.

"You may be seated," she says. She spends a minute arranging some files and stationary, while she regains her composure. I am sitting mesmerised.

"I am a psychologist, and I have come to do an assessment of you," she tells me.

I haven't seen a woman for about a hundred and seventy thousand years. She has dark brown silky hair which is cut short, but in a feminine style. Her large brown eyes are graced with thick long eyelashes, and her quizzical gaze simply melts me to a puddle. She is handsome rather than pretty, with a strong jaw, full lips, and a soft creamy skin. I can smell a faint alluring whiff of a citrus based perfume, and I notice that she is wearing tiny pearl earrings on delicate ears which look like pink seashells. My attention is drawn to her small shapely hands and her slim fragile-looking wrists, with fine bones, and I have to make a concerted effort not to stare at them. Her observant eyes notice that I am studiously scrutinising her physical attributes. Thank God there are women in the world; what an unbearably brutish place it would be without them. It's as if I have come from the gunpowder room to a kitchen of freshly baked bread.

She asks for my home address, and stupidly I tell her I do not have one. "Where do your parents live?" she asks me in puzzlement.

"I do not know, the last I heard of them they were staying with my grandmother, but I doubt they are still there." It occurs to me that this is not a good beginning. The shrink is kindly and speaks with soothing dove coos. I find myself beginning to be unmanned by the situation, and I must make an effort to get a grip on myself. I so want to put my head on her bosom and cry like a baby; I want to be comforted, to feel solace.

She asks me about my military service. "What was it like in Kimberly? Did you have a rough time?" she enquires. She fixes me with her frank gaze the way lovers do, and I have to ask her to repeat the question.

"No, it was much easier than I expected. Physically anyway. I was fit when I started my service."

"Was it mentally difficult?" she asks, searching my eyes for the truth.

"No, not really, I was in an Afrikaans boarding school for three years. That school had girls, and that was about the only difference to the army," I reply with a smile, but she does not find my analogy amusing.

"You were on the Mozambique border," she says checking her file, or should I say my file: her eyes are again locked on mine, waiting for me to comment.

Her neck is elegant and so delicate, it would be so easy to snap it. Some of the gorillas in here would be able to wrap one hand right around it. The brutish male heart is sometimes softened by such a slender sight. Her soft mouth evokes tender feelings which well up from some buried depths. My mind has been in war mode, in grim survival mode, and in that state the gentle blossoms are so easily forgotten. All memory of tenderness fades.

"The border? I loved it there. A beautiful place. Like a holiday camp but without a swimming pool," I say, though once again she fails to respond to my attempt at humour. She is searching intently for the true state of my mind, and she knows that I have my defences up.

"So what made you turn against the army?" she says more as a statement than a question.

"It's nothing personal. I have turned against the system which claims that their actions are sanctified by God. I will not have God's will dictated to me." I find myself starting to preach, and have to bite my tongue, because I sound like a religious nutter, even to myself. She makes notes for the first time.

"Are you a pacifist?"

"No. I do believe in self defence. I believe that evil is sometimes necessary," I add. "I believe the war between the Christ and the Antichrist is being waged. The war between the sacred and profane." I can't help myself, even though I know it probably sounds bonkers to her. I have been isolated for far too long and I have lost control of my tongue. Stuff just spouts out of me unbidden.

For a brief moment it occurs to me that maybe I should let her think that I am insane: it could extricate me from the punishment cell but then again it could land me in a loony bin. She is wonderfully non-judgmental. She is not outraged or incensed by my ridiculous beliefs, nor does she seek to dissuade me or deride me. I have no need to be fanatical in the face of such acceptance. She asks me a bit about my childhood, where I went to school and so on, and I effortlessly put an overly positive spin on the narrative of my youth. Loving parents, close to my sisters, enjoyed school by and large, played sport, sang in the choir, etc.

A guard knocks on the door and asks her if she would like some tea, and she orders tea for two much to the guard's consternation. There are some chocolate biscuits brought in with the tea, and she insists that I eat them all, which I do.

Out of the blue while I am in mid-sentence about my ideal childhood she says, "Are you against apartheid?"

I sense danger in this question, but I do not want to hesitate too long before replying. Psychologists are very suspicious of hesitations. "I have mixed feelings about apartheid," I reply, and she just stares frankly waiting for me to elaborate. "I do not like the fact that black people have no rights, nor the way they are treated, but I am not sure that they are ready yet to govern the country. Anyway, my reasons for objecting are religious and not political," I say, and I hold my tongue. It is perhaps only my imagination, but in her eyes I read agreement with my sentiments.

We must have spoken for about an hour and a half, but for me it was all too soon when she indicates that the interview is over. "Am I sane, captain," I ask her rather facetiously as I stand up.

Again she shows no response to my attempt at humour, and she stares at me gravely for a few moments before replying. "I think that you are of sound mind, and I wish you well," she says, and finally she allows herself a brief glimmer of a smile.

Back in my cave I think of the interview over and over and over. She is so not my kind of woman, yet I am still besotted by her femaleness, her gentleness, her compassion, her slim neck, her large brown eyes. Eventually the darkness swallows her up, and the images from within rise up and come to visit uninvited. The child in me is still alive, he walks down dirt roads, he is surrounded by people but very alone. "The child is father to the man." I think it was Wordsworth who wrote that, my darkness, and now I understand what he meant.

CHAPTER THIRTEEN

1964

Siesta Guest Farm was a sort of kibbutz, and the inhabitants were mainly young working couples with children. We all resided in red-roofed bungalows arranged in a large double circle facing inwards towards a communal park. There was a large canteen which served breakfast and dinner, a day crèche, and a communal swimming pool. Once again I had to walk down a long dirt road to catch the school bus, for we always seemed to live off the beaten track. I learned to swim with the help of earplugs, made friends with Queeny who has ginger hair and skin like milk, and I learned to ride on Rikki's bike. Rikki's dad had a car accident and lost his right arm, which fascinated me, and I offered to try to find it. I had my first real fist fight there; it was with an Afrikaans boy, and some adults had to tear us apart. That was the first and the last time that Dugald ever gave me some praise. The boy's father came around to complain and Paula told him to stuff off, then Smuts bit him on the calf muscle. Ben and Jill Sayers moved in next door to us, and they became Paula and Dugald's best friends for the next eleven years. Jill is from England, she is five years older than Ben, and she has two children from a former marriage, dark-haired Isabelle who was seven, and blonde blue-eyed Patrick who was two years younger. Jill was a conventional housewife and she became a second mother to me. She is sweet-natured and kind, motherly, and good–humoured, and I would spend a lot of time with Patrick who became the little brother I had always wanted.

One night I was awoken by the racket the drunken adults were making. I could hear Paula and Ben arguing, and my ear pricked up when I heard my name mentioned, so I sneaked down the passage and stood near the lounge door. Paula was telling them about my real father, and Ben was arguing to the effect that I should be informed that Dugald was not my biological father, with which Paula vehemently disagreed. I had already intuitively suspected that he was not my dad, but still I felt bereft to hear it spoken out loud and remember feeling sad for weeks after that.

I turned seven at Siesta Guest and we went on our first real holiday. We hired a bungalow at Shaka's Rock on the coast of Natal, and I saw the ocean for the first time. That first sight of the ocean was a stupendous experience, which filled me with conflicting emotions of fear and awe. A short while later a neighbour came around to complain about the racket, and Paula and Ben ganged up on the fellow and told him to piss off. The result was that the Sayers and we were evicted, and we all moved to Yeoville, which is a large town that borders the city of Johannesburg. There we shared a double storey house with the Sayers. They stayed upstairs, we lived downstairs, and Patrick and I went to Yeoville primary school together, which was just a three block walk from our home.

I am in a tunnel under the ground walking with some trepidation. The tunnel is something like a mole's tunnel with earthen walls that have roots coming through. There is no obvious source of light, but I can see my way. Then to my surprise I see a little man, no more than two foot tall; he is dressed in a green suit with a blue shirt and yellow boots, and he puts a finger to his lips to indicate that I should keep quiet. He waves me to follow him, and he disappears through a hole in the wall which I had not noticed. I follow him through the hole, and come into a large living room of a farm house. Again I am astonished for there is another little man sitting on a bookshelf way above the floor, next to a cuckoo clock. He too is in an elaborate outfit, a blue suit with a green shirt and red boots. This Noddy character is apparently being punished. I bump against something, making a noise in the process, and a stern male voice comes from another room, and says, "What are you up to?" In a voice quivering with fear the little man on the shelf says, "Sorry, I just bumped my foot." "You be still, do you hear," barks the farmer from another room. The little man in the green suit leads me on tiptoe to a serving hatch in the wall. This serving hatch connects the kitchen to the lounge. I leap through this hatch and land in the kitchen, and again I am surprised. Sitting at the table is a florid-faced farmer who is in a bad mood. With him is a large woman, and yet another little man with a fancy outfit who sits quietly at the table. The glowering farmer's wife says to me, "I know why you have come." She stands up and offers me a chocolate cake. "Here, this is for you," she says, approaching me. I put my hand to her chest, to keep her at bay; her eyes become red with rage, and at the same time I take a knife from my pocket, and in a patricidal act I stab the farmer in the neck.

My seven days are up, and today I will have breakfast, and then lunch and then dinner. I don't think I can go on any more, please let this be the end. After breakfast I wait hopefully to be taken for a shower but no one comes until my lunch is brought. It's Snake Lips and Cadbury. "I am supposed to see the major," I say to Snake Lips. "He is not here today," replies Cadbury, much to the annoyance of Snake Lips. "You will see the major when he wants to see you!" says Snake Lips. I am not sure if it is three or four days that I am kept waiting to see the major but finally Pug Nose and Acne Head arrive and they take me for a shower and shave. My eyes struggle to see clearly, and my ankles are very sore. I look in the mirror and my gaunt face keeps blurring out of focus. There is a new lieutenant present at the trial, by the name of Brand. He has studied law, and now he is a lawyer for the defence force. Like Lieutenant Grim, he too commands me to stand to attention. The major tells him to leave it be, and he seethes with fury. He seems to have an aura of black and red about him which reminds me of the German flag. Blotches of white and red pulsate on the skin of his beaky face like some agitated octopus.

There is no greater sin for this type of person than insubordination to the state. I know this type well: they are very easily prone to righteous indignation. They go to church regularly and they regard themselves as devout Christians, but they will happily torture you if given half a chance. It is these Christians who put blowtorches to the faces of recalcitrant black people, and feel they have done God a service. It was German Christians of the same ilk who slaughtered six million Jews and felt righteous in doing so. From the age of six white children of this land are taught about how the barbaric black people had killed Piet Retief and his comrades, who had come to bargain with the Xhosas in good faith. We are repeatedly taught about the Battle of Blood River, where a few hundred God-fearing Voortrekkers had with the help of the Almighty repulsed the onslaught of over 30,000 heathen Zulus, and in so doing the God of the trekkers had indicated that this was now rightfully their land. We had it drummed into us that black people were lazy, stupid, and predisposed towards criminality. We were also reminded over and over again about the atrocities that were committed by the British during the Boer War. The British had indeed killed many thousands of women and children, burnt crops and farmhouses, slashed and burnt entire communities, and they did put tens of thousands into concentration camps. However, this ceaseless scratching at the wound of defeat created an enmity between English- and Afrikaans-speaking

South Africans which I had experienced personally many times. It was the English-speaking South Africans, well, a few of them, who tend in the main to stand up for the rights of the black people, and it is the English press that is most critical of the apartheid regime. It is the English kids who grow long hair, smoke pot, wear bell-bottom jeans, and protest. Here I stand an Englishman and a rebel in a bastion of Afrikanerdom, a traitor to the cause. The major looks most unwell to me. Like a stranded blowfish he gasps for air. He cajoles and pleads, he bribes and tempts me, he is paternal and kindly. His approach is hugely effective, for I waver and feel myself beginning to give way, but then Brand cannot restrain himself and intervenes. "Prisoner, do you think you can defy us?! You are nothing but a traitor, you deserve to be shot, and yet you spit on the major's kindness!" "That's enough, lieutenant," says the major. Brand's Adam's apple bobs convulsively; the blotches on his face and neck roam like the blobs in a lava lamp. He would so love to smash me with his baton, but I am grateful to him for strengthening my resolve. There are few things I loathe more than a bully. The major is not a bully, but I am sentenced by him to another seven days in the punishment cell.

I fall to my knees and pray fervently, and desperately. "My God, my God, I am falling. My Father, I am tested beyond what I can bear, I am tempted beyond what I can bear. My enemies see that I am becoming weak and they circle me like vultures, I beg you please to strengthen me, to support me. I deserve nothing, but I am your child, I am your willing servant. Please, please help me!" The silence is resounding, my despair envelopes me, and I cannot help but roar in anguish. I shout and scream even though I do not want to, for if they hear me they will know I am breaking, I am melting. "Where are you, Father? Where is your spirit? Are you dumb! Are you deaf? Where in hell are you, great and almighty God! Are you sleeping in your egg? You are still enjoying your Sabbath? Wake the fuck up! I am suffering here! I am dying. You give no sign. Oh forgive me please, forgive me for my anger and my stupidity. Perhaps you are weak, you need sacrifice, you need help, you need praise and worship and adoration. You demand obedience from the inherently disobedient. Are we really made in your image? If that is true then you too are weak, you too are ambiguous. You demand devotion. Why? Are you not sufficient unto yourself? Forgive me, I am angry and there is no one here but me and the silent darkness. Please give me a sign, or better, a quiet voice, that I am on your side. Please I beg you, forgive me for my sins. Amen."

> *I am standing on a long beach looking out to sea. The moon is rising from the sea and I am aware that the sun is setting behind me. I look to my left and here comes a young woman who is the same age as me. She smiles and I realise that I have always known her, from even before I was born. She holds out her hand, I take it and we walk in absolute bliss along the beach, with the moonlit sea to the left, and the setting sun to the right. Now and then I look at her, and we smile at one another. We do not need to speak for we know what the other is thinking and feeling. I feel deep love for her, and she for me. In this blissful state we walk for a nearly an hour, it grows dark, the indigo night falls, and she says to me, "Remember, I am always with you," and I ask, "Who are you?" "Do you not know? I am your sister and daughter, your mother and your wife. I am your soul."*

I am bitterly disappointed when the dream ends and I find myself not on a beach but back in a cold cell. I remind myself of her words, that she my soul is always with me, and I am comforted. She is here in the darkness with me, we still walk hand in hand. She can never be apart from me. She cannot offer me much solace for I must suffer, we all must suffer, we must be melted by fire, forged in the flame without light, and by the hell of our own dichotomous being. She has but given me a glimpse of the future to fortify me. I am not so alone now.

I remember the divine light that was born in the darkness. This is an amazing mystery, that the divine light rests in the darkness of our own being. My soul, my white swan, my blue hyacinth.

My mind is all over the shop, it's turning to slop, I can't keep my brain on one subject for more than two minutes any more. It is a very worrying sign. Soon I will be gibbering and drooling, howling at the unseen moon. Perhaps it is the lack of food. I recall reading somewhere that the brain uses up to twenty-five per cent of the energy we ingest. Assuming you use your brain that is, and mine seems to be spluttering. I practise the nine times table, I recite poems I can remember, which is embarrassingly few. I think about the history and biology I learnt at school, but find my mind keeps going off on tangents, wandering down strange paths. Slipping and sliding, weaving like a drunk in a labyrinth. The past wants me, the river flows backwards, and I am drawn irrevocably into the terrifying void. There is nowhere to go, only the deepening blackness darkening still blacker. Darkness at one with darkness, utterly dark. I must take the journey to oblivion and die the death, the long and painful death that lies between the old self and the new. My body has fallen, bruised, badly bruised. I am animal, sweating and stinking, my saliva froths. I grunt and moan, whimper and tremble. I could kill for a steak, happily cut someone's stupid head off. I could tie up Steyn and smash his knee caps with a bat. No, I must not think such gruesome things. Why do such thoughts come to me when I do not want them, like an evil that comes to choke me. I am a lion, hunting, stalking, and sniffing for warm-blooded prey. I will snap its windpipe and chew the living flesh while its heart still beats. Has my brain or my heart a will of its own? Are my thoughts my own, or am I a victim of my thoughts? I could stick a screwdriver into Youngblood's beady eye with impunity. I am an eagle spying the land and I swoop for the kill. Go away, please go away, please Father help me, save me from my animal bloodlust, from my violence, please save me from my evil, my Father. I am falling into my evil, that which I do not want claims me, and now there is a black goat with me in the cell, I can smell him, his rank humid breath, his musky coat; I see his flaming red eyes glowing with a Luciferian fire. Go away! What do you want with me! Get behind me Satan, in the name of Jesus get behind me! I stand up and a force propels me violently against the wall, and I fall to my matt in sheer terror. I curl up in a foetal position, my hands clasped between my legs. I am pouring with sweat, shaking like an earthquake. I swoon and faint from horror.

CHAPTER FOURTEEN

1964

Yeoville is a busy and buzzy part of Johannesburg. Such an adventure, for since Honey Street we have always contrived to live in isolated places. The town which borders the golden city had a cinema which Patrick and I frequented as often as we could, and I decided that I wanted to become an actor. I was sent home from school for having holes in my shoes, and Ben kindly bought me a new pair, then Dugald beat the shit out of me with a piece of hosepipe when he saw me wearing my new shoes after school. I told John that I did not want to be bathed with my sisters any more, after I noticed Stella staring at my penis.

Dugald and Ben were arrested after a pub brawl, and they both came home after being bailed with swollen lips and black eyes. Dugald was offered a job in Swaziland and we all went together on the journey. We arrived in the capital Mbabane as the sun was setting. Stella and Laurie were asleep on the back seat next to me, and Samantha was on Paula's lap. We were hit by a car at high speed; it smashed us from the side, fortunately hitting the front of the car, and we were spun a full 360 degrees. Paula and Samantha were flung from the car, and I saw them lying sprawled in the road. Crowds assembled to gawp at the carnage; ambulances arrived and took us to hospital, the sirens wailing dismally. Samantha had a huge purple bump on her forehead, Paula had a broken arm, a broken nose, and a cut to the side of her face, and the rest of us were miraculously fine except for shock. The man who hit us apparently died, and Dugald never did get to his interview. I cannot remember how we returned home. For years after that Paula told people that we were hit by a twenty ton truck. Ben and Paula had a drunken row one night, more vicious and personal than usual and the Sayers moved out in a huff. Not long after that we moved to the isolation of Oliver's Farm and I became a pupil at Aloe Ridge primary school.

I am still on suicide watch, and every so often they open my cell and command me to stand up. The door is opened and I am surprised to see Lieutenant Brand. He does not have a guard with him and this is against regulations. After all, I might attack him, though he knows that I am now greatly weakened. I stand and come cautiously to the door, squinting my eyes to cope with the light. Brand stands back from the door to evade the worst of the foul odour emitting from my den, and probably as a precaution against sudden lunges. He surveys me intently for a while, points his baton at me and says, "I would like to know why you are doing this, prisoner?" This man is deeply troubled by me, that's for sure. I evoke something within him. I am not sure what to say or where to begin. I know that anything I say will only enrage him and my hackles are up, which tells me he is in a combative state of mind.

"Are you a communist?" he asks bluntly. These guys are so paranoid about communism.

Here I feel on safer ground. "No lieutenant, I am not a communist. Communism is a religion, just like nationalism, socialism, and materialism. In my opinion no political system or political ideology has the right to the souls of its citizenry." Brand ponders my reply, and I perceive it has annoyed him. His allegiance to a totalitarian regime with its apartheid policy does not demand atheism, but it does demand a certain brand of Christianity, which opines that the state is sanctioned by God.

He changes tack and says, "If some criminals attack your home and your family will you just stand by while they are slaughtered?"

"I am not a pacifist, lieutenant, and I would defend myself and my family, but I will not be part of a system which claims to do God's will." There, I have done it. I have provoked him, his face lights up with flashing blotches and the bridge of his nose becomes a pinched white. He is straining to keep his composure which as a student of law he is expected to cultivate.

Then he really surprises me by taking out of his pocket an edition of the New Testament, and opening it he reads a scripture to me. "It says in Romans chapter 13 verses one and two, 'Let every soul be in subjection to the superior authorities, for there is no authority except by God; the existing authorities stand placed in their relative positions by God. Therefore he who opposes the authority has taken a stand against the arrangement of God, those who have taken a stand against it will receive judgment to themselves.'" Brand has come with the sword of scripture, and he looks pleased with himself. It is a scripture he knows well; it has been hammered into him from the year dot.

I reply, "What, lieutenant, if you found yourself living in the communist Soviet Union, would you obey the authorities if they said you could not be a Christian? Jesus said render unto Caesar what is Caesar's and unto God what is God's. What if Caesar demands something that rightly belongs to God? What if there is a conflict of interests?"

"Our government does not demand you give up your Christian faith!" he snaps, and his Adam's apple begins to convulse.

"It demands I give up my interpretation of the scriptures, which says you must love your neighbour as yourself."

"You twist the scriptures to suit yourself, and you will receive judgment!" he shouts, and with that he ends the conversation and locks me up.

I have a love-hate relationship with Christianity. I love the Christian myth, the idea of God incarnating in man, but I loathe the sanctimonious organisations it has spawned. Christianity began as a living myth that deeply touched the souls of many, but it has become worn out and jaded. A collective belief rather than a personal one. I also take issue with the other monotheistic religions of Islam and Judaism. I feel that they too have largely fallen prey to literalism. I have no problem with Buddhism, or Hinduism, probably because I do not understand those faiths, though I have tried. I have no quarrel with pantheism or ancestor worship. It is the religions that claim to have the only authentic truth that freak me out. I love all religions, for the very fact that they have manifested themselves through the divine experiences of certain individuals and yet I cannot stand the dogmatic and domineering religious institutions which now predominate. What was once true does not remain so eternally, and what was once meaningful inevitably becomes meaningless. Even the Divine One is evolving and has not had its final say. I do feel that the divine source behind all religious experience is the same. Jesus, Buddha, and Mahomet all touched and quickened the same divine matrix. The divine manifests itself in individuals, and as such it is an individual experience, which gives rise to an individual interpretation, making divine truth relative. How I despise orthodox Christianity which has become so superficial, so literal, they have frozen the lifeblood out of our ancestral myth by making it rigid with no room for growth. The evolution of Christianity ceased centuries ago and the flock have departed from the house of death. The clergy preserve the house they have inherited, and it has become cramped and mouldy. They do not know it but there are people even now who see the burning bush and hear the quite voice. There are those who meet the Dark Lord, who is also an essential part of the divine fabric. If Jesus were to come into this world now I feel sure that he would denounce Christianity as rationalistic, dogmatic, realistic, and dead. The clergy are still feeding off the divine experience of those early Christians, and they have fallen into the trap of realism. I am angry that the pope not only encourages, but demands that the poor have more children than they can afford, more than Mother Earth can carry. I think it boorish that he insists that his flock remain chained to disastrous relationships in matrimonial agony. I am sickened by the cardinals and bishops all living in the lap of luxury, consorting with politicians and capitalists, obscenely striving to be part of secular society. I abhor the bishops in their ostentatious frocks, their obsessive love of choirboys, and their sanctimonious cover of celibacy. To me the Catholic Church and its hideous Protestant offspring have become a monster with ten heads, a "dwelling place of demons and a lurking place of every unclean exhalation, and a lurking place of every unclean and hated bird! The kings of the earth commit fornication with her and the nations have fallen victim to her" (Revelation 10.2, 3).

Christianity has put up a bulwark against any experience of the divine. Its scribes insist that God has had his final say for once and for all time and will never ever speak again. He spoke freely to the many prophets of old, but He maintains a dreadful silence for us, for we supposedly have His never changing, stagnant word. That is why God has died. The myth has died. Gentle Jesus would make another whip and flay them. It is plain to see that Christianity has rigor mortis, it has become stale, tired, and dogmatic; mired in outworn tradition, it has become a house of death. I have no respect for the Christian sheep, the sleepwalking bleating masses who docilely accept whatever rubbish they are told, so that they may live in a fool's paradise. I know some Catholics who do not believe in eternal damnation, who do believe in evolution, who do believe in contraception, yet still they cling to the skirts of a corpse. These

Christian sheep have blindly stumbled into two world wars, the Holocaust, the gulags, and the atom bomb. The Christian nations rape the earth, make ever greater weapons of mass destruction, and demonise those of other faiths. I feel that the monotheistic religions have become a danger to humanity, even though they were originally inspired by the divine ground of all being. I have never yet heard the Church leaders speak out against the obscene amounts of money that their governments spend on armaments? Do they ever speak out against the exploitation of Mother Earth? Even pot-smoking hippies do so, but the shepherds remain deathly silent while the planet is laid to waste. I despise them all and long for the day of their demise so that the Divine may be born anew in the human soul. If Christianity is to survive then she needs to reform. She needs to accept the feminine side of the Divine, to acknowledge the dark and terrible aspect of the Divine, to understand that we need direct contact with the Divine in order to have a true faith.

CHAPTER FIFTEEN

In 1965 we left the hectic city life and moved to the solitude of Oliver's Farm where I was reacquainted with solitariness and the night music of crickets. Aloe Ridge is a beautiful part of the bush veldt, bejewelled with numerous rocky hills called kopjes. At first, I felt bereft of my city friends and I especially missed Patrick, Jill, and Isabel. Once again I had to traverse a dirt road for two and a half kilometres to catch my school bus, which was no hardship, but it heightened my sense of loneliness, and I once again I resumed my relationship with the inner world. We did not do any farming as such, apart from a small vegetable patch and a couple of free-range chickens, as Paula and Dugald had full-time jobs in the city. They departed at the crack of dawn each weekday while we children were still asleep and they returned from work when we were already in the realm of dreams, so we only tended to see them at the weekends. It was John who fathered and mothered us, bathed us and fed us, and we children rapidly regressed to our feral ways.

There was a retired circus horse on the farm called Cinzano, who was completely white except for a small black blotch on his chest. Occasionally I took the radio out to him, because he liked music, and sometimes when a sort of marching type tune was played he would remember his circus days, and go up on his hind legs and dance. I often took him carrots, apples, or sugar lumps and we gradually became close friends. One time Dugald mounted Cinzano who promptly reared up, flinging him to the ground, and he sprained his wrist quite badly. Soon after that I tentatively climbed from the farm gate onto his back, and he walked about with me calmly, which thrilled me to absolute bits.

I made friends with Bobby and Janet Baker who lived on a nearby farm. One day we were playing hide and seek, and Janet and I hid in a cupboard while Bobby tried to find us. There was a light in the cupboard and Janet switched it on. She was sitting on the floor and she had pulled her dress up, and then she pulled her panties aside to show me her fanny. "Would you like to touch me?" she asked. I was about to touch her when Bobby came into the room and opened the cupboard. I felt deeply ashamed for reasons I could not comprehend.

Anthony came to visit us a few times while we lived out there. He would always arrive out of the blue without warning, and he invariably came bearing gifts and masses of grog. One time he brought me a hunting knife which became my special treasure, and he always coached me to box.

One weekend we had a large party, and about seventy city people pitched up. The Sayers came, and rather eventfully even Jack and Noreen arrived. There were other reporter friends of Paula's as she now worked as a journalist for the *Rand Daily Mail*, the newspaper that took the photo of me and John at the Ship House. We played cricket on the lawn and there was a massive barbeque, most of the adults drank to excess, fireworks were let off, and then Paula came riding naked on Cinzano, like Lady Godiva. He reared up and threw her off, she lay sprawled on the lawn with legs akimbo, and a broken arm.

Anthony came again one weekend; it was a full moon night and while he and I were sitting on the stoep just chatting idly about this and that, I asked him, "Do you think humans will ever walk on the moon, Anthony?" "No, my boy, it will never happen," he replied. Just four years later Neil Armstrong did walk on the moon and Anthony lost a chunk of his hero status.

On a farm near us lived five Afrikaans children ranging from six to thirteen years old. One day their school bus dropped them off at the same time as mine, so we were all walking up the dirt road in the same direction. I do not remember the reason, but they attacked me and beat me up, pushing me into a barbed wire fence, causing multiple cuts down my back and on my arms. I arrived home with a ripped and bloody shirt which deeply distressed John. He bathed me and tended my wounds, but even he could not repair my shirt. When Paula and Dugald came home that night an anxious John told them what had happened, so I was awoken and my wounds were examined. Paula was incensed so she and Dugald drove off to accost the parents of the five children. It turned out that their mother had died, and the father was paralysed and bedridden.

> *I am walking in a field of green grass, carrying William my black cat. Then in the grass I see a huge black mamba coiled and waiting. He is watching me and his purple forked tongue is tasting us on the air. William leaps from my arms and approaches the snake. "No, William!" I cry, but too late, the serpent strikes, and bites William in the shoulder. I am horrified. Then William turns into a woman.*

I have tried so hard to be pure, to be good, but evil keeps coming from me. Like the black cat and the black snake, evil is part of me and cannot be purged by all the will in the world. The blackness needs to be humbly accepted. Darkness belongs to the light; there cannot be one without the other. There is no yin without yang. If I am made in the image of God then God too is evil. I must accept the evil along with the good, or I must reject both. Maybe that is what the Buddhists mean by the middle way. They endeavour to succumb neither to good nor bad. Jesus succumbed to the good. After all, how many terrible things have happened in the name of goodness. How I loathe the self-righteous, those who want to force goodness on everyone. Those godly men of the Inquisition who tortured tens of thousands in the most diabolical of ways were so certain that they were doing good. Those who burnt so-called witches at the stake, those who burnt the heretics like me, those who insist that adulterers must be stoned to death, those who chop off the limbs of thieves, they are all certain that these are good works, pleasing to God. All these good people who burn those with different opinions, in the name of good, commit absolute evil out of their enslavement to virtue. They sanctimoniously take the child away from its mother because she has given birth out of wedlock. They say it is for her good, and for the good of the child. Evil is a destroyer, but it often clears the way for new growth. It is the shaker and stirrer that prevents stultification and stagnation. If there is creation then there must be destruction. Without darkness there can be no light. Now I comprehend the frightful Kali, the destroyer revered by the Hindu's. When the Dark Lord comes to visit me again, I will submit and accept him as part of the divine matrix. Come Satanael, I am waiting to receive you.

I see something, or are my eyes playing tricks? It is like a cloud of luminescent bees swarming near my cell door. The Dark One has come as I requested but now I am utterly terrified, I sweat coldly, curl up in a ball, and close my eyes tightly. I will not resist; let the Dark One do what must be done: "I am waiting Dark Lord." I feel the Evil One draw closer; I am panting like a sprinter, my heart pounding against my ribs. I am lifted into the air as if I am a down feather and a completely unexpected bliss of ecstasy overcomes me. I am being held in someone's arms like a child, and danced in circles. I dare to open my eyes; I am facing away from the dancer, looking out on a large swirling room. There are marvellous objects with many patterns, shapes, and colours, but I do not know what they are. I merely drink them in with wonder. The dancer takes me to a window, and directs my attention to the world outside. It is a sunny day, and in the garden sits a man on a reclining chair under a tree; he looks up and sees me watching him from the window. Then he stands up and walks away down a driveway with his back to me. My bliss vanishes and I become enraged; my hands bang on the glass pane, and I bite at the pane with my toothless gums. Suddenly everything vanishes and I am floating in my cell. My absolute terror returns; I am fearful of falling to the concrete floor, appalled and panicked at what is coming. A light appears in front of me and I stare at it with fascinated horror, my heart thudding in my chest; I can hear my rasping breath. The light spreads, and there appears a large head of a man, but no ordinary man. The head is square, almost a block, like the Easter Island statues, but it is a long living face, of flesh. A tremendous power emanates from this being who is staring at me intently. He is grim, so very grim, and extremely powerful, his skin is swarthy, his hair is dark; I look into his dark eyes, and to my astonishment I see kindness emanating from them and with that a shock flashes through my body, like an electric shock of high voltage, and I find that I am lying on my mattress, curled up in a ball, with my body drenched in sweat.

This vision leaves me stupefied. Was I taken back to the time when I had no teeth? Now I remember all the wonderful things I saw as I was danced about the room in motherly arms. They were normal objects, like tables and chairs, lampshades and paintings, but I did not recognise them as I had no words for them. I was preverbal. Who was the man in the garden, could that be my biological father who turned his back on me and walked away? Is that why I have felt bereft of God? The absent God and the absent father. Can a child with no teeth know that it has been abandoned and suffer rage as a result? Have I carried that rage at my real father and the unknown God, without knowing it all this time? And who is the Grim One? Is that the Dark Lord, or was it God both grim and kind, good and evil? Was it Adam? Who danced me around the room, and infused me with such ecstatic bliss? I think it may have been my mother, or was it Mother Nature?

The door is unlocked, and here are the two guards with a prisoner who carries my bread, potty, and water bottle. The prisoner winks at me, or are my eyes fooling about? I am disappointed to see that it is white bread today. It gives me much worse heartburn than the brown bread, and of course it is less nutritious. I hand him my sweets, and he winks at me again and gives me a smile. I discover that this prisoner has squashed his hard-boiled egg flat, and hidden it between the slices of bread. I am profoundly grateful for this daring act of human kindness. "Here and there a heart stays warm." "I am truly thankful, Grim One with kind eyes. Most truly grateful."

I became increasingly aware of nature's wonders on Oliver's Farm. After the first summer rains, huge swarms of flying ants would arrive, and I would watch in fascination as they landed and tore off their own wings. The butcher birds would hang baby birds they had stolen from other nests on the barbed wire fence to mature. Nature red in tooth and claw. I learnt where to find snakes, and I made friends with a large bullfrog who sat near the kitchen door at night, under the outside light which attracted swarms of moths, and she would take titbits from my hand.

One day a huge storm rolled in, and a crack of thunder released hail the size of chicken eggs which created an unbelievable din as they crashed down onto the corrugated iron roof. I stood at the window watching the multiple flashes of lightning streaking down, and the very earth shook from the perpetually rolling thunder. A streak of lightning struck a dead tree with a fantastic flash, not even thirty paces from the window where I stood, and for about half a minute I feared I had been blinded forever. The tree burst into flames, and burned for a while until the rain doused it. The storm passed and was supplanted by a gigantic double rainbow with intensely vivid hues.

I saw a bull mating a cow, and began to understand the mechanics of reproduction, and I witnessed a sow giving birth to her piglets on Bobby Baker's farm and began to comprehend how I had come into the world.

One day as I was standing waiting for my school bus to pick me up a car pulled up and the driver beckoned to me. I assumed that the man wanted directions or something, so I came to his car. He rolled down his window and drew my attention to his lap. His fly was undone and in his one hand he was holding his erect penis. Instinctively I ran from him and he drove off at speed. I did not tell my parents about the incident, but from then on I kept my hunting knife on me, and I became very wary of approaching cars.

From time to time we went into the wilderness to camp for a weekend, but in '66 we went on holiday to the Transkei coast and we camped on the beach of Port St. Johns near the great Umzimvubu river where I caught a fish which we ate for dinner. It was the second and the last holiday we ever had as a family.

One Saturday I walked the two miles to visit Bobby and Janet, but they were not at home. On my way home I was enticed by a small rocky hill that I had often walked past. On that particular day it looked more alluring than usual and I succumbed to its silent invitation. Between the boulders were tall aloes armed with spears of scarlet flowers, and lizards were hunting on the rocks. A bird of prey was gliding on the thermals, and I sat dreamily on the summit surveying the wide stretch of surrounding countryside when suddenly it happened. That feeling I had experienced next to the river at the Ship House came back. All my senses were suddenly heightened and the landscape looked even more remarkably beautiful than usual. The same deep sense of peace and calm came over me as a kind of grace, and all my fear, loneliness, and anxiety dissipated and blew away in the gentle breeze. I wondered if God was present or an angel perhaps, and as if in answer a serendipitous gap opened in the clouds and a shaft of sunlight beamed down directly onto the little kopje where I sat, and the aloe flowers blazed even more brilliantly. This coincidence seemed utterly extraordinary to me. The grasses shone like copper streaked with gold, and I was a part of the landscape, a piece of nature, looking at nature in awe and wonder. I was "happier than green grass", and I felt deeply blessed. "I will never forget this. Never ever," I said aloud to the wide world. I have had that experience a few times since then, those moments when all things glow with a holy light, but never for much longer than five seconds at a time. There is a downside to becoming sensitive to beauty, in that one also becomes aware of what is ugly. The one always goes with the other.

Stella broke her arm one afternoon, and we had to wait until eight that night before our parents returned home and finally took her to hospital. It was the first time I experienced deep compassion for another being.

Ben and Jill came to visit us with their new baby who they named Bubsie. Jack sent me five pounds for my eighth birthday and Paula borrowed it—forever. Anthony came to visit and as usual Paula and he had a drunken row; this time Dugald became embroiled and they had a fist fight. I did not see Anthony for another six years after that. About that time, the adults were all discussing the assassination of the prime minister by some Greek madman.

One afternoon a large black car arrived at the farm with four suited men wearing sunglasses. I went out to ask what they wanted and the one man said to me, "Are you the son of Paula?" Naturally I was most surprised by the question but I replied in the affirmative. The four suits stood around me and spoke in a foreign language for a while, and I knew they were discussing me. They asked what time my parents would be home and I told them I was not sure as I was usually asleep when they returned home. This reply generated another discussion, then the one man shook my hand and they departed. That night I woke up and I could hear adult voices talking, and with my name mentioned more than once, I could not resist the urge to sneak down the passage and eavesdrop near the living room door.

"He will have the very finest education, and he will go to the best universities … and naturally you would be handsomely remunerated …"

"Yes but he is my child, I can't sell him like a cow."

"… but you will have access to him, he will fly back here at least twice a year and stay with you for holidays, and you can phone him and write to him …"

Dugald mumbling … Paula again, "Yes but I can assure you that although George and I had a brief affair the boy is not his child."

A foreign voice, "He looks remarkably like George … and the timing of your affair is right."

I had heard enough and was frightened of being discovered so I snuck away. A few days later Paula did speak to me about the visit of the four foreign men.

"There is a Greek millionaire who I was once friends with, and he is unable to have children. He wants you to go and live in Greece where he and his family will look after you, and give you all the best things in life. You would be able to come home twice a year during school holidays to visit us, and you could phone us and write to us. Would you like to go?"

My answer was an emphatic no and the subject was not discussed again until I was seventeen, when I brought it up. It transpired that while Paula was having her affair with my biological father, Paul Cluer, she also had a brief fling with one George Lavranos, the only son of a shipping tycoon. The family got wind of this affair, and when they heard that Paula was pregnant they summoned him back to Greece. It turned out that George was homosexual, the family finally realised that he would never produce any heir to the dynasty, and then they remembered his affair in Rhodesia and came looking for me, assuming that I was a product of the liaison.

"How do you know he is not my father?" I asked Paula.

"Because we only ever made love Greek style," she replied.

"What the hell is Greek style?" I asked. "Oh darling, he only did me anally, so you cannot belong to him."

> *I am walking through a city when suddenly there is a massive explosion inside a building, the windows are blasted out, and there is fire everywhere. I run to the scene to see if I can help, and I venture into the destroyed building. There is dense smoke and rubble everywhere, bodies lying about. I see a badly wounded man and taking him under the arms I drag him outside onto the pavement and prop him up against a wall. I kneel in front of him to see if I can tend to his wounds. His clothes have been blasted off and the flesh on his arms has come away revealing the bones in his forearms. With considerable surprise I notice that his bones are made of steel. His shin bones on the one leg are also exposed and I notice that they too are made of iron. I use a piece of cloth to bind his arm and as I do so he says to me, "You are a healer, a very good healer." I suddenly realise with holy terror that this is Grim Man, and I say to him, "You are powerful, very powerful."*

My Grim Man has been wounded by our encounter, and it seems to fall to me to heal him. He is powerful yet also weak. He is grim yet also kind. The old God is dying, or is it my particular image of God that is dying? I read somewhere that God has to die every two thousand years, and that he has to be reincarnated. The history of humankind is essentially the history of God's evolution, the ongoing incarnations of the Divine. I too am grim, grimly determined yet I am weak, so pitifully weak. I too am wounded by the encounter. The grim God of the Old

140

Testament and the kind God of the New Testament is dying. I now see an old man, he has a heart attack, and as he is falling I catch him. I can feel his heart breaking in his chest and I lay him down. She takes his head in her lap, and I hold his feet. He looks very surprised to be dying.

My seventh week of solitary is complete but I am kept in my cell for ten or twelve days on full rations. I kick up a fuss every time my meals are brought but I am treated dispassionately. I suspect they are fattening me up, and this hunch proves to be more or less correct. Finally they come to take me for a shower and shave. My legs are uncertain and jelly-like and my ankles are very painful. My eyes cannot hold focus; I look at a face and see it clearly for a few seconds and then it seems to melt and blur. I walk like a retard because the ground looks further away than it is, then it looks nearer than it is. Noises and sounds seem exaggerated, and make me feel crazy, so I put my hand over my good ear. Once again I see myself in a mirror: I have a beard, my skin is pale, almost translucent and my sunken eyes look deranged.

CHAPTER SIXTEEN

I am taken to the medical bay, and there I sit for nearly two hours until the doctor has dealt with the other prisoners who have been sent to see him. I manage to ask one of the prisoners what the date is, and find out that it is the ninth of April, and work out that I have been in the punishment cell for sixty-three days. It feels like I have been there for many years, even for a lifetime. I give urine, my blood pressure is taken, and I am weighed. Even with the last twelve days of normal food rations I am still thirty pounds down on my original weight. I tell the doctor that I am struggling to see properly and that my ankles are painful. He uses a little torch to look at my eyes but makes no comment. He does not seem interested in my ankles. Then he gives me a huge brown injection and tells me that it is vitamin B12. After the medical I am returned to my cell, and for the next few days I am given full rations. I was just starting to believe that my spare ration days were over when I was again taken for a shower and shave before being escorted to the major, who once again sentences me to seven days on spare rations.

I think this is it, my darkness, I am done for. I can't take it any more. Mother of God I cannot take any more! How lonely is it possible to feel, how hungry? The suicide watch has been terminated, winter is approaching, the nights are growing colder, and I ask for another blanket every time my bread is brought but with no success. Strangely the tormenting visions of food have ceased; perhaps my body is beyond caring. I think I have gone beyond caring any more, my darkness. I think about cannibalism. Would I eat another human? A bit of raw thigh!

I wake up and there is a regal woman sitting on a large marble throne. She has incredibly thick silver hair braided with living emerald vines. She wears a royal purple dress but is naked from the waist up, and she has six breasts. She smiles at me, and I stand up and walk to her. Her eyes are yellow gold like those of a lioness, and they completely transfix me. She is ancient and young at one and the same time. I go down on my knees before her and put my head upon her lap. She smells like honey and wet earth, like ocean breeze and summer hay. She puts her soothing hand on my head and I am filled with a tremendous erotic excitation. "I want to be in you Great Mother," I plead. "Not yet, my child, not yet," she says gently, and I start to cry. She strokes my head consolingly, and a deep peace imbues me. I fall asleep and dream of a woman with a beard who is singing the most beautiful song to me.

I perceive that God is light and dark, yin and yang, male and female. I cannot any longer endorse the idea of an all male Divinity. The monotheists are strictly patriarchal, their God is all male and the feminine aspect of the Divine is banished to material nature. To sinfulness. The black snake and the black cat of my dreams held the feminine side of the Divine. If God is made in our image then surely the Divine has a female aspect. Or behind God lies the female source, the mother of God. "Mother, my Mother, I long to be extinguished in you!"

I wake up and see some light. On closer investigation I realise that there is a small door in the cell wall, and the light is coming in through the gaps at the top and bottom of it. I wonder how it is that I have never noticed this door before. I feel the door, and find a handle which I turn and pull: the door opens. I have to crouch to see through the door, and to my astonishment there is a large and very beautiful park bathed in glorious sunlight. Many children are playing there, some are kicking a ball about, while others are chasing one another. Some are climbing trees while others are playing on the shores of a blue lake. I am about to go through the hatch when I become suspicious. Something in me tells me that if I go through this hatch that I will never come back, I will be in that playground forever. I am torn in two. I stick my head through the hatch and watch the children play. Then I see a procession of adults coming along a pathway. There is something mournful about them; they are dressed in cassocks and they sing a strange dirge in what sounds like Latin. I realise that this is a procession of the dead, the catatonic, and I am struck by the fact that the children do not seem to notice them. Rather reluctantly I pull myself back into the cell and close the door and it vanishes instantly. It was a close call.

I am being pursued across the Sahara desert by a large army which is steadily gaining on me. I come to the Red Sea and I realise that I have no alternative but to try to cross it. I wade into the sea and I am startled to find that the water only comes up to my chest. Eventually I reach the other side of the sea, and when I come out of the water I find a huge crowd of people waiting. I am given a large drum with shoulder straps. All of a sudden I find myself walking behind Nelson Mandela who has a similar drum. I walk twenty or thirty paces behind him beating my drum to the same rhythm as him. There are thousands of people lining the streets and they are cheering Mandela.

Then I find myself in a boat on the ocean and nearby is another boat with four men. One of the men gets out of the boat and stands on the water, and he is followed by another man and then a third. The fourth man hesitates but he too climbs out of the boat, but he seems unsure about his ability to stand on water. The first man begins to walk and the others follow him. Suddenly I am the fourth man, walking with great uncertainty, wondering if I can stay on the surface of the water. Just as I am becoming comfortable with walking on water, the first man begins to climb into the air as if walking up invisible steps, and we all follow him. I am very uncertain as to whether I can do this but to my amazement I find that I can, and we climb up into the heavens.

I find these dreams comforting for I feel that I no longer need to fear that I will drown in the psychic ocean.

I awake to find a magnificent owl looking at me with its huge eyes. The owl stands as tall as me and its magnificent plumage is black and white. It spreads its wings, and the feathers of its left wing touch my face. I feel deeply honoured by this. I am then distracted by something and looking to my left; I see an African grey parrot who nibbles at my left hand. "What do you want?" I say to the parrot. I look back to the owl but it has gone; I look for the parrot, but it too has gone.

The parrot is all the stuff which I have learnt from others, all the collective ideas I have accepted as gospel. My preconditioning and indoctrination distracts me from the angel of insight. The one who is black and white, the one who can see in the dark. That angel of wisdom who combines the opposites, and so transcends them. I am guilty of imitation, and I am a parrot in a large flock. I must relinquish my indoctrination, I must be open myself to what is revealed. For the spirit has touched my face.

Usually when I climbed onto Cinzano he would just carry on grazing as if I was not even there, but one day I climbed on his back and he began to trot, which rather alarmed me. I held onto his mane tightly and he picked up speed until we were galloping across the fields. It was both exhilarating and terrifying all at once. Finally he came to a stop and just began to calmly graze once more, and I slid gratefully from his back. To my disappointment, he never did that again.

Paula bought us new clothes, and we drove 100 kilometres to the town of Springs. We were going to meet Paula's mother, her grandmother and her great grandmother, none of whom we had ever met before. It was my great great grandmother's 100th birthday, and there was a huge family reunion for the occasion. Paula hated her mother so we had been deprived of the privilege of ever meeting her before, but Mom did have some affection for her great grandmother, Granny Cook. It was simply astonishing to see how numerous our extended family was; nearly 300 clan members were gathered for the celebrations. Granny Cook had the first of her children when she was fifteen years old while on the third and final Great Trek. These were the pioneers who tried to escape British rule by setting up a homeland in the Transvaal, and they travelled more than 1,000 miles in ox wagons over land and mountains with no roads. Now here she was surrounded by her extended progeny, with jet planes roaring overhead. In all Granny Cook had fourteen children, fifty-three grandchildren, more than 100 great grandchildren and numerous great great grandchildren. We all had to stand in a long queue to meet the great matriarch who was sitting in a chair in her large garden. Finally our clan came before her. She was a tiny woman, about four foot six inches tall, with thick silver hair and bright cornflower blue eyes which still did not need glasses, and she was visibly delighted to see Paula. Dugald was carrying Laurie as she had a large cyst in the sole of one foot, and was shortly due for an operation to remove it. "What is wrong with the girl?" enquired Granny Cook. She was duly informed and she then instructed someone to call her gardener, and when he came she sent him to fetch the leaf of a castor oil bush. The leaves of this noxious shrub are maroon. Laurie's foot was put into Granny Cook's lap, and she personally bandaged the leaf over the cyst. "Do not remove it for five days," she commanded. When the leaf was removed the cyst came away leaving a clean hole. I also met my grandmother Violet and my great grandmother Nan, not to mention a bewildering horde of cousins. There was a feast the likes of which I had never seen before, with whole lambs and pigs on the spit, and huge trestle tables groaning under the weight of food. Grandmother Cook eventually transferred out at the age of 106.

I often heard Paula referring to our landlord Mr. Oliver as a tyrant and a miser. Rumours abounded that he had more than once set his pack of six bullmastiffs on black people who had trespassed on his land, but no bodies had ever been recovered. He was a tall man with a sunburnt pate, and never once did we see a smile cross his stern visage. The floorboards under Stella's bed had partially collapsed, and Mr. Oliver came with some of his black labourers to do the repairs, so the girls were all moved into my room. A large pile of building sand was heaped on the good part of the floor, presumably for repairs to the wall through which the damp had come. It was while Mr. Oliver was in the basement that the floor gave way, and he was buried under this pile of sand. His labourers scrabbled desperately to try to save him, but to no avail. That was the first dead person I ever saw. "There is some justice in the world after all," said Paula. Shortly after that I turned nine, Jack gave me a Timex watch, and we moved to Craighall Park.

Steyn and Youngblood open my door. "Come prisoner, bring your pot and your blanket," says Steyn. I find my water bottle, my potty, my blanket and come to the door. Hope springs up in my heart; will they take me to a normal cell, one with a window and a light? I emerge into the corridor and Steyn points to the cell next door, the one where the prisoner killed himself. "That is your new home," says Steyn with a broad smile. Youngblood punches me to my lower back as I am walking into my new cell; I feel a rush of rage, and it is all I can do to restrain myself from smashing him with my potty. Later they bring a prisoner to wash and scrub my old cell. My new cell has three unexpected delights. First, the air vent is more efficient and the atmosphere is less stifling, but even more wonderful are the two tiny sources of light that find their way in. The board that covers up the window is not as snugly fitting as the one in my old cell, and in the one corner a tiny sliver of ethereal light penetrates the dense blackness. This fragile holy beam, thin as a needle, sends a ray across my cell and makes a minute star like a spark on the far wall. There is also a fragment of pale light finding its way in under the cell door so I can now tell if it is day or night. I am further astonished and elated to find a blanket that has been left in the cell, so now I have two. I am aware that the light might save my eyesight to some degree; it certainly cheers me up. What is more, the foam mattress does not stink as hideously as my old one. They had intended to be evil but had done good. I take it as a sign, my darkness.

She has come smiling and lies down next to me. Hanging on her neck by a fine necklace of silver is the Star of David, her ear-rings are crescent moons with a star in each, she wears a tiara of blue diamonds which has a ruby crucifix in the centre, and her dress is made of living green gossamer. Her large eyes are spring green like fresh peas and her hair is red. I see that she is heavily pregnant and wonder at this. She unbuttons her dress to reveal her stomach, and she takes my hand and puts it on her wondrous swollen belly. She is pregnant with God. He has died and is to be reborn. My grim all male God has died and is now being incarnated in the womb of my soul, for this is the miracu-lous virgin birth. I feel deeply contented, and lie with my head on her shoulder and fall asleep.

CHAPTER SEVENTEEN

1966

Although Craighall Park is an upmarket town, we probably inhabited the most run-down house in the entire suburb. It had a massive back garden, about an acre in size with an overly mature fruit orchard, a number of large trees, and lots of over-blown shrubs. The relatively small front garden was planted with about 100 rose bushes which Paula adored and they made for a magnificent sight in summer.

I became close friends with Andre Sullivan, a serious and intelligent boy who lived just three houses away, and he taught me to play chess, Monopoly, and various card games, and together we made a box cart which we raced down Water-fall Hill regularly until one day the brakes failed, we had a crash that left us heavily scraped up, and a ban on box carts put in force. We bred silkworms in shoe boxes with holes in the top. Fortunately we had two massive mulberry trees in the garden because these black and white worms can devour astonishing amounts of food. I watched for hours as they munched the leaves, and they make quite a racket as they chew. I watched for days as they spun their wondrous golden cocoons. My friendship with Andre was all the more precious because for reasons I could not comprehend, I found myself to be generally unpopular with most of my new classmates. They soon found out that despite my scrawniness, I did not tolerate being bullied and that I was always prepared to fight any boy who dared to try. Perhaps I was a bit rustic for their liking.

Paula and Dugald were both gainfully employed at that time, and numerous drinking friends, mainly journalists and jazz musicians would arrive almost every night with a bottle or two in hand. It was an open house, and on Friday evenings the real parties would begin, often only fizzling out towards dawn on Sunday morning. Granny Stella took a break from playing golf and came at least once a month for a civilised lunch. We had developed the wonderful habit of having a roast every other Sunday, and even Jack and Noreen came once. Noreen with her genteel background was probably appalled by our dilapidated abode, or perhaps Paula became a bit too smashed and vulgar, but she never made the mistake of coming again. Paula has a tremendous knack of alienating the extended family.

One weekend we drove through the Orange Free State when the sunflowers were in bloom, and the land was golden yellow from horizon to horizon. We journeyed to the town of Welkom where Granny Violet lived with my great grandmother Nan. I thought that my grandmother Violet was very attractive, for a woman of forty-seven, and I was intrigued by her dark brown hair and large brown eyes, as Paula and her progeny all have blonde hair and hazel eyes. Violet never did remarry after her disastrous thirteen-year marriage to Jack, and I often wondered why this was so. While visiting Nan that day, it dawned on me that Nan is married to an Afrikaans man and therefore Violet must be half Afrikaans. Then I drew the conclusion that Paula must be at least partially Afrikaans, and by extension so must I. This realisation was significant because Paula is so scathing and demeaning of the Afrikaans tribe, and often speaks of them with the greatest disdain, which I had naturally imbibed like a parrot. I once asked her why she called them "Slopes". "Haven't you noticed darling, that their foreheads

recede sharply from the brow like Neanderthals," she replied.
I only ever saw one man with a sharply receding forehead and
he was English. On the way home I said to Paula, "Mom, your
Granny is Afrikaans." Paula became extremely agitated by this
remark and gave me a long and distorted history of her lin-
eage. Granny Cook was the child of French Huguenots who
had fled religious persecution in France, and she had married
a Scottish Presbyterian priest. This much was more or less true
but Paula left out the vital bit about Nan's Afrikaans husband.
Later I was to learn that the French Huguenots were absorbed
into the Afrikaans fraternity anyway. It turns out I have French
and Dutch blood and as such I am partly Afrikaner. Until now
I had only been indoctrinated with the notion that Jack came
from English aristocracy, which was not true, for at best his
father came from the middle classes. It was in our first house
in Craighall Park that I had a seminal dream at the age of nine.
I had a rich dream life and often pondered the meanings of my
dreams but this dream was much more significant than usual.
The meaning of my dreams were often obvious to me, like
those of being chased by Dugald and my legs failing me. This
dream, however, affected me profoundly and for many months
I could not shake the feeling it left me with. In the dream, I was
walking through a beautiful garden in a state of wonderment
and awe. It was laid out something like a park, with a long
central path lined with an avenue of glorious blossom trees.
Everything was clothed in a sacred light and I marvelled at
each tree, indeed at every leaf and flower. Then up ahead I saw
a magnificent fountain which tumbled down many tiers into a
large raised circular pond. As I drew closer, I saw that the pond
was bejewelled with hyacinth blue water lilies, and it was so
breathtakingly beautiful that I gasped. I approached the pond
and at first I gazed closely at the deep blue flowers, and then
at the lily pads which glowed with a luminescent green light.
Then I looked into the water and noticed that under the lily
pads were some dark objects, and stepping closer I peered into

the depths of the pond to see what they could be. With horror I realised that those objects were the corpses of my parents and my sisters, and I woke up in a great fright. I pondered that dream often and was deeply worried that my family would be killed. When they had not died after three months I decided that there must be some other explanation for the dream. It turns out my family were spiritually asleep to the beauty of it all and so, too, oblivious to the horror of it all. Oblivious to the invisible sacred background.

We began to go camping more frequently, usually in the Magaliesburg area, and Dugald would tramp about with his geologist's hammer prospecting for gold and diamonds. He has a passion for geology, and apart from jazz music it is the one subject which he can talk about almost intelligibly. We never camped at official campsites but always in wilderness areas and often we trespassed on private land. One weekend we went camping in an area called Pelindaba, and there the fields are littered with gneiss rocks abandoned by a long-gone ice age. These mica-flecked rocks have the most appealing shapes and all kinds of striations, and Paula insisted on taking some of them home to put in the rockery. This turned out to be a fateful occurrence. At that time Dugald was working as a draughtsman for a highly successful advertising agency, and it seemed that he had at last found his calling in life. He was earning more than he had ever done before, but Paula was deeply displeased because his job increasingly demanded that he go out to parties and dinners, generally without her. Dugald, with his pitch black hair and jet blue eyes, was handsome, and he looked stunning in a suit which aroused Paula's ever-present green-eyed monster. She would lie awake until he returned home, and then have a huge row with him when he returned, and deprive him and myself of at least two hours of vital sleep. "I suppose that harlot Jane was there, you reek of cheep perfume!" "Mumble, mumble." "I swear by God Almighty Dugald that if I find that you so much as hugged her I will commit suicide and leave you to bring up the kids." "Mumble, mumble." "I have a good mind to have an affair!" "Mumble, mumble." When Paula was jealous she could be merciless. Sometimes I was amazed that he did not give her a smack. She called him the most demeaning things, and cruelly hacked away savagely at his manhood. "Well, she will soon find out that you think sex is a dirty business. That you are essentially asexual!" "Mumble, mumble."

Anyway, one of our many visitors noticed the Pelindaba rock, and asked if we could sell him some, and so began a small business. Rockeries had become all the rage in Johannesburg back then. We began to go camping even more frequently, and each time we brought back as much stone as the old Buick could tolerate. Then a landscaper saw the rock, and asked Dugald if he could supply him a few tons of the stuff. Dugald hired some hands and a truck, procured a heap of stones, and made a tidy profit. More orders rolled in and other landscapers started to call up. On the way back from Pelindaba, Paula called in at a garden centre and showed them the rock. They immediately put in a large order, and so it came about that Dugald left his successful trajectory in advertising, bought a truck on hire purchase, and began to wholesale Pelindaba rock. This was to be the pinnacle of Dugald's success. Initially the business was storming along, and he could barely keep up with demand. The parties grew more fabulous, and the circle of friends became greatly expanded.

I was given a bicycle for my tenth birthday which thrilled me nearly as much as my tricycle had. I also received a cricket bat, a rugby ball, and best of all a two-man tent. I hardly knew what to do with myself, as there was suddenly so much choice. I would camp in my tent in the garden, never dreaming that we would be using that same tent eight years later on our flight from Philippi pig farm.

I was still receiving regular beatings from Dugald for habitually being in breach of some rule I had never heard of before.

On one occasion I played with his collection of crystals, and I did not put them back in the box correctly, for which I was soundly whipped with his belt as if I had sold them. I came from Andre's house at about five one afternoon which was my usual ritual. Dugald was home early for a change, and decided I had come home dreadfully late and I received another brutalising. I dropped a plate and broke it. I gave Paula some backchat. There were tens of hidings for outrages I cannot even remember. Then I experienced a particularly brutal beating for tricking Stella into tasting a chilli. Worse was to come.

One day Andre and I were walking home from school, when the topic of fanny came up. I think he said something like, "I wonder what a fanny looks like." I was somewhat astounded by this. Until recently I had bathed with my sisters; they still ran around the house naked, and until about the age of nine, I use to take things to Paula while she was bathing. I would top up her wine, or bring her a glass of water so the fanny was no mystery to me. "You have never seen a fanny?" I asked in disbelief. "Surely you have seen your mother!" It transpired that he had never seen his mother naked, and I was perplexed by this. He asked me to describe a fanny, and I found myself at a loss for words. It dawned on me that the best solution to the problem was to show him one, so I took him home and I asked Stella and Laurie to show Andre what a fanny looks like, and they were most obliging. Andre ogled the exposed fannies for a while and left looking rather disappointed, however it led to dreadful results.

Andre told the story to two of his friends and they told other boys and soon I was inundated with requests. I was not used to such ingratiation, but more importantly I also saw the chance to make a bit of money, and informed them that it would cost twenty cents to see a fanny. About six boys came around, and they duly paid their twenty cents which I had agreed to share with Laurie and Stella. We went into the garage, the boys sat on the floor in a semi–circle, and the girls lifted their dresses and pulled down their panties, when of all things Dugald walked in. The boys scattered, Dugald took me by the arm, lifted me off the ground by my wrist, and hurled me into the garden. Then he snapped a gnarly branch off a peach tree and whipped me all the way into my bedroom and then some. The back of my legs were streaming with blood, and I did not go to school for nearly three weeks until the wounds had sufficiently healed. I felt his moral indignation; I was made to feel like a disgusting filthy pervert. "Your child is depraved!" I heard him say to Paula. I looked up the word "depraved" in the dictionary and I felt deeply ashamed in his presence for a year after that.

Dugald was finding it increasing difficult to poach rock so he approached a farmer in the Pelindaba area and offered a fee to clear his fields of rock. The farmer probably would have been glad if he had taken the rock away for nothing. The business grew rapidly, and Dugald set up a camp on the farm with John as the supervisor of a gang of twenty men, who gathered the rock and loaded and unloaded it. John earned well and even bought himself a second-hand car with the result that women buzzed about him like a swarm of midges. Much to my delight Dulgald would sometimes stay out in Pelindaba for a few days at a time.

In 1967 we moved to a new house, still in Craighall Park, and acquired two maid servants. It was the biggest and newest house we ever lived in, with large bedrooms, two bathrooms, and a colossal kitchen. Paula's greatest passion after sex, reading, parties, gardening, and alcohol is cooking; she devours cookery books by the score, and whenever we could afford it she would make exotic dishes. So she decided to give up her job as a legal reporter for the *Rand Daily Mail* and start up a cookery school. The walls of the huge kitchen were bedecked with copper pots and long-handled pans of various sizes. A large stove and an enormous fridge were installed; this was the first time we had ever had brand new appliances, and the last. Paula advertised her new venture and discovered that she had found a real gap in the market. I would return home from school to find the kitchen packed with about thirty students, mostly the black maids of very wealthy households who probably felt their cooks could do with improving, but she also had a class of wealthy bored white women twice a week. Paula drank wine while she lectured, and with her rather profane sense of humour she was quite a hit. We ate like kings almost every night, and for a brief period we children were not malnourished. The parties grew yet bigger and wilder, and at times the house felt like a railway station. Paula would feed the multitudes with the produce of her cookery classes, and so gave away all her profits and probably more.

One fine day Dugald was coming down Sylvia's Hill with a heavy load of rock and five of his labourers, when the brakes of his truck overheated and failed. He lost control on a bend and went careering down the hill, smashing through a large garden wall; the truck tore through some flower beds and ended up in a swimming pool. Amazingly no one was killed, but some of his men were badly injured and needed long hospitalisation. Dugald broke his collarbone but that was the least of it. It transpired that there was a problem with Dugald's truck insurance: he had forgotten to pay it for two months, or something idiotic like that. It also turned out that he had no personal indemnity insurance and would have to bear the cost of repairs to the pool, the wall, and garden, the removal of the truck, wrecked beyond redemption, and the removal of the six tons of stone from the pool. Added to which he also found himself liable for the injuries to his men. In short everything went to hell in a basket, and overnight we were not only bankrupt but found ourselves owing large amounts of money. Summonses were issued, creditors were bashing on the door, friends dried up and vanished, the parties ceased. Paula was presented with a huge tax bill on her cookery school and it turned out that she had not put aside any money for the inevitable day. She sold the stove and the fridge and as much furniture as possible, all her copper pots and pans, and bought airline tickets to Cape Town. Paula took Smuts to the vet and had him put to sleep without telling me. That was my first true experience of deep grief. Paula actually put her arms about me and cried with me, and that was the first time I ever saw her cry. My second experience of grief came just two days later when it devastated me to say goodbye to John. I clung to him sobbing and he kissed me on the head. He was a good father to me, and I have never stopped missing him. I had to leave my bicycle, toys, and sports gear, but I did manage to take my beloved tent, and to my regret I did not get a chance to say goodbye to Andre. I wonder how he is, my darkness, I wonder if that funny little man ever thinks of me.

It all happened so quickly and unexpectedly. Suddenly we were on an aeroplane fleeing the Golden City. Paula chided Dugald who was sick with fear as it was the first time any of us except for her had ever flown. We landed in Cape Town at nighttime, and Ben Sayers was there to collect us. It was a hell of a squeeze to get us and our suitcases into his small Anglia. Samantha sat on my lap, Laurie sat on Paula's lap, Stella sat on Dugald's lap and there was baggage poking into us from every direction. The Sayers had moved to Cape Town the year before, and now we were going to live with them until we were on our feet again. I was partially mollified for the loss of John and Smuts when I saw Patrick and Isabelle again, who are among the few constants in my life.

CHAPTER EIGHTEEN

My seven days of punishment are complete, and again I am brought full rations for an entire week before being collected for another trial. It is early winter now and the shower is bitterly cold on my skinny body, causing my teeth to chatter like a machine gun. The icy wind turns me blue all over, and my feet ache on the frozen concrete floor. A prisoner I do not recognise greets me by calling my name as we walk by, and is told to shut the fuck up. Others prisoners stare with brazen curiosity, and it seems that I have become something of a celebrity among the punished ones. While I am waiting outside the major's office various guards pop out of the charge room to have a look at the prisoner in black underpants. Pug Nose sticks his head out of the office and jeers at me.

Even now that his office is cold the major still sweats like cheese under the African sun, and his fan continues to work on the double. Brand is again witness to proceedings, and the hatred in his heart shows clearly in his face and demeanour. It is the usual drama, with the major softly appealing to me to be reasonable, offering temptations, telling me that his hands are tied by due process, and inevitably he winds up by giving me seven more days on spare rations. I am returned to my cell with dread in my heart as if I were being taken to the gallows.

I am walking twenty paces behind a holy man in the Egyptian desert; we have been walking for many days. He is clothed in a deep blue robe and headscarf, and his head is bent forward in contemplation. Eventually we come to an oasis with many tall palm trees and some cultivated fields, which look wonderfully inviting. We do not stop but pass by and begin to ascend a steep mountain pass. After some hours of climbing I am extremely tired and it is becoming tremendously hot. We come to an overhanging cliff that casts some shade, and there we sit side by side in silence to rest for a while, looking down on the verdant oasis. When I look again the holy man has disappeared. Suddenly I am standing on the slopes of Muizenberg Mountain next to Baily's grave. The town of Muizenberg has gone, as has the neighbouring town of St. James. It is post Apocalypse, and nature has reclaimed the land so that almost all former traces of humanity have disappeared. I am hugely relieved to see that Mother Nature has survived the catastrophe. Then I see a huge herd of elephants walking along the beach towards me. It is a magnificent sight, making me joyful to find that the majestic elephant species has avoided extinction. They reach the foothills of the mountain and traverse the slopes below me. I hear a noise behind me and turning around I see a female elephant coming down the slope directly towards me. I decide it would be prudent to give way, and move slowly to the right. There I notice a cave, and decide that it would be the perfect place to find protection in case the elephant should become hostile to me. As I am nearing the cave a Stone Age man comes to the entrance. He is naked as a psalm, except for his smile. I walk up to him and put my hands on his shoulders, he puts his hands on mine, and we smile at one another.

We may forget the past but something in our mind and soul never does. Something in us remembers even the most mundane and banal of happenings. Our past is alive in us all the time, an ever dancing flame. We have an elephant, indeed a herd of elephants that remember everything, even the hostile things we want to forget. They have certainly come back, my elephants, many peacefully but some dangerously so. We carry our primitive ancestors deep down within ourselves; they live in our evolved bodily fabric, and we need to honour them, our forebears, for many lived short and brutal lives to bring us to this point in time, where we have walked upon the moon. We may consciously have forgotten them, lost touch with them, but something in us remembers them always; perhaps the dead live in us, in our inner universe. The Stone Age man in me still sees the spirits in everything, in the sea, in the rivers, in the animals, in the thunderstorms. My pagan ancestor is glad to see me, and I am so very pleased to see him, who is so close to nature that he is very nature. What have we lost? We have been sundered from our natural roots and our rightful inheritance as children of Mother Nature and Father Spirit. We have ceased to be children of the gods, we have lost our Mother, and we have walked far from the Garden, deep into the wilderness of death and bareness, since we lost our Edenic animal innocence. The divine wants to be conscious, wants to reach the light of day, and we are her vessels, his agents. We suffer in God and God suffers in us till we can find Eden again, together, this time consciously, knowing good and bad. God needs me to suffer his good and his evil, to suffer her paradoxes, so that good and evil can be reconciled in her and in me. This is my sacred service. To heal the divisions in my God who has been split asunder by his act of creation.

Oh my sunbeam, a human being can endure great suffering when there is a purpose to it. How many have gladly been burnt alive or crucified for the cause of bringing the Divine One out of the dark and into the light? The holy spark lives in me and leads me; it is a hard journey through parched lands, but over time there is shade and shelter. I am weary now, my light and my dark, smitten with a great weariness, I have been taken way beyond my own strength and willpower.

I am utterly exhausted to the very core of me. I surrendered completely, I have become a sacrifice. Please Mother, have mercy on me.

> *She comes dancing out of the black in a dress that is blue, green, and silver; her long hair is braided with ribbons of gold and green. I leap up and dance with her, an ecstatic almost frenzied dance. We leap high and we twirl, we sway and spin. Eventually we stop the dancing and she hands me a rod. As I take it, I feel power pass from the rod into me. She says to me, "I love you, if only for your mission." I reply rather disdainfully, "You do not know my mission." She vanishes and I immediately regret my words. "I am sorry, my soul."*

1968

I remember that first day in the Cape like it was yesterday. I awoke in the morning, having shared a bed with Patrick, looked out of the kitchen window and there was Muizenberg Mountain soaring into the sky, and the sight of it sent a thrill of excitement through me, as I am crazy for mountains. Muizenberg has everything a boy like me could possibly want. There is the great blue living sea with waves ceaselessly pounding; there are grand ships and little yachts sailing across the great blue. Whales come leaping in the grey winter sea. The town is blessed with a lake, mountains, a large exciting swamp land, and all of it free to the likes of me. To white people that is. The Cape is so different; the people, the houses, the landscape, and the climate are so utterly foreign. We had left the summer rainfall bush veldt which lies 6,000 feet above sea level, for the green mountainous Mediterranean with its winter rainfall. It is all so marvellously new and different. In this, the oldest of the colonised provinces, live the so-called coloured people of whom I had never even heard. These people of mixed race are generally speaking a cross between the early Dutch settlers and the indigenous San people, who were known also as the bushmen or the Hottentots. They also have some Malaysian blood from the slaves the Dutch brought from the Far East to the Cape. To my mind the coloured people are noticeably extroverted, engaging, and humorous. They are a people given to dancing and singing wherever and whenever the opportunity arises.

Muizenberg itself is a town like none I had encountered before. Very wealthy people live on the slopes of the mountain and along much of the beach front, the middle classes are mostly grouped on the other side of the lake, and in the middle of all this is the sizeable ghetto, where in the natural order of things we resided. Even though we had moved from a big house in a posh suburb to a grotty little house in a ghetto, I was enthralled by the Cape from the outset, and could hardly believe my good fortune.

We lived with the Sayers for about three months in which time Paula acquired a job with the *Argus* newspaper, and Dugald landed a part-time job on the Cape Town Docks operating a crane. Then we moved to our own flat in Maxton Buildings in Church Street, across the road from Diamonds Butchery and Café Mons. We lived in Maxton for two and a half years which was the longest period we would ever live in one abode as a family. In fact we would move no less than nine times during the five years after leaving Maxton Buildings. Normally because we fell behind with the rent. I turned eleven and started year four. Jack sent me ten rand and Paula borrowed it on the never–never. My teacher, Miss Dring was very pretty and more importantly she liked me, and I in turn was so totally besotted I would happily have jumped through fire for her. She was my first crush, which amused Paula immensely, and she would tease me remorselessly about it. Three months after we arrived in Cape Town I had to undergo yet another ear operation in an attempt to restore the hearing in my right ear. It was unfortunately for me another failure.

The ghetto itself has a very cosmopolitan make-up with a good sprinkling of immigrants from diverse countries, and there were numerous other poor families like ours, so we were not as conspicuous as usual. One drunken man shot his entire family just four houses down the road from us, making us look rather tame.

The more salubrious parts of Muizenberg possess a sizeable Jewish population, the town sports a large and active synagogue, and I made a number of Jewish friends. During the summer holidays Muizenberg is filled to absolute bursting point with visitors, and the long golden beach heaves under tens of thousands of people, creating a wonderful carnival atmosphere. Every summer was a holiday without going on one. I often climbed the mountain, which is riddled with exciting caves; I fished in the lake, swam in the sea, played on the beach, explored the swamp, which has flocks of pelicans and flamingos, and very rapidly came to regard Muizenberg as the most marvellous place I had ever lived in, even though I never lost my love of the bush veldt.

Dugald was dismissed from the docks and found work as a beach constable. The job paid a pittance and he was obliged to wear a fascistic brown uniform. Paula would greet him with a Nazi salute when he came home, but his workplace was less than three minutes from the flat, and he had zero work stress. I then underwent yet another ear operation, in which the surgeon attempted to reactivate my ossified ear bones and to graft me a new eardrum, but the operation was a failure, and it dawned on me that I would be deaf in my right ear for life. I acquired a spirited fox terrier whom I absolutely adored, and named him Max. He slept at my feet and went everywhere with me except the local Empire Theatre. I took piano lessons with Mr. Lehman who looks like a little old lady.

About this time I became increasingly interested in theological questions, or should I say obsessed. One day I looked up from the newspaper which I was reading on the lounge floor and asked Dugald if he believed in God. At this question he became unexpectedly angry, his face clouded over, and I realised that I had inadvertently touched a raw nerve.

"No I do not believe in God! It is just superstition," he shouted angrily.

I was perplexed and even amazed by this furious reply, but I persisted. "Why do so many people from all parts of the world believe in a God?"

He then lost his rag and began to rant at me. "I could have brought you up as a Catholic and you would be a Catholic! I could have brought you up as a Muslim and you would be a Muslim! Or I could have brought you up as a Hindu or a Jew. It is all indoctrination and superstition! There is no proof of God!"

"But you can't be sure," I said defiantly.

Dugald slammed his huge hand hard on the table. "I am telling you! Religion is a crutch for the weak!"

I did not mean to say it, or even intend to, it just came blurting out. "So is alcohol a crutch!"

Dugald leapt from his chair and gave me a resounding crack across the face that had me cartwheeling.

For a long time after that I considered his statements. I could see that he was right to some extent, in that most people who persist with a religion stay with the one they were indoctrinated with. Humans have a tendency to tribalism, religiously, socially, and politically. Our family have never been part of a religious, social, or political community. We are our own little heathen tribe. Us against the world. I think that is why I have such loyalty to my family. We have drifted about on the periphery, always on the outside, so I know tribalism when I see it. Even so, I too have been indoctrinated, but with what? With pointlessness and nihilism. With the myth of science and reason. The belief in realism and rationalism. Though it has brought us great discoveries and material benefits, rationalism is vastly overrated. What is rational to one person or tribe is completely insane to another. The atom bomb was made by highly rational men, and dropped by rational men on the people of Japan. Rationalism only believes in what can be proved by experiment in a laboratory, and personal experience is dismissed as inconsequential. Rationalism on its own has a nihilistic trajectory. My parents are essentially hedonists who live for the weekend, the next drink, the next visit to the racetrack, the next party. Perhaps I am always looking for meaning to compensate for this meaningless existence. Maybe I loathe narrow-minded tribalism because I have never belonged to one; it's a sort of jealousy. Perhaps that is why I can never embrace one ideology. I am conservative and liberal or I am neither. I am rational and non rational, actor and priest. Thinking and feeling. Hedonist and devotee. I insist on being a paradox. We need all these ideologies, but it seems to me that too many people become enslaved to just one or two ideals, and become hostile to all the other isms. I always rebel when I feel that I am being made to conform; perhaps that is why I actually refuse to continue with military service.

At Muizenberg primary school we had religious instruction once a week, which consisted of being read Bible stories, interesting in themselves but not enlightening in any way. They are just grand stories that do not reify the spirit any more than any other good stories. We learned nothing about Christianity and zilch about other religious faiths. My Jewish friends were sent out of the class when we had religious instruction, and I started to become aware of the conflicting claims and beliefs of different religions. Added to that Ben Sayer became at about this time a devotee to some esoteric Eastern religion originating in India, and he was in thrall to some turbaned swami, who looked remarkably like Mahatma Gandhi. During the weekends Ben took to wearing Eastern wrap-over robes, burning incense and practising meditation while enjoying the occasional joint, the odd cap of acid, and playing Pink Floyd at full blast. Jill in her frivolous empty-headed fashion went along with this fad, and a gulf began to widen between them and my parents, who felt that they had gone dotty. Jill still ate meat when Ben was not around, mainly hot dogs.

The winter is deepening and my cell is now perpetually cold. Even with my extra blanket I never feel warm, so in some desperation I decide to put on the overall at nighttime and take it off in the morning, when I keep it wrapped around my feet. When my seven days of spare rations are up the powers that be keep me in the cell for another five days before taking me for a shower and shave. The water is bitterly cold, and my bony body turns corpse blue. Then I am taken to the major's office but I find that he is not there; instead a Captain Viljoen has taken charge of the military prison. He is in his mid–forties, with prematurely silver hair and severe black eyes adorned with thick jet eyebrows. Blotchy lieutenant Brand is there to witness proceedings, and so is my good friend Corporal Steyn, which is an unusual development. The fan has been relieved of its duties, and stands at ease, and I thank the Lord for this small mercy. The captain surveys me venomously, and then commands me to stand to attention. Here we go again. I remain mute and hold my stance. Corporal Steyn moves in swiftly and punches me to the ribs, putting me down like a ninepin, and once again I experience shocking pain. He pulls me by the arm to my feet while roaring into my deaf ear. "You will stand to attention, prisoner!" He pulls my arms to my side, and then boots my shin causing me to buckle to the floor. He grabs the nape of my neck with his huge hand, and yanks me to my feet roaring. "This is a military order, stand to attention, prisoner!" He dearly wants to impress Captain Viljoen with his dedication to the cause. The captain has now come to the party. He puts his furious face close to mine, our foreheads almost touching; he grabs me by the throat with great menace, and orders me to stand to attention.

I am suffocating, my eyes are bulging from their sockets, my vision becomes spotty and fades, but inside I am strangely calm; my fear and doubt have inexplicably vanished. Instead I feel I am in the presence of divinity, in a sacred place. Something about this little drama is age-old. It takes on an impersonal nature. This is an eternal battle, that takes place over and again. A comforting warmth spreads from my heart through my entire being even though the pain in my ribs and shin remains.

The captain releases his grip on my throat as I am about to pass out, and I gasp for breath. The lieutenant loses his fragile composure, and brings his baton cracking down on my head, and I collapse to the floor a little theatrically. I roll my eyes back in my head and throw in a couple of body spasms, and the thespian in me tells me not to overdo it. This action seems to sober the captain up a bit, and he calls for restraint. Even so Steyn, who is in something of a frenzy, again stands me up by the neck and gives me another punch, this time to the stomach and I fall winded to the floor, fighting to breathe. "Leave him!" says the captain who returns to his seat, his face swollen with fury. I kneel on the floor for a while until my head clears sufficiently before I somehow manage to stand up, and resume my objector's stance. Legs apart, and hands held together. My vision is all over the place, my eyes are full of dancing dots, but I am calmer than the doldrums. The captain is giving some tirade about traitors and treason, cowards and communists, but not much is going in, as there is a ringing in my head, and I feel horribly nauseous. The captain sentences me to another seven days in solitary on spare rations, and I am taken back to my cell by Steyn and Pug Nose who has been standing guard, or is it keeping watch, outside the captain's door. I more or less know what is coming, but I am not afraid. As I reach my cell, Steyn yanks my arm behind my back and twists it upwards till it feels like my arm socket is going to pop. I so don't want to scream, but a genuine shriek of agony escapes me. Pug Nose has lit a cigarette which he presses to my neck, and I can smell my own burning flesh. His cigarette is extinguished, and he has to light it again before he once again crushes it to the back of my neck. Sergeant Major Liebenberg arrives unexpectedly on the scene, and calls them off. He reprimands Pug Nose, not for torturing me, but for doing it in a way that it leaves marks. Steyn informs me that he will be back to pay me a visit in the near future, before locking me up. I have a thumping headache, my arm is partially paralysed, and I vomit up my precious breakfast.

He is standing here, the holy man in blue robes. His skin is swarthy yet his hair is golden. He has unusually large eyes and he gazes at me solemnly. "Is it my time to die?" I ask. I am in a temple reclining on a divan. A marvellous light pervades the great hall. Through the large arched doorway comes a golden-haired young boy of about four, who is dressed in a celestial white robe. He holds his arms out when he sees me, and I sit up to receive him. He comes to me smiling, and we hug one another. How I adore this radiant child; to touch him fills me to overflowing with blissful love. He disengages himself from my embrace, and points over my shoulder laughing. I turn and there she is, surrounded by a sublime silver aura. She smiles at us with great joy and the vision fades. I have become the child I was. God has come as a child, this time born in a cell, in my own being. My God is a radiant child.

CHAPTER NINETEEN

1969 was one of the happiest years of my life. Dugald found a job as a drill master which required him to be away from home for weeks at a time, and I revelled in his absence. Granny Stella moved to the Cape and she came often to visit. My year five teacher was Miss Hickman. She was fantastically sexy and wore the most daring miniskirts and long false eyelashes, but those delights aside she was the finest teacher I had ever had. She taught with passion and enthusiasm, and for the first time in my life I worked hard at my studies. I started to actually enjoy going to school and it made a massive difference to the quality of my life. When Neil Armstrong stepped onto the moon Miss Hickman brought a radio to the classroom, and we were listening when Neil said those famous words, "That's one small step for man, one giant leap for mankind." I was keenly aware of the historical importance of that occasion and felt a part of history in the making.

I had somewhat outgrown Patrick by then and had cultivated a few friends of my own age, though I still visited the Sayers regularly because I loved Jill, and Ben was always willing to talk about his new-found beliefs. He often lent me literature on Buddhism and Hinduism. Paula drank less while Dugald was away, and she tended to be a more attentive mother. Over dinner she often regaled us with romanticised stories of her youth on the shores of Lake Nyasa. We would regularly go on picnics to the lake, and sometimes we walked the few miles to Kalk Bay to snorkel in the tidal pools. At that time Paula gained quite a reputation for her fortune-telling and she was for a while doing well at her job.

Granny Violet came to stay with us for two weeks. How that came about I do not know. She slept in my bed while I hunkered down in the dining room. Violet dressed smartly every day as if she were off to church, and every evening I would walk her down to the beach, where we would sit on a bench eating ice cream, watching the surfers carve up the endless waves. She spoke very softly, and even now I cannot recall her saying a single thing of interest except that she too had once been a journalist. She never mentioned her childhood or her past, nor did she seem interested in my life or what I thought. I ached to communicate with her but did not know how. She lived in her own quite sad world, with beautiful sad brown eyes, and I wondered how such a fragile person could have produced someone so hard-arsed and brash as Paula. It was only a few years later that Paula told me that Violet was continually bombed out of her skull on prescription drugs, withdrawn into some kind of cotton wool fug. We never saw her again, and I only found out about her death two years after she had died. When I told Paula that her mother had died she said, "Oh. So the old girl is gone," and she resumed reading her book.

Dugald came home for a weekend. I was in my bedroom reading when he came thundering through, and gave me a brutal beating with a belt. I had no idea what heinous crime I was supposed to have committed. He was shouting something about swearing. It turned out that Stella had used the word "cunt" in his presence, and when he asked her where she had heard the word she immediately blamed me. I was enraged by the injustice of this hiding like I had never been before. After all, Paula swore like a trooper, as did many of her friends, not to mention that Stella had some very lowlife friends of her own. When Dugald was gone, I warned Stella that if she ever did such a thing to me again she would pay very dearly for it. "I will pour boiling oil over your shitty face! Do you hear me? People will vomit in the street when they see your deformities." I was very menacing and Stella ceased her habit of getting me into trouble with Dugald from that day forth, except for one occasion. I also had a conversation with Paula about the thrashing, and made it clear to her how outraged I was. "Next time Dad beats me for nothing, I will come with a hammer while he is asleep and smash his fucking skull in," I told her, and she was genuinely aghast and she called me malicious. "I have been taught well by a brute," I replied.

One night as I was sitting in the lounge doing my homework, the building began to sway and rattle in the most alarming fashion. There was a strange rumbling sound, and ornaments fell from the mantelpiece. I looked up at Paula and we just stared at one another until the earthquake had subsided. The epicentre was 100 kilometres away in the town of Tulbach where a number of people were killed by falling houses. We went down to the beach to see if a tsunami was coming, but fortunately none did. The streets were crowded with people and I wondered if the end of the world was coming.

Paula made friends with a Norwegian man called Greg, who was a lifelong whaler until the South African government banned whaling. He had long flaming red hair, and a fulsome fiery beard. He was a huge man in his mid-fifties, who could drink like a fish, yet he never appeared to become drunk. Greg had great charm and was good with us kids, but looking back I realise that he was positively ingratiating. I liked him enormously, and he frequently told me fantastic tales of his whaling adventures, and his time fighting the Nazis during the Second World War, most of which was probably highly exaggerated.

When Dugald was home, the three of them would go off to the racecourse together. One weekend Ben and Jill came around, and Ben made some remark about Greg, Paula, and Dugald being a right old ménage à trois. A fight broke out between Greg and Ben, who was about thirty-four years old at that time. It was a royal battle considering Greg's age, and they both had to be hospitalised. Much of our second-hand furniture in the lounge was absolutely trashed, there was blood spattered on the walls, and bits of red hair all over the place.

Shortly after that I was on the beach when I noticed a commotion, and went to investigate. A middle-aged man had drowned, and a man was trying to resuscitate him, but to no avail. This corpse set me to thinking about the claims of Christianity about life after death. I asked Paula if she believed in the afterlife, and she told me that the very idea appalled her. She could not imagine that booze was allowed in that worthy realm, and that image struck her as infernally boring. I pointed out to her that Jesus had made wine from water. Then little Max with his huge heart was run over by a truck, leaving me grief-stricken. I carried his small body up the mountain and buried him there. I prayed to the silent God to receive his dear soul.

I finished primary school with good grades, and decided I wanted to go to boarding school. Paula was in agreement as she was finding me increasingly difficult to handle without Dugald about. I was entered into a school about 200 kilometres from Cape Town, in the village of Villiersdorp. Two days before I was due to go to Villiersdorp High School, Stella came to my room and told me to come and see something, and she indicated to me that I should be quiet. She took me to the window of her bedroom which looked out onto an enclosed courtyard where we dried our laundry. I looked in the window and there was Paula lying on Stella's bed, her arms thrown back and her glasses off. Greg had his head buried between her naked legs.

It is becoming increasingly difficult to imagine the world out there, my Divine Child. People shopping, going to the movies, walking on the beach. The world carries on, busy, busy, busy. Everyone frantically chasing goals, searching for fun and charging about madly. Flying planes, teaching pupils, driving lorries, performing ear surgery, fighting on the border, protesting, and loving. Is it real? Does the world really exist, or is it just a fantastic dream? I think the Buddhists call this illusion of reality Maya. Maya is the great spider who weaves us into her web of life, so that we think the dream is real. When time folds in on one and collapses, everything becomes opaque, and loses substance. Einstein's theory of relativity says that time is relative. Time apparently warps and wraps around gravitational matter, slowing down to the point of ceasing. It seems to me that in absolute darkness time can even go backwards, at least in the mind it does. I seek the beginning, I wander back through the eons, before Adam and Eve, before the first bipeds, back through the Triassic and Permian ages, the Devonian, Silurian, and Cambrian ages. Back to the molten newborn earth, and then further, much further, to the explosive birth of our dear sun. Back, ever back. In the beginning there was no-thing, absolutely nothing. The great maternal nothingness pregnant with all possibilities. Yet now I perceive that no-thing is in itself something, just as zero describes a state of things. If nothing is something, then something is nothing: I comprehend that now. Nothing and something are two sides of the same coin. Both are real and unreal in relation to one another. They only exist in relation to one another. The nothing is infinite, but as needs be the something is finite. Therefore the nothing is mother of God and all that exists, the manifest and the intangible. To be reborn we must touch that void, and be extinguished for a while in the no-thing. I am falling. Falling into a vortex that takes me towards the no-thing. Nothing cannot be described, for it has no opposites. No good or bad, no male or female, no light or dark. In the nothing, the opposites of the manifest cancel each other out. They do not exist at all. In the nothing there is no small or large, no here or there, no up or down. Creation is a dream of the pure bright nothing. I am falling, plunging, I can no longer resist the void that draws me.

Ah! The snake has come again but it has changed: it is now white and black, and it makes me dreadfully fearful. "What do you want with me, great serpent?"

The serpent rears up and with a booming voice it speaks to me. "I am the poison-healing serpent, I am everywhere but few find me. I am creation and destruction, I am death and healing. I am fire and water, and from me you may extract the mysteries. I give to you the powers of the male and the female, and also those of heaven and earth. From me you may extract compassion and wisdom. Many long in vain to find me, the egg of nature, but I am given only to few. I am father and mother, young and old, visible and invisible, hard and soft, very strong and very weak, death and resurrection. I am the highest and the lowest, the lightest and the heaviest. I descend into the earth, and ascend to the heavens. I am dark and light, I come from heaven and earth. I am known and yet do not exist at all. All colours shine in me. I am the jewel of the sun."

"Oh Mother and Father, you who are poison and healing, you jewel of the sun, how am I to be saved?"

"As you have redeemed me from the ever sleeping, I will give to you, if you persevere, the subtle diamond body that endures forever."

"How do I know that you do not mislead me, as you did Adam and Eve, you creator and destroyer?"

"I gave them the knowledge of good and bad. I gave them the Tree of Knowledge, or they would have walked sleeping in unending unknowing. I made them god's. I make you a Christ."

"But my Father and Mother, Adam and Eve were expelled from Eden, and with them unending humanity."

"They did not know they were in Eden; like beasts of the field they lived in blissful ignorance, until I brought them the light and the fire of consciousness."

The serpent becomes a man, a tall Oriental, with grand robes, and a hat with four peaks. He takes me to the North Pole in an instant. I see a large clear crystal on the ice and pick it up; immediately the ice begins to melt, and I sink to my waist. "Save me death and resurrection. Please save me!" Suddenly I am on a mountain overlooking a magnificent harbour. It is the North Pole but the ice has gone, and the land is now forested and the valleys are carpeted in emerald grasses laced with numerous flowers. I marvel at the transformation and the beauty of it all. The Oriental one takes me along a road; I am barefoot, and the stones on the road hurt my feet tortuously, but I keep walking and after some time the pain disappears. We come to a magnificent temple surrounded by walls and a moat. The Oriental hands me a stone which is egg shaped. I look closely at it, and see that the shell of the stone is clear like glass or crystal. In the stone are thousands of layers of sediment, and as I gaze into the egg stone I see the eons of evolution in one profound glance, the stupendous amount of time it has taken for the flower of consciousness to come into the cosmos. We are the vessels through which God can become conscious, and I put the sacred egg stone in my pocket.

CHAPTER TWENTY

I do not know how it happened. My mind is turning to mush. I have one foot in each world. They bought my bread as usual, and swapped my potty, but they did not bring me my two litres of water, and I did not even notice. So here I am with an empty water bottle, and so crazy with thirst that I could happily massacre children. As it is, the two litres I am given each day is not sufficient. I am perpetually thirsty, and every time I am taken for a shower, I drink to the point of popping. It is difficult to eat my dry bread with a parched mouth, and I have to gulp it down my throat like a pelican. How could I have been such a bloody dolt? It does not take long for the images of water to surface. Rivers clear, lakes deep, waterfalls thundering, rain pouring. Why do my instincts torment me like this? There is nothing I can do to alleviate the situation, except to try to keep my mind off the subject of water and thirst. The hours pass, and as the thirst intensifies I begin to feel increasingly vulnerable. If Steyn saw me now he would know that I am on my knees, out for the count, all the fight in me has evaporated. I would crumble and submit pitifully, if he just prodded me with his finger. The hours drag on, my tongue has grown a fur coat, I cannot summon any saliva, and it is increasingly difficult to swallow.

What a magnificent waterfall, it tumbles in slow motion into a deep pool. I run into the pool and stand beneath the foamy white liquid which cascades down luxuriously over my body. I put my face into the delicious avalanche with my mouth wide open. The water washes over my face, down my body, but it simply will not go into my desperate mouth. I cry with frustration, I curse the beautiful water. I realise I am shouting, and collapse to the floor. If they come now, they will know I am broken to smithereens. All by a stupid and moronic accident. I am defeated now, after all this, I am undone. I lick the salty tears that have run down my face. "Oh God what an imbecile I am. I have no strength left, I have absolutely nothing left. My God! My God! Why have you abandoned me? Why, my radiant Child. Why, my Mother, Father?" The day and night are perpetual torture and I can feel the last vestiges of strength draining away. I want to cry but cannot.

They are coming, and I stand up to meet them. They have brought my bread, and a bottle of water. The guards survey me with interest, but do not seem to notice that I am finished, or that I am crushed to dust. It is all I can do not to drink the entire bottle of water in one go. I resolve to make the water last but after just a few hours I have finished it all so that by the next day when they come again, I am still crazy with thirst, and the next day. Finally comes a day of food, but still only two litres of water. I am in deficit and simply cannot be replenished until they take me for a shower. Only after five or six days on normal rations do they finally come and take me for a shower. I will never ever take a drink of water for granted again, I swear it.

My eyes are buggered now, and I cannot cope with the light, so I have to keep them almost shut. I find that if I squint my eyes for a bit they can see things clearly for a few seconds, but then the world goes all glassy again. I am giddy and uncertain on my feet, my legs are turning to jelly, and my ankles ache more than ever so that I hobble like an arthritic old tramp. I have sores on the rims of my ears, and cannot lie with my head on the side for the pain. My teeth feel loose in my gums, and I peer at myself in the mirror but my eyes cannot keep focus for more than two or three seconds. I drink till bursting and feel nauseous, and fortunately for me they take me back to my cell.

Only after lunch do they collect me for my trial. I feel like one being taken to his execution. I stand before the captain for a long while on my infirm legs as he talks on the phone to his wife about some repairs being done to their house. It sounds like she is deeply unhappy with proceedings as she cannot access her kitchen. Brand keeps himself busy by reading some document, and I am considerably relieved that Steyn is absent from proceedings. My shoulder still hurts like buggery where he twisted it. I am feeling faint, my gums tingle, and I am worried lest I pass out. If they detect the minutest sign of weakness, I will be finished. The captain finally ends his lengthily personal call, and turns his irritable attention towards me. All he has to do is shout "Boo!" and I will fall down in a pitiful heap, grovelling at his feet. I feel tears of rage ready to flood, pressing at the back of my eyes. To my surprise the captain gives no lectures, no commands; he merely fills in the paperwork, sentencing me to another seven days on spare rations and disdainfully dismisses me. I return to my cloister feeling like a dreadfully old man.

> I am sailing on a tall ship up a loch. The water is choppy and the breeze is stiff. I am wearing a kilt with a sword at my side, and apparently I am a commander. We come to shore where there is already a desperate battle raging. My people are in trouble and have been forced back to the shoreline; the reinforcements have come not a moment too soon. We leap ashore and engage the enemy. It is a fierce and bloody battle that rages back and forth, and at one point I am wounded to my right shoulder. Gradually we push the enemy backwards, and I manage to lead my men to higher ground where we regroup and make a counter-attack which repulses the enemy, and my men give chase to the fleeing

soldiers. I am standing in a field taking stock of the situation when two women dressed like peasants of old approach me. The one woman addresses me. "My lord, we are thirsty, do you know where we might find water to drink?" With my sword I point down the valley and say, "Down there is a grotto with good water." They thank me and depart. Suddenly about four or five handsome youths of about fifteen years of age come charging at me with their swords. I am distressed, because I realise that I will have to kill them. I cut the infantile youths down, and am sore at heart about it. Then I notice that I am dreadfully thirsty, and I walk down the valley to the grotto. There amongst a copse of ancient oak trees is a cave, and from the cave issues a small clear living stream. I put down my weapons, take off my shirt and enter the cave. At the back of the cave is a hole through which the water issues, and it tumbles down into a natural stone basin, where I kneel. I drink the water, and it is the most heavenly water I have ever drunk, so sweet, so fortifying. I splash some of the water onto my wounded shoulder, and I am amazed to see the gash heal before my eyes. Just then I hear something, and looking out of the cave I see the two peasant women who had approached me. The one woman has picked up my shirt, which is drenched with sweat and blood, and holding it above her mouth she squeezes the shirt, so that the bloody sweat pours into her mouth. I say, "Why are you doing that? Come, there is water of life right here." Suddenly the scene changes. I am in a stone castle on the top of a mountain. Around me stand my captains, and my troops, and in front of me stand four kilted women holding candles. They are singing a song of praise to me. I feel honoured but at the same time I feel unworthy of such praise.

1970

De Villiers Graaf High School was founded by Sir de Villiers Graaf who was born of English and Dutch stock. Mindful of the deep divisions between the English and Afrikaans citizens of

South Africa, he had established the first bilingual, coeducational boarding school in the country, and to my knowledge it remains the only one. In reality nearly eighty per cent of the students were Afrikaans speaking while I was there. The charming town of Villiersdorp is set in a fertile valley surrounded by tall mountains, which have colourful sandstone cliffs. The farmers there grow soft fruits, table grapes, wheat, and vegetables, and raise dairy cows, pigs, and sheep. The school itself only had 450 students, most of whom were boarders who came from far and wide. I arrived at my new school three days late, which had some significance, as I became the focus of attention. Dugald had been held up at work, and came home two days after the Greg incident. So when they dropped me off at my hostel in Dugald's badly battered and ancient Jeep, I was under the intense scrutiny of my eighty or so hostel mates.

The school is governed by an ethos that children kept busy to the point of exhaustion cannot cause much trouble or mischief, and this policy did work to some extent. We were awoken at five-thirty in the morning by a ghastly clanging bell that would regulate every hour of our fleeting lives. We sixth formers would dress hurriedly into our track suits, assemble outside the hostel before the sun had risen, and then we would jog for a few kilometres up into the pine forests where we would cut down a few tall trees with hand saws. Then we would be jogged to trees that had been felled some months before, and cut one or two of them into metre-long logs, which we heaved onto our shoulders and carried back to the hostel. The logs were thrown into a large boiler known as the donkey which heated the hostel's water. After stoking the donkey we would run to our dormitories, change into our uniforms, make our beds, tidy our cupboards, and polish our shoes. Like most boarding schools there was a fag system. All those in year six were called new shits, and each new shit was appropriated by a tenth former, who expected you to make his bed in the morning, polish his shoes, and pack his cupboard after you had stoked the donkey and done your own chores. A tall gangly chap called Dixon came to claim me as his new shit. Being the weakest boy in the tenth former pack, he was the only old boy without a new shit, and I had now stepped into the firing line. He pointed at his bed, and told me to make it. My rebel demon arrived unexpectedly in my chest, and I calmly refused to make his bed, or to polish his shoes, or to wash his socks and underpants. His three Afrikaans room-mates were outraged by my dissent, and clubbed me about for a while, and then they gave me a caning for my rebelliousness. Dixon himself did not partake in the punishment meted out to me, in fact he tried to restrain his room-mates. He, poor sod, would have let me be, but his dorm-mates were incensed by my lack of obedience, and chided him to call me again and again. They even fetched me on his behalf, so for about two weeks in a row, I was beaten about each morning until finally they relented. So it came to be that I was the only new shit in the entire school who did not fag for an old boy, probably in its entire hundred years of existence. Dixon went on to become an Anglican priest, bless him.

We would begin lessons at seven-thirty in the morning and after school we would have lunch, and then depending on what day it was we would either run the two kilometres to the sports fields and partake in sport, or we would be expected to be involved in choir practice, drama practice, or cadets. I chose the former two. We also had duties to perform, like garden duty, and those of us who took agriculture as a subject tended the vegetable patch or the orchard. After a shower we would have dinner and then we would go into the study hall and study for three solid hours. Finally, at ten in the evening we could go to bed, stunned with exhaustion. You would close your eyes and three minutes later that bloody bell would be clanging again.

For all that there was much I loved about the school. I had three regular meals a day, every single day. I enjoyed the sport, the choir, the drama club, and the camaraderie of my dorm-mates who were all likeable chaps. On the down side there were 10,001 rules to be obeyed, and it was simply impossible not to break some of them during that first year. If you whispered to someone during study time, if you ran down a passage, or if you had a fight, then after dinner each evening a list of offenders, pencilled by the numerous prefects would be read out, and all those summoned would wait outside the hostel father's study to receive corporal punishment, while the non-offenders ate their sago pudding within hearing distance. There was always a preponderance of sixth formers on the list, and my name featured very often during that first year. Scurvy, our hostel father, who would have been good-looking had he not contracted smallpox in his childhood, had an array of canes on a specially made rack, and he would make his selection based on the severity of the crime. When I came home on holiday during that first year, Paula would insist on me showing my black, blue, and yellow butt to her bemused friends. Eventually the myriad laws would filter through, become ingrained and entrenched, and as the years wore on one learnt to become a reasonably well-behaved automaton. I resented this moulding into conformity, and breaking the rules made me feel individual and alive. I clung to the words of MacNeice who wrote, "I am not yet born; O fill me/With strength against those who would freeze my/humanity, would dragoon me into a lethal automaton,/would make me a cog in a machine, a thing with/one face."

On Saturday mornings we played sport. Sometimes we were taken by bus to distant schools to compete, and often we did not return until dinner time. If we were back in the afternoon then we used the time to read, write letters, and wrestle on the lawns. On Sundays it was required of us to attend church twice, once in the morning and again in the evening. We would assemble in front of the hostel and march down to the Dutch Reformed church in a crocodile. The church was massive and apart from the 400-odd boarders, about 700 to 800 villagers and farmers would be in attendance. We were kept entertained by Rev. du Rant who would boom his sermons like some old-time prophet. I had never attended a church service before, and was astounded by the whole thing. He bellowed and roared, spittle flew, and he repeatedly thumped the rostrum. During that first year I barely understood a word he was saying as my Afrikaans was rather poor, but I nevertheless sat spellbound as he implored, threatened, and cajoled us to ever-greater righteousness. After the Sunday lunch some of the lucky boarders were allowed to spend the afternoon with their parents, who could take them for a picnic or to a restaurant. My parents only managed to come about five times during the three years I was there. Then in the evening after dinner we were again treated to the thunderous admonitions of Rev. du Rant. I loved the hymns; with over 1,000 voices and good acoustics, the singing was a tremendous rush.

CHAPTER TWENTY ONE

I catch myself. What have I been thinking about? I have been lost in deep thought about something, but it has vanished like a dream that slips away as you are recalling it. Perhaps I was thinking and dozed off in a reverie. What the hell was it? This trend of lapsing into a comatose state is happening to me more frequently now. Maybe the brain is starving, and it shuts down in parts to conserve energy. Feels like that, like I am only using a small part of my brain at a time, and on dim at that.

Oh yes! I recall! I was thinking about the mysterious words of sage Tao Te Ching. I read his fascinating book at least ten times and always found it incomprehensible. Yet somehow or other I perceived that this oriental sage had something important to say. He wrote, "In the beginning was the Tao. All things issue from it; all things return to it." It sounds very nice I thought but what the hell is the Tao. Literally speaking it can mean spirit of the valley, or winding silver river, but those are analogies which I could not fathom and Ben could give me no satisfactory explanation. The book of Genesis on the other hand says that in the beginning God created the heavens and the earth. The apostle John and his Christian followers say that in the beginning was the Word and the Word was God. That's seems easy enough. The Word is consciousness, and the naming of things, the classification of things, and for humans and for God that would be a sort of beginning. Before we homo sapiens were blessed and cursed with consciousness, our ancestors wondered about in Edenic blissfulness, unaware of good and evil, oblivious of the past or the future, and unaware of their nakedness just like the innocent animals.

Consciousness and the world is a manifestation of the Divine, but not all things issue from consciousness, nor do all things return to it. Now I understand that the Tao is the source of the divine child. Tao is the nothing that gave birth to everything. Even God was born from the Tao in some sentient beings. Tao is the nothing from which everything comes. The master Lao Tzu said, "Seeing into darkness is clarity, knowing how to yield is strength. Use your own light, and return to the source of light. This is called practising eternity." I think I begin to comprehend now that with the light of our consciousness we find the source of divine light in our own darkness. We must yield to the darkness to gain clarity. It is in our own deepest, darkest selves that we find the black sun of clarity, the divine spark. The divine source lies sleeping in the Tao and in me until I venture to meet it. I must touch the void, the silver river of life, that is called the Tao.

Lao Tzu said, "The great Tao flows everywhere. All things are born from it. Yet it does not create them. It pours itself into its work, yet makes no claim. It nourishes infinite worlds, yet it doesn't hold on to them. Since it is merged with all things, and is hidden in their hearts, it can be called humble. Since all things vanish into it and it alone endures, it can be called great. It isn't aware of its greatness; thus it is truly great."

The great nothing that is the mother of all things, nourishes even God. She is hidden in our hearts, she resides in all of us and in all things. Even Steyn carries within his darkness the sleeping light. The Tao is mingled in his heart and being. What was I thinking about? Perhaps I dozed off, or maybe I was dreaming. Ah yes, it was the water of life. It is in us, it is in me. A place of perpetual nourishment and healing. A hidden spring that waits to be found in each soul. Jesus said, or rather the divine light in him said, "Whoever drinks from the water I give, will never get thirsty at all; but the water I give him will become in him a fountain of water bubbling up to impart everlasting life." In the Bhagavad-Gita of the Hindus, the divine light says, "I am the Atman, O Gudakesha, seated in the heart of every being; I am the beginning, the middle and the end of all beings." We all carry the divine within our own being. We all have the Tao, the Atman, the light, the water, the kingdom, in our own dark selves. My darkness, how the light shines in you!

The door is being opened and I hurry to remove the overall from my feet and put on my underpants. It is Lieutenant Brand: what does he want? I stand squinting in the doorway; it's so good to feel the breeze and see the light of day. It seems he has come to assess the state of my mind. He stares at me for a long time before speaking, and I notice that his truncheon is at the ready. "You do realise that you are damaging your health, prisoner?" he says to me.

"I realise that the military police are damaging my health," I reply.

"You have broken the law," he snaps back. I hold my tongue, I am not going to get into the old argument of God's law versus man's law. "You do realise, prisoner, that when we are finished with you here, you will spend many years in a civilian prison."

"I believe they have proper beds and warm water in those prisons, lieutenant."

"You think this is a joke. You will serve three years minimum, and when you come out the army will call you up again, and if you persist in breaking the law, you will do another three years and another, do you understand? You do not belong to any religious group, so you have no legal standing to declare yourself a conscientious objector."

"I belong to all religions, lieutenant. I am a Jew and a Christian, a Hindu and a Buddhist, I am a Muslim and a pagan, and I am also a Jehovah's Witness."

The lieutenant snorts in derision. "You cannot prove that you belong to any religion, and for that reason you will spend most of your life in prison. Have you ever been to a synagogue?"

"Yes I have, lieutenant."

"You fucking liar, have you been to a mosque?"

"No, but I have read the Koran."

"You are full of shit prisoner, but don't think you can fuck with the army and get away with it!" He is becoming very angry and I try to quell my anarchist. "The psychologist's report states that you are of sound mind. I think she was wrong, you are definitely not right in the head, prisoner. You have shit for brains. Get back in your cell!"

Nothing like a dash of intellectual stimulation to get the old brain cranking into action. I spend the next hour thinking of all the clever things I would like to have said. It is so much easier to be wise after the event, when the anarchist in me has abated.

It was strange to come back to Muizenberg for the Easter holidays after my first fourteen weeks away in boarding school. We had moved into another flat with the grandiose name of Melrose Mansions. These apartments had long since lost their lustre, and they had become run-down and dilapidated by the salty winter winds and a chronic lack of maintenance. My sisters were a bit like strangers to me, and for the first time in my life I found it awkward to communicate with then, but they hung around me whenever they could, and spoilt me rotten. I saw them a little more objectively. I noticed that Stella had a permanent frown which puckered up her large forehead, and she had developed the apotropaic habit of pulling at her top lip. I realised that she was in a constant state of nervous anxiety, and who could blame her. I was particularly struck by Laurie, who I realised had features that none of us other siblings possess, her almond eyes, her large bones, and her unusual tallness in spite of being born so prematurely. It dawned on me that she could have been fathered by someone other than Dugald. Perhaps that was why Paula persecuted her. Laurie survived by being somewhat detached and withdrawn, and I noticed that she seldom had much to say. Samantha is the favourite with both parents, and she still retained her sunny disposition. I had lost touch with most of my primary school friends, and I spent a great deal of time alone during my holiday breaks, reading, walking on the beach, climbing the mountain, and listening to my records. I read *Mila 18* about the Jewish resistance in the ghettos of Warsaw and was shocked to my naïve core. I tried thereafter to find all the Holocaust literature that I could, and on one occasion I discussed the genocide with Paula.

"Well, the Jew's do bring these things upon themselves you know, darling," she stated callously.

"How can a group of people living in more than twelve countries bring mass genocide on themselves?" I asked.

"They demand their pound of flesh. Read Shakespeare's *Twelfth Night*. Even back then the Jew's like Shylock were known to be greedy and avaricious."

I was astounded by this fantastical prejudice, even though Paula habitually said racist things. For her the Italians were Wops or Dagos. The black people were Munts or Wogs. Her conversation was littered with Kikes and Spicks, Chinks, Yids, and Coolies.

"None of the Jews I know are greedy," said I.

"You do not do business with them, and if one day if you do you will find that they will screw you."

"And you think that justifies the gassing of children!" I shouted. I visited the Sayers once or twice, but I now found Patrick particularly childish and beneath me. Naturally everyone was astonished at how much I had grown on three meals a day. That first year in Villiersdorp boarding school was marked by four major events for me. The Drakensburg boys choir came to our village while on a tour of the Cape. One Saturday our entire school and most of the villagers and farmers from the district came to hear this, the country's most famous choir sing in the town hall, and it was truly inspirational. Myself, Vervits, and Tait had been practising a Latin psalm with the school's choir master for weeks, and at the Sunday night service the three of us stood and sang to the congregation, which was extra-large because the Drakensburg boys choir was present. I regarded that event as one of the highlights of my life. All three of us were invited to join the Drakensburg School on the basis of our excellent performance. The choir was due to go to Israel to take part in the World Choir Competition. Tait did not want to go, Vervits did and departed shortly thereafter. I did want to go to Drakensburg School but my parents could not afford it, which is just as well, as my voice broke only two months later.

During mealtimes a tenth former sat at the head of each table, and on either side of him sat ninth formers, then came the eighth formers, and so on down to the new shits at the bottom of the table. The three chaps at the top of the table would serve the food. Having arrived late for the school term I sat at the very bottom of the table. The head of my table was a ninth former called Bronkhorst, and he was unusual in one respect, in that he was considerably overweight, which was a substantial achievement in a school like Villiersdorp where one was run ragged. As a result of his slothfulness and gluttony we new shits at the bottom of the table were deprived to some extent of our rightful rations, which embittered us no end. Bronkhorst had a hole in one of his molar teeth, and while eating he would suck noisily at this aperture to release the trapped morsels. We would all cringe inside when he made this disgusting sound, but otherwise pretend not to notice.

One evening after being particularly short-changed in the food department I, on an impulse, imitated the suction sound he made and regretted it immediately. He glowered at me from the top of the table while my table mates tried not to giggle. He pointed his knife at me and muttered, "You are going to shit." I kept my face to my food and hoped that he would forget about my wild indiscretion. After dinner while we were waiting for the study bell, a number of us were playing King Stingers outside when suddenly I was punched violently to my back, and went sprawling to the ground. I was instantly gripped by a blinding rage and the world turned red. Bronkhorst came at me presumably to give me another thump, and I instinctively barraged him with a combination of four punches to his face that had him reeling back in shock and surprise. Even I was surprised. Immediately a frenzied throng gathered about us chanting "Fight! Fight!" He came lumbering at me again, and received another rapid fire combination to the face, and another. The crowd grew larger, and more frenzied as boys came running from all over to witness the action. My rage was disappearing rapidly, to be replaced by a fearful concern for the shape of my face. I knew that if Bronkhorst got his corpulent hands on me I was going to receive a panel beating. I danced to the left and to the right, I came forward and danced away, keeping always on the move. He charged like a bull intent on grabbing me and getting me to the ground, where he would have the advantage, but I was ready for him, I was all desperate focus. I weaved one way but stepped the other unbalancing him, and punched him with all my might to the nose; I heard it crack, and thick blood poured freely from his nostrils. This drove the crowd berserk, and the screaming reached a new crescendo. I could see the fear and doubt growing in Bronkhorst's eyes. Someone pushed him in the back, "Go and get him!" He lumbered in again, his cumbersome arms flailing like a windmill, but I side-stepped and smacked him to the temple so hard that my hand hurt, he stumbled, went down on one knee and I could not resist giving him a kick to the kidney which put him down. I always fight dirty, because I have never yet fought someone smaller than myself. He put up his hands, walked away, and I was mobbed. I was lifted onto someone's shoulders, and paraded about like a hero with boys cheering their approval. Here was a thirteen-year-old new shit beating a seventeen-year-old bully boy. After dinner, during which a puffy faced Bronkhorst desisted from sucking his tooth, the inevitable list was read out. "Graff for running in the passage, two cuts; Stokholm for climbing over the fence, three cuts; Smit, Nouwers, and Viljoen for talking during study time and Klein for reading a novel during study time, three cuts. Mackenzie and Bronkhorst for fighting, six cuts. We duly assembled outside Scurvy's office to receive our due. I went in third or fourth, while Bronkhorst was still awaiting his turn.

Scurvy looked at me and said, "This is your fourth fight, you know the punishment."

"Yes sir."

Then to my amazement he smiled at me. "I hear that you fought very well." This nonplussed me, and I did not know what to say, so I stayed dumb. "Mackenzie, I am going to do something I have never done before. If you tell one person about it you will receive six of the best for three nights in a row, do you understand me?" I did not know what he meant, so I just nodded in agreement. He then proceeded to give his leather chair six of the best, while I stood watching him agog. He gave me a wink and pointed to the door. I was simply stupefied by the incident, and walked out with my head down. When Bronkhorst came out of the office he had tears streaming down his face and he could not help rubbing his ample rump, which was viewed by the students as a shameful sign of weakness.

Villiersdorp held its prizegiving ceremony in the third term of the year, and as an incentive to entice parents to come long distances, the boarders could go home for the weekend if their parents attended the function. We had to put our names in a specially assigned book if our parents were coming, so that the hostel knew how many boarders to cater for. It transpired that there were only about three of us in my hostel whose parents would not or could not come. A friend of mine called Alvin told me his father would be prepared to give me a lift to Cape Town, so I took the chance, and put my name in the book. The prizegiving took place in the town hall as the school hall was not big enough for the event, and that Friday evening we all marched down to the village. Five hostels' worth of pupils and all the parents were milling about waiting to go in to the town hall, so Alvin and I took the opportunity to slip away to an appointed rendezvous, never for a moment thinking what would happen if we were awarded a prize. His father was late, and we hid near the village café for nearly an hour before he finally pitched, by which time I was having terrible misgivings about the whole venture.

Alvin's father arrived in a battered old Beetle with only one light working, and once we were in the car and on our way, I realised that he had been drinking, and was a bit worse for wear. Even more alarmingly the sole functioning headlight would occasionally go out when we went over a bump, and then take a few nightmarish seconds to come back on again, so I was becoming increasingly anxious. We drove over the Franschoek Pass which climbs to about 800 metres, and all the while my heart was in my mouth.

As we came over the top of the pass, I was sitting in the middle of the back seat holding the two leather strap handles on each side of the car, like someone on a crucifix. Coming around the top bend the headlight went out, and did not come back on. Alvin's father drove off the road and over the edge of the cliff. We went into a sickening free fall, and then there was an almighty impact which burst all the windows, and sent the car spinning, until we landed on the slope. The car rolled for an eternity, and I could hear the dreadful tearing of metal. I blacked out and when I came too I could smell petrol, and fearful of a fire I was desperate to get out of the car, which only had front doors. I had to push Alvin's seat forward to get out, but he was critically injured and unconscious, slumped

197

forward in his seat, so I had to squeeze out over him. I was struggling to see as it was pitch dark, and warm blood was pouring from numerous gashes in my forehead into my eyes. Once I had made it out, I tried to pull Alvin from the car but his one foot was jammed. Alvin's father was also slumped in his seat making strange gurgling sounds; stumbling around the car, I managed to pulled him out and lie him down. Putting my hand to my forehead, I could feel shards of glass embedded there, and I pulled a few of the larger pieces out. Then up the slope I saw a torchlight coming. Someone had seen us go over the edge, he had sent his wife to the nearest town to summon ambulances, and he himself had bravely climbed down the mountain to help us. Alvin's father came round, and when the torch was shone on his face, I saw that he was missing his nose. The man with the torch shone his light on my face and told me to sit down away from the car. Alvin's dad started to hunt about for his nose, seemingly oblivious to the fact that his son was dying. "Where is by dose, I must find by dose." Finally the rescue workers arrived, and putting me on a stretcher they heroically carried me up the 300 metres we had come tumbling down.

I was rushed to Wynberg hospital, and during the trip the medic was trying to extract my details from me. "What is your address?"

"It is the house opposite the Porto Bello Café in Muizenberg," I replied.

"What is the number of the house?"

"I do not know. All I know is that it is opposite the Porto Bello Café."

"What is your parents phone number?"

"I don't know, they just moved there about two weeks ago."

I was taken to the emergency ward, some doctors came to examine me, and after some discussion it was decided I would need plastic surgery. I was very fortunate that one of Israel's finest plastic surgeons was in South Africa to teach the local doctors the very latest techniques in his well-honed art. He worked on me for nearly three hours while I was awake, and inserted 180 minute stitches into my lacerated head. Someone had to drive to Muizenberg to inform my parents of the accident. That kind fool had my blood-soaked blazer in his hand when Paula answered the door.

Come the end of the year when the tenth formers had finished their final exams, we had a departure party the night before they took leave of their home from home. Some had been in Villiersdorp since the age of six, so it was a rather emotional occasion. Scurvy and his wife even had wine on their table. The food was fabulous, we were fed large steaks, and there was trifle pudding. Each of the tenth formers gave a speech, and some even proudly confessed to the crimes they had got away with. Then it came the turn of Scurvy to stand up and give his speech. He was to be leaving the hostel as hostel father after seven years in the post, and he too was surprisingly emotional, and furthermore his usual inhibitions had been loosened by alcohol. Then to my great surprise he said. "Where is Mackenzie?" I put up my hand. "Ah, there you are, stand up my boy. No stand on your chair." I stood up on my chair blushing like a girl, not knowing what to expect. Scurvy raised his glass to me. "You all saw Mackenzie when he came here. I took one look at this skinny little boy, and I thought to myself, this one will not last even one term. This place will be too hard for him. But I was wrong. He did well in athletics, in the choir, in the school play. He made the under fourteen rugby team, he played in the cricket team, he swam in the gala, he always stood his ground. That is what this school is all about: here we make men out of you. I want three cheers for Mackenzie." The speech absolutely amazed me, and my head was spinning. Of all the sixth formers Scurvy had singled me out for elaborate praise, the likes of which had never been heaped on me before, or since for that matter. I loved Scurvy for that speech as it was the greatest thing anyone had ever done to alleviate my well-developed inferiority complex.

Jack once said to me that those who feel inferior are inferior. I have often pondered those words. They struck a chord with me, in that I often have a feeling of being inferior. On the other hand I have noticed that every now and then I am puffed up with a huge feeling of superiority. This always comes unexpectedly, taking me by surprise, and afterwards I wonder what the hell has overcome me. I have concluded that those who, like me, feel inferior have a deep and hidden feeling of superiority, and that those who feel superior and act superior probably feel inferior deep down inside.

CHAPTER TWENTY TWO

It is nighttime and I am standing on a high plateau with a woman and two men. She seems to be an astronomer, and she is telling us the names of various stars. I am entranced by the night sky, and wander away from the group, but I hear her say, "Sometimes it is possible to see the full moon from here." Suddenly I see the full moon hanging in the sky, and the beauty of it causes me to gasp in astonishment. A constellation of stars drifts behind this three-dimensional orb, and for some reason I happen to know that it is the constellation of Aquarius. I sink to my knees at the wonder of it all. Then I turn to draw the attention of the group to the sight, but the dream ends.

What an amazing thing the brain is. What an even more incredible wonder is the mind. I did not know that within us we have a universe. In us fly huge flocks of birds, great rivers meander, colossal mountain ranges doze. The mind is like a vast tropical jungle seething with life; we have sun, stars, and moon; we have deep oceans. We have angels in us, and serpents too. Life and death perpetually dancing, the mind never ceases to dream. From the magical mind come dreams that contain phenomenal wisdom and prescience. Our soul speaks to us with her dreams, when we are in her realm. The inner universe wants to take part in the outer one, and reaches out to us in dreams. Dreams can root us to the dark rich soil of our very being, if only we pay them respectful attention. Truly God and the angels have spoken to many in their dreams. I know this to be true.

In Joel chapter two, verse twenty–eight, the God of the Jews says: "And after that it must occur that I shall pour out my spirit on every sort of flesh, and your sons and your daughters will certainly prophesy. As for your old men, dreams they will dream. As for your young men, visions they will see. And on the men and on the women in those days I shall pour out my spirit". Those days have surely come.

I have lost all track of time. I'm not sure how long I have been in here. It is somewhere between eighty-eight and ninety-four days. I think. When they come with my bread I ask the prisoner what the date is, but the guards forbid him to speak. It's a food day. Won't be too long till I have another freezing shower: I long for it, as my body is itching all over like a rash. I am feeling a bit feverish, and fear I am becoming sick. It seems now to be routine that I am five to seven days on proper food, and seven days on rations. Again I ask the prisoner what the date is. He says he does not know, and receives a crack across the arm from Snake Lips with the baton for speaking. My underpants don't fit me any more; they want to fall around my ankles, so I have tied a knot in the side which no doubt looks amusing; they certainly made Cadbury snort and chortle through his gaping mouth. I am increasingly frightened that my sight is going to be irreparably damaged, and I keep my eyes virtually shut when the door is open. I watch my sunbeam whenever it penetrates, which it does for about three hours a day. When it is gone I gaze at the pale sliver of light that comes under the door. Ah, the simple things in life. A warm bath, a good book, a walk on the beach. A sun beam.

I hear people coming so I take the overall off my feet and make ready to stand up, but it's not for me. Another prisoner is going into a punishment cell. He knows I am adjacent, and once the guards have gone he tries to communicate with me, but even though he is shouting the sound is muffled, and I cannot make out a word he is saying. I shout back, "I cannot hear what you are saying," but he keeps on shouting for a while. With the neighbour comes a regular suicide watch, and pretty much every three hours from dawn till late at night they open our doors and check we are still alive. I hear my neighbour complaining of terrible toothache. Good ploy that; perhaps I should try it: I might get an hour or two in the waiting room. My neighbour is fairly quiet for the first few days but then on about day four or five he goes a bit barmy. He shouts and roars, and bangs on his door. Whenever the suicide watch comes he angrily remonstrates with the guards. On his last day in punishment he goes particularly bananas, and produces an unending wolf howl which is eerily disquieting. I am so grateful when he has done his time, and the great silence is restored. We are taken to the showers together, but I am taken alone to see the captain and Brand to be resentenced.

I have always wanted to live but now I also want to die, to have cessation. Death no longer seems like such a terrible thing to me, in fact sometimes it now seems the most perfect of things. What could be more peaceful or more tranquil than death? I have thought often about death; I could even be accused of being somewhat morbidly fascinated with the topic, but I always thought of it with horror or dread. That has gone now. Death seems to have its upsides, and they have become increasingly apparent to me. Death is the nothing from which everything grows, it is the matrix of matter. It is the profound stillness and peace of the goddess, the nothing. We merely return to the source. "Energy cannot be created or destroyed, it can merely change from one form to another." I do not fear death any more, and find that this bestows an unexpected freedom on me. I have submitted to death. Dylan Thomas was wrong to rage against the dying of the light. "Death, where is thy sting?" I do not know if there is such a thing as an afterlife. I reckon that the rational mind can never be totally certain, but then again it cannot be certain of the alternative. We need to accept uncertainty. However, I do not live for me, but for God, who lives through me, suffers through me, is reborn in me. For this reason my life is not my own, but it is in the service of the Divine, that dwells in me, and as yet, I cannot accept the notion of my own suicide. I am at peace with death, but I will not kill myself with this razor that Steyn gave to me.

In 1971 Villiersdorp high school turned 100 years old, and we were subjected to a more frantic routine than ever. Life went by in a blur of hyperactivity, and in general things were easier for me as I learned to speak Afrikaans and to obey most of the rules instinctively. Apart from school and studies, there was the endless sequence of athletics practice, rugby practice, gala practice, choir practice, play rehearsals, church attendance, gymnastics, cadets and more. The only time I ever had free was on Sunday afternoons when many of the boys would be out with their parents, and I would use this precious time to read. I did most of my reading during the holidays, and that year I discovered Steinbeck, Solzhenitsyn, Tolkien, Bashevis Singer, and Chaim Potok. I broke my collarbone during a rugby match, and later in the year I broke my nose on the diving board. I came back on holiday twice to a new home, and one time Anthony came to visit. He wanted to go skydiving, and I went with him to the Ottery airfield. He went up to 14,000 feet for his jump, and afterwards while we were having lunch outdoors, watching the jumpers, a female parachutist developed a roman candle and fell to her death a mere 200 metres from us. I was surprised when her body did not bounce.

With each spell away from my family, the more like strangers they seemed to me. I turned fourteen that year, and finally it dawned on me that my parents were immature, irresponsible alcoholics. Stella was becoming increasingly neurotic, smoking like a trooper, and pulling her lip so much that it became permanently distended. "Stop pulling your dammed lip, Stella, for goodness sake, you will end up looking like an orangutan!"

Paula would shout. Then to my shock one of my friends told me she was screwing around with lots of different boys. I told Paula what I had heard, and was shaken when she replied, "I know, darling, that is why I have put her on the pill."

During the third term a well-known hypnotist came to perform in the town hall, and we pupils were allowed to go and see him. He enticed some students onto the stage, hypnotised them, and made them do the craziest things, and we laughed till our bellies ached. I became fascinated by hypnosis, and tried it on all my dorm-mates with varying degrees of success. When I came home on holidays, I naturally tried it on Stella. Some of her friends and some of Laurie's were present as an audience. At first things went very well and Stella obeyed every request no matter how absurd, but when I tried to wake her she seemed to stay in a trance. In desperation I poured cold water over her, and that more or less did the trick. That gave me a huge scare, and I gave up hypnosis after that, when my attention turned to fortune-telling and astrology. I still wonder if I did some lasting damage to Stella. That year we performed the musical *Oliver*, and I became confirmed in my desire to be an actor. On stage my reticence and reserve vanished, and I basked in the attention of the audience.

In 1972 during my last year in Villiersdorp I turned fifteen. Paula upended herself and the girls and went to live in Saldanha Bay over 120 kilometres from Cape Town, where Dugald was working on a drilling rig. They moved into an isolated house called Big Diamond which was surrounded for miles on end by bleak windswept sand dunes. It was situated about ten miles from the village, so there was precious little for the girls to do in that remote outpost, and they were consequently bored stiff. I spent two holidays in that backwater, and loved walking for miles along the beach, reading and listening to my records. I learnt to drive on the country roads, and would occasionally drive Paula to the shops. Anthony, who was about twenty-nine years old at this time, came to visit with his girlfriend Vera, who was fifty-five years old. They are still together as far as I know. Paula reckons he is looking for the mother he never had.

It was at Big Diamond that I nearly killed Dugald, and it came right out of the blue. I had come back from a long walk, and I was sitting on the toilet. I had unstrapped my hunting knife which I had put on the edge of the bath beside me. Two rooms away the girls became embroiled in an argument, born out of frustration, and Laurie, who was lying on her bed, kicked Stella in the stomach and she promptly screamed like a stuck pig. Dugald came charging through from the lounge and said to Stella, "What the hell is going on?" Stella replied, "Rod kicked me in the stomach." "Where is he?" shouted Dugald and Laurie pointed to the bathroom door. I was pulling up my pants at this stage, when Dugald kicked down the bathroom door and came bursting in to manhandle me. Instead he found my hunting knife pressed point-first into his neck, and I backed him up against the wall. "I did not touch your precious Stella, I was on the fucking loo, and you come in here to hit me. You try and touch me and I will cut your fucking head right off!" I knew he was contemplating whether to try and grab my arm or not, so I pushed the blade even harder into his neck. "You fucking bully! Just give me the excuse! If you ever think of touching me again you must know that I will kill you!" Dugald never did lift his hand to me again, for he had seen deep into my eyes that day, and he knew I truly meant it. In those days I still valued my black horse.

In '73 we performed *A Midsummer Night's Dream*, and I played the fabulous role of the jester, Puck. To my eternal shame I took a new shit into service. For some reason there was a dearth of tenth and ninth formers that year, and a glut of new shits, so I bagged a runt Afrikaner to be my fag. To his credit he put up a bit of resistance at first, but a bit of brutality on my part soon cowed him. I discovered that the Villiersdorp valley is littered with Stone Age implements, and on some Sunday afternoons I would search among the foothills for these enigmatic objects. I built up a wonderful collection, which Paula sold without consulting me. That year I discovered C. S. Lewis, Laurens van der Post, Fowler, Paul Gallico, and Lawrence Durrell. I had now become so fluent in Afrikaans that I sometimes even caught myself thinking in the language, which actually appalled me. In spite of the fact that I now had close Afrikaans friends and had myself morphed into being substantially Afrikaner, I still was infected with Paula's deep-seated prejudice against this tribe.

By that stage I could completely comprehend Rev. du Rand's sermons. His image of God was that of an extra large, white male Afrikaner, who was continually outraged by the sinful disposition of his creatures whom he had allowed to become conscious. This was an angry God, apoplectic with fury at the iniquitous behaviour of his progeny, and hell-bent on wrath. We heard a great deal more about the niceties of hell than the joys of heaven. To some extent I imbibed this grim image of God the father. Now it is absurd to me, even ridiculous, to think that God will roast sinners for hundreds of millions if not billions of years even for the most sinful of transient lives. The diabolical Hitler himself does not warrant, say, more than two to three hundred years of intense and unrelenting fiery agony. This God of Rev. du Rand had no sense of proportion, and a badly skewed form of justice. Du Rand had far more of an affinity for the dark God of the Old Testament than the light one of the New Testament, where He is largely portrayed as all good and merciful, until the book of Revelations, where he regresses to his smiting ways, and lets rip with Armageddon. In the light of our evolution from primates, it is time we accept that the good and the bad in us has its place. There was no fall from perfection, but there was an awakening. We were bequeathed the fire of consciousness. We children of nature are not to carry the burden of becoming conscious, of being inherently good and bad.

At first I had loved the order and even the discipline of boarding school, but in my third year there I found that being ruled by a bell from early morning till ten at night was becoming tedious and irritating. The fact that there were girls in the school helped enormously, and I took every opportunity to sit with a gang of girls during break times rather than hang out with the guys. In truth, I would not have assented to go to Villiersdorp if it had been a single sex school. Towards the end of eighth form I was feeling stifled by the rigid and hectic routine, and by the uniformity imposed. During the school holidays I became acutely aware of the Sixties youth movement that was only now in the early Seventies starting to really catch on in South Africa. I longed all term to get back to my records, especially Bob Dylan, Leonard Cohen, Cat Stevens, and Pink Floyd. I was beginning to smart at my prison style haircut which was compulsory at Villiersdorp. The schools in Cape Town allowed the boys much longer hair, and long hair was then the in thing. All the hippies hung out at Surfers Corner in Muizenberg. "There was music in the cafés at night, there was revolution in the air," and it was contagious. How could they not look cool, with those bell-bottom trousers and bead necklaces? I felt that I would have looked cool in my new bell-bottom jeans if I did not have a crew cut. In the quiet backwater of Villiersdorp we were still deeply rooted in the 1940s. Only a week before the end of my third year in Villiersdorp did I finally decide that I was not coming back. The school had been a saving grace for me in every way. Most importantly it had removed me far from my badly disturbed family, and this had allowed me to view them more objectively. It had given me discipline, order, and some continuity. I now understood the dream of standing on the outside of the hyacinth pond looking at my family as they all lay asleep under the water. Leaving Villiersdorp, however, was to prove a fateful decision.

I wonder how many people reflect intensely on their past? It may be in the past but it always lives. The life one has lived is not dead and gone, even if you want parts of it to be. In many ways this past which lies recorded in us needs and wants to be remembered, pondered, and relived. Yet life out there in the physical world is so distracting and enticing, so hectic, and for many so fraught with worries. When most people do have spare time they want fun, distraction, or entertainment, and who can blame them. Yet the inner world is neglected and even forgotten, and then the roots to the soil of our being wither and die. It is not a matter of recalling the past, it's a matter of digesting, reliving, and understanding it, otherwise it remains like a lump of undigested food in the stomach that makes you ill. The child is father of the man, for the child who once was still lives in us, always lives in us, but in most people this child wonders lonely, neglected, and forgotten.

Paula often reminisced about the past; she would become quite sentimental at times, usually between the third glass of wine and the fifth. The sixth glass would normally see in the aggressive and abusive stage. She would relate to whoever would listen anecdotal tales of her youth, and fables about our family life. She tells these tales with glowing inconsistency and sometimes the most trivial event would be expanded until it became an epic saga. The truly epic events like robbing building societies were never referred to. It would be putting it mildly to say that she is prone to gross exaggeration, and a generous distortion of events. Even the most diabolical happenings were transformed into something hilarious by twisting the truth more than just a little, but she could make people laugh. She is prone to painting a rosy picture that simply did not exist. Paula never relived her past, she merely recreated it. As a result of her propensity to mutilate familial history, when Paula spoke about her youth I always took her narrative with a cup of salt, and I enjoyed pointing out her inconsistencies. When she was five Jack went to fight in the Second World War in the deserts of north Africa, and was gone for six long years. This is actually true; he once told me to my shock that those were the very happiest years of his life. He was a captain, and due to happenstance he never saw any serious action personally. When the war was over he continued in the service of the army for eighteen months in Italy and Austria in an administrative cleaning-up operation, and won the Luger in a game of cards. According to Paula they lived in a fabulous mansion on the shores of Lake Nyasa, with fourteen servants attending to their every need.

"Last time you said ten servants!"

She and Anthony were educated by a tutor who had "gone black under the skin" and was mad as a snake.

"Last time you said you had no schooling at all. Not till you were twelve!"

"Well it was as good as no schooling, he was completely inept."

Violet was hopelessly inebriated seven days a week.

"Oh come on, Mom, I have never seen her drink one drop of alcohol."

"That's because she lives on prescription drugs, darling, didn't you notice that she was perpetually bombed out of her cranium?"

"Can't say I did, I was eleven when I last saw her, and she seemed the model of sobriety."

"Don't talk utter bilge, Rod. When she was down at the beach I looked in her drawers, and she had packets and packets of uppers and downers. You saw her for God's sake, a walking zombie! Once when the Queen Mother came to visit, shortly after Jack came back from the war, we all stood on the grand stairway of the house along with all the servants to greet Her Majesty's arrival, and Violet's panties fell down around her ankles, and she stumbled down the stairs as the royal visitor and her entourage arrived. She was absolutely smashed out of her bracket. Poor Jack, he was utterly mortified as you can imagine. That is when he decided to divorce her, you know?"

"Why would the Queen Mother visit Jack, you never told me about that before?"

"He was the district commissioner, darling, you know, the major domo of the area. Anyway the dear Wogs scooped Violet up, and carried her away, and being an aristocrat the Queen Mother pretended not to notice."

I never heard Dugald speak about the past. I asked him about his youth once or twice when he appeared approachable, but received one-liners that were ambiguous, like "I went to boarding school from the age of five." He scarcely spoke about anything in fact. He was a consistent one-liner man. I doubt I heard him string more than twelve sentences together more than twice in eighteen years, and on both of those occasions he was very drunk, and his rambling speeches made not the slightest sense to me. If he read a book it was Mickey Spillane or Peter O'Donnell.

CHAPTER TWENTY THREE

I am on a high mountain peak, and far below me lies the ocean. Before me stands a stone, and in my hands I have a hammer and chisel. A voice commands me to chisel a piece from the stone. I put the chisel to the rock and hit it with the hammer, and I am surprised that it cuts through the stone as if it were butter. A piece the size of a chicken's egg comes away, and I notice that it is the colour of gold with a green tinge. I pick the egg stone up, and immediately I feel a surge of power coursing through my hand and then my entire body. I look down at the ocean, and am astonished because I can see to the very bottom. The water has become crystal clear, and strangely the light of the sun can now reach great depths. I can see the currents flowing and sea creatures living. I hear a voice calling me from a distant place. "I am coming," I reply with my mind, and in an instant I travel hundreds of kilometres to another mountain, and there on the slopes are two women who live in a cave. The one woman asks me for some of the green gold. I break off a piece the size of a grain of rice, and give it to her, then the other woman also asks for a grain, and I give her one as well, and immediately I realise that I have given them more than they can bear.

The sunbeam has come! What a welcome sight, this blessed beam of light. Fragile, ephemeral, I put my hand right through you. Powerful, you pass right through me! Let there be light!

I find myself talking to you, shining beam, you have come 93 million miles from Father Sun, and you have found your way into this sealed-off tomb. You effortlessly pierce through the darkness and it cannot repulse you. I have tried to hold onto my own light, but it burns low now, my sunbeam. My flame now flickers and splutters weakly like a candle in the breeze. I know I am dying, that my body is eating my body, and my being is saturated with the toxins of my body's meltdown. Precious beam, you have come to visit me, to cheer me up. You remind me that there is a world, with billions of beings who live in quiet desperation. Who live without living, who are caught up in the thousand and one things. Who do not know of the treasure, the hidden gold that lies within each human breast. It is lonely to die far from the madding crowd, but you comfort me, my sunbeam. I will be talking to my potty next, bowing down to it in worship.

I have bedsores on my butt from lying around on a sweat-drenched mattress, and they are sufficiently painful to make me want to shift around constantly. A lassitude has taken me, a deep lethargy, and I just want to stop bloody thinking and remembering. I am so terribly sick of it, so very tired of myself. If I manage to clear my head of thoughts, then images appear, the images make me remember, and remembering makes me think. This unstoppable cycle drives me ever closer to the brink of the void.

It is a food day! "Food glorious food! Hot chocolate and mustard!" It can make you sing. I remember the various hostel fathers all said a prayer before each meal. It was always the same boring prayer said by rote. "For what we are about to receive may the Lord make us truly thankful." The prayer was essentially a meaningless ritual, for none of us felt in the slightest bit thankful. No matter how many times the prayer was said the Lord never managed or bothered to make us truly thankful. To achieve the state of being most truly thankful, it is starvation which works absolute wonders. One is so truly grateful for food after a prolonged bout of terrible hunger, that I am sure that even a person of the atheistic religion will wish they had someone or something to thank. When starved, a good meal can produce such a profound thankfulness, that it overcomes you with tears of gratitude. They flow freely down my face and plop into my lap. You swear to yourself you will never ever again take a meal for granted. Mother Father, for what I am about to eat, I am so deeply appreciative, so truly thankful, so utterly grateful, may you be praised! Amen.

There are many people who are constantly starving, and I do not mean the poor people of Africa. No, it is the fat people, the morbidly obese, who are never satiated. They can eat till they burst, but still they are starving. Starved for meaning and love, starved for the divine in themselves. It seems that the vast majority of us are terrified of our inner world, of our own souls. We do everything in our power to ignore our psyche. "Don't worry, it is only a dream," we say and banish the inner world to nonsense. Yet within us is the source of power, the source of light, the provider of sustenance. Jesus said, "Love your neighbour as yourself." What I think the Atman in Jesus meant was, learn to love yourself first, and then you will naturally love your neighbour for the divine spark that lies in them. I was searching for God and I found myself. Our dire problem, which threatens the very existence of humanity, is that so few people actually love themselves or their own souls, which in the main lie sleeping beautifully in our own darkness.

My day of judgment is coming. The end of my world is upon me. The Pleiades have been set loose. My Armageddon is coming to claim me as I have long suspected and anticipated. I thought it was coming to the world at large, but it was coming to me. To my world. It was the death of my own inherited God that I foresaw; it is the death of my own ego as king, that I have anticipated and intuited. The Armageddon I have so dreaded is my own death. The end of my ego's rule. My ego has died for it is now the divine spark in me that has become my king and queen. In me the Christ and the Antichrist have waged a terrible war. My religious self and my rational self have slaughtered one another, and now a third has arisen to rule. I must subordinate myself to the divine spark that has emerged from the depths of my own dark being. "Come Great Mother, I am waiting, I am prostrate, I am ready. Please take me into your maternal nothingness that gives birth to all. Take me beyond God the creator, to you, the very source, to what I was, before I was. Take me please to the all-knowing non-existence, to the all-seeing sleep. Take me to the ocean of coming to be, and passing away."

When I came home to stay in '74, the year I became afflicted with the Armageddon neurosis, we were living on the ground floor of a large double-storey house called St. Ives which had been divided into two dwellings. The Sayers lived upstairs and we lived downstairs. Isabel had sprouting breasts, Ben had grown his hair long and cultivated a swami-type beard. Janis Joplin, Led Zeppelin, and Ravi Shankar poured from the Sayers windows along with incense and cannabis at the weekends. St. Ives was an elevated house with a small lawn which lay level with the top of seven-foot retaining walls. Granny Stella lodged with us while we lived there, and Dugald spent about one week out of six at home, so I found myself in a very female house. The girls all shared one massive room, Granny Stella had a large room, Paula made what was supposed to be the lounge into their bedroom, and I slept in what had presumably once been a pantry and painted the walls blue.

Muizenberg high school was as much of a shock to me as Villiersdorp had been. It was a tiny school of only 170 pupils all housed in a single three-storey block of a building. The school was situated on the lower slopes of the mountain, and it had the most spectacular views of False Bay and the coast. We looked straight down from our classroom windows onto Surfers Corner, where we could see the surfers free as Jonathan Livingston Seagull, dancing on the curvaceous waves.

On my first day at my new school, I walked through the gate and onto the small tarred playground, which also doubled as the school's hall, and was stopped dead in my tracks, with my jaw dropping in total disbelief. There were pupils who were not even wearing school shoes, but sports shoes and leisure shoes. I was incredulous at this. Some had their ties flagrantly loosened, and the top button of their shirts brazenly undone. None of the pupils had their blazers buttoned up, the girls had very short skirts, and to my astonishment, some of the kids were actually chewing gum. In Villiersdorp all these offences would have cost you very dearly. A loose tie would have earned a severe beating or a thousand lines for the girls. I was genuinely shocked to my core by this anarchy. The bell rang and no one ran to line up, instead some even carried on playing football, while others ambled and chatted their way to line up, something inconceivable to me. Mr. Nathan, the headmaster, emerged from a door with his Hitler mustache and to my disbelief he was actually smiling. Jug Head, the headmaster of Villiersdorp, would have had a thrombosis if he saw this shambolic assemblage of Philistines. Then the teachers emerged from the building chatting and laughing. When the teachers at Villiersdorp filed into the grand wood-panelled hall for assembly they were grave, even funereal. All the while pupils were still talking and laughing freely among themselves, and the whole situation seemed utterly unreal me. Nathan stood on a rather weather-beaten box the size of a linen chest, which had a little rostrum hammered onto it. The teachers all sat in one line on sixteen chairs that had been put out, and I was agog. We did not sing the national anthem, nor did we sing three hymns, and we did not sing the school song. We were not reminded forcibly of the school's long list of rules, and the dire consequences of transgression. There was no Bible reading, no hair inspection for the boys or dress length inspection for the girls. Nathan spoke for no more than about ten minutes. Affable, charming, weak, he welcomed us back, and wished us a prosperous and

217

successful year, and we were dismissed to go to our classes. Pandemonium erupted as the pupils charged for their classes, hoping to bag the best seats, the ones at the back of the class or near the windows. There was a bottleneck at the main door, the only door, and pupils scuffled and shoved for supremacy; it was scene out of Bedlam, and I felt slightly crazed as I was crushed in the hysterical melee. I finally found my class, and here again was chaos and insubordination. My new classmates were all talking and laughing loudly; some of the guys were arguing about a desk near the window. I sat at my desk quietly the way I had been programmed to do. The teacher came in about five minutes late, with an apologetic smile. I bolted to attention as she came into the classroom, and this caused the pupils to roar with laughter, and some were even chirping at me. They had all remained disrespectfully seated. I wanted to sit down but could not, my legs simply refused as my years of Villiersdorp training held me up. The teacher smiled at me, which was rather surprising as teachers in Villiersdorp did not smile as a rule. Miss Potgieter was our class teacher, and our Afrikaans teacher. She held up her hand, and gradually the din subsided. She addressed me in Afrikaans, and asked me which school I had come from, and was most impressed by my answer.

"What made you come here?"

"I had enough of boarding school, miss."

"Yes but why to this school?"

"My family live in Muizenberg, miss."

"What is your name?" ... "But that is an English name."

"I am English, miss.

"You may sit down," she said, and the class laughed again. "That is what you all should be doing," she said to the class.

I had longed for more freedom, but it took me months to adjust to it. I was still standing up for teachers when they came into the class five months later. Some of my primary school-mates were in Muizenberg High, and I knew many of the pupils by sight, so in spite of the incredible difference to Villiersdorp, I quickly felt at home. I liked most of the teachers, especially my biology teacher, and found that they were refreshingly open to discussion, and we pupils were allowed a generous measure of individuality. It was not a sin to have a personal opinion. I now had so much more free time, and during that year I discovered Herman Hesse, D. H. Lawrence, the Upanishads, the I Ching, and the Bible. Granny Stella bought a spaniel dog and named him Punch; it quickly became evident that he was my dog, so Gran bought a bitch and named her Judy.

Everything went well for the first six months in my new school, then suddenly and inexplicably the wheels came off me. For the first time in my life I experienced acute depression; a heavy melancholy settled over me, and I struggled desperately to understand the source of it. "What the hell is wrong with you? You go around wearing a hair shirt. You play those mournful dirges endlessly, you have become an old man before your time, you are so bloody serious," Paula would say in moments of exasperation."

I got drunk a few times with my friend Gunnar, but it always made me sick as a dog, as my body has no tolerance for alcohol. It was always a very short high, and I paid too dearly for it with the most horrific of hangovers. I was visiting Ben one morning, and he was dressed in his sari as Paula called it, extolling the virtues of vegetarianism while puffing on a joint. He absent-mindedly proffered me the joint, which I took and I inhaled two puffs. In just ten seconds the black cloud that had enshrouded me lifted, and the world once again took on a wondrous sparkle. I noticed things I had never noticed before. I was entranced by the weave in the table cloth, and by the play of light in the aquarium. My conversation with Ben suddenly seemed elevated to a higher level; every statement he made now sounded utterly profound. I laughed for the first time in months, laughed till I wept, and when I left there, I walked down to the beach and felt free and alive.

Naturally the drug wore off and my cloud of gloom returned with a vengeance, but at least there was no hangover. It seems we must pay for every high with a low. Thereafter I would hang out on Saturdays at Surfers Corner, get stoned, and talk pseudo philosophy, politics, and Eastern religions with the hippies, some of whom thought of themselves as my mentors. Bjorn, who had been to India for three years, tried to persuade me to try LSD, but something in me baulked at the idea. As it was, two puffs of a joint made me so high that I was stoned for up to eight hours. My depressions deepened, and I was possessed of an existential crisis which I could not articulate to myself. What the hell was the meaning of it all? Everything was suddenly meaningless, pointless, and a drudge.

Midway through the year of '74, during the three-week winter holiday, I decided on an impulse to hitchhike up to Johannesburg and go to see Jack whom I had not seen for seven years. Paula freaked out, had a cadenza, forbade me to do it, threatened me with the wrath of Dugald, but it was water off a ducks back, and when I came with my rucksack to say goodbye she relented, gave me a tearful blessing, and ten rand. My friend Gunnar decided to come with me as his mother lived up there, and two days later we were in Johannesburg.

Jack was very pleased to see me, and I was surprised to find that I was taller than him. One day Jack and I were chatting in the sitting room while Noreen was out having her hair done. I asked him if he believed in God.

"My dear fellow, I am an agnostic," he replied. Then he truly stunned me. "My mother was a Jew, not a very devout one, but she had her superstitions and rituals; my English father was raised as a Christian, but never went to church in his life."

"Your mother was a Jew, but that makes you a Jew," I said, aghast.

"It makes me half a Jew. Did Paula never tell you?"

"She has never mentioned your mother to me ever. What was her name?"

"Ethel. Ethel Cohen," he replied. Suddenly Jack stood up from his chair, and came and stood before me, with his usual military bearing, his hands clasped behind his back. "I have something I wish to tell you, something I think you ought to know," he said rather gravely.

"Is it about my real father?" I asked. Jack was taken aback by this question. "Yes it is. I presumed that your mother had not told you."

"No, you are right, she has never told me, she has always tried to portray Dugald as my father."

"Yes, we always disagreed about that, how is it you know?"

"Conversations I overheard, the fact that I was born in Rhodesia and Dugald has never been there, the fact that he has black hair and blue eyes. The fact that he never liked me."

"Yes. Well I am pleased you know. Your father came from good stock, a very good Scots family, but he was a rogue."

Now it was my turn to be astounded. "You knew him? What was his name?"

"Oh yes, I knew him well, all too well. His name is Paul Cluer."

"Paul Cluer? How did you know him, what was he like?"

"Well, that brings me to something else I wanted to tell you. Perhaps you know about that too? It is something I am deeply ashamed of. I was in prison for nearly four years for fraud. I got into some gambling difficulties and borrowed some of the firm's money hoping to return it before anyone noticed and well, you know, it did not work out. Paul, your father was the prison commander. He was very good to me. He had charm and he was intelligent. We played chess, and he brought me sugar and other niceties, books and so on. Only later did I find out he was taking advantage of Paula, and had made her pregnant. As you know, Paula was seventeen when she fell pregnant with you, and he was forty-five at the time, a year older than me. I must confess I did encourage Paula to have an abortion, and when she had you I encouraged her to give you up for adoption."

All this information had my brain bobbing about. "What did Paul look like?"

"You have his mouth and something of the shape of his head. He was baldish, about your height. You have bigger shoulders than him. He was a cad, a married man with two children who were about six and eight years old when you were born, so you have a half-brother and -sister somewhere. He and his brother Roderick inherited a tobacco farm in Kenya when their father died. Their father, that is your grandfather, was at one time chief justice of the Cape. They made a hash of the farm, and Paul shot off his left thumb to try and obtain insurance money. However, the insurance company charged him with fraud, and he was compelled to flee Kenya. He was a bad egg, that is all I will tell you, he was a nasty piece of work."

That little conversation certainly had me reeling. To think that my real father was now about sixty, and that I had a half-brother and -sister. That Paula the anti-Semite was at least quarter Jewish, that my respectable well-spoken grandfather had spent four years in the chooky.

A few days later I tried to broach the subject again from a different angle. We had come back from a spell of shopping and we were in the kitchen making tea and matzos with Marmite when I said, "What was your father like, Jack?"

"Oh, he was a very nice man, with a great sense of humour, but he travelled a lot, and I did not see enough of him."

"Where was he born?"

"Bath, in England. He made his money in Argentina raising beef, and when he came here he started a canning factory for meat products, like bully beef. He met my mother on the ship coming over here."

"How old were you when they died?"

"The old boy pushed off when I was twenty-two and the old girl lives in Durban."

"Your mother is still alive! Why have I never heard of her or met her?!"

"Well, she disinherited me, old fellow. Irreconcilable differences, you know?"

"No I don't know, that's why I am asking you."

"When the old boy shuffled off he left me and Freddy a tidy sum. I rather foolishly gambled it away, dropped out of university, and married that appalling woman."

"Violet? What was so appalling about her?" said I in surprise.

Jack suddenly slammed the sink with his hand and flushed an angry red, something I had never seen him do. "I do not want to speak about that damnable woman!"

I stared at him amazed.

"Sorry, I did not mean to be angry. I was engaged to be married to Noreen when my father died. We were deeply in love. Then I lost my head, and went on a mad and prolonged bout of drinking and gambling. Lost everything including Noreen. Met Violet while I was drunk, and married her drunk. Ran away to the war for six years and left that alcoholic to bring up Paula and Anthony. Came back to find that they were wild animals. Divorced her, and tried to raise them myself. Tried to instill some decency and sense into them, but as you know I failed hopelessly."

We discussed the political situation, and I was shocked to find that Jack was in favour of apartheid. I still had very mixed feelings about it.

I went with Jack to the Turfontein race track, and we spent the afternoon gambling. Noreen Royce, who came from a wealthy family, gave him a weekly gambling stipend. The incident became something of a farce. Jack introduced me to his bookie who looked like Rupert Bear, and then we sat on the terrace eating steak, salad, and chips for lunch and examined the form book.

"You going to take a flutter? Go on, you must, here is five quid for you," said Jack. I selected a horse at random because its was named Siddhartha. "It is a rank outsider," said Jack, and he gave me his choice. I went off to the bookie to ostensibly place our bets, but I refrained from taking a bet myself as I needed the five quid. Sod's law, Siddhartha came storming home by about seven lengths, and Jack was slapping me on the shoulder with delight. At twenty to one he thought I was quids in.

I met up with Gunnar and we hiked back to the Cape together, and that was quite some adventure. I said nothing to Paula about my discussions with Jack as I felt I needed time to digest the implications of everything I had learned. It took me a while to register that I was grieving for my real father. I was also furious with him for abandoning me, and intrigued as to his personality and character. My depressions grew more severe, and I began to bunk off school on a regular basis. My grades were atrocious and I just did not have the will or the motivation to study. Paula was worried about me and we did have some lengthy discussions about my state of mind. I brought up the subject of her drinking and gambling addictions, the fact that we kids walked about in rags, our school uniforms were too tight, our diet not nutritious enough. I told her how much money her cigarettes, booze, and gambling cost per month. Yet in truth I had the deep suspicion that my depressions and my lassitude were not related to these issues. I could not put a name to the depressions, and I was fobbing Paula off with guilt.

She suggested I take a few months off, and go back to school the following year. At first I did not want to but I realised after a while that it would take a Herculean effort to catch up on my neglected studies and I relented. I found a job selling newspaper subscriptions which kept me busy from five in the afternoon till nine at night. The days were mine and I would go for long walks or lie on my bed and read or listen to music. I bought a flute which I took up the mountain to play and then I bought a guitar. One day I was sitting on the beach, reading a book when a tall sinewy girl with long straight blonde hair walked up to me, sat herself down next to me, and said, "Hi, I am Deneen, are you bunking school?" When I asked her if she was bunking she laughed and said she had completed school. It turned out that she worked at the Chris Snaith riding stables. She invited me to come riding, so at least once week, sometimes twice, I would walk the five kilometres to the stables, and we would take racehorses down to Sunrise beach and gallop them. She was always pleased to see me, yet she was the quietest girl I ever met and she could go for hours without saying a word. I never got to know her or anything about her beyond her work and her passion for horses. I bet she is galloping now, my sunbeam, flying like the wind down that long glorious beach, so in tune with her horse she appears to hover above the saddle.

Paula was now struggling to keep a job for more than five months at a stretch, as she started to lose the war on her drinking problem. Dugald being away so much of the time was wearing her down, and we children were now all bigger and becoming ever more difficult to handle. Stella was smoking like a chimney, hanging about with dubious characters and further distending her lip. I was smoking pot more frequently and none the happier for it. The inevitable fight broke out between Paula and Ben and the friendship finally came to a terminal end. We moved to a house in Clovelly and Granny Stella moved into her own flat with Judy.

One Saturday some man gave Paula a lift home from the racecourse. She invited him in for a drink which became five drinks. Stella came to my room in the cellar, and told me she felt the situation was getting out of hand, so I went up to check things out. He was a big man with a foolish yokel grin on his sodden face, and he stood to shake my hand. I did not take his hand but said, "Thank you for bringing my mother home, but I think it is time that you were on your way."

"We are just chatting, darl," said Paula with a slur.

The stranger's face changed and became aggressive. "I don't think you need to be telling us adults what to do," he said with some threat. I walked out of the room, returned with a wooden pole and told him to leave immediately or I would batter his stupid head in, and he became most obliging.

"I am so lonely, Rod, I just long for a bit of company sometimes, you know," said Paula plaintively. "He wasn't here to chat, Mom."

My terrible depression slowly lifted, and I started to gain the will to live again. The despondency would still come to possess me now and then, and still does. I met Bjorn on the beach, and he invited me to his flat overlooking the sea. There were some hippy girls there, making herbal teas and cookies laced with pot. Bjorn's girlfriend and I hit it off, and we became deeply engrossed in an animated discussion about life, the universe, and everything. I did not notice for quite some time that Bjorn was pissed about it. Bjorn obtained revenge by lacing the tea with LSD. I was walking home when it dawned on me that I was tripping out of my tiny mind. It was a bad trip, and it was all I could do to keep myself remotely grounded. I was hugely aware of a little red light at the back of my brain that was flicking on and off. It was a warning to me not to succumb to the bombardment of images and emotions that were afflicting me. Needless to say I never visited Bjorn again.

CHAPTER TWENTY FOUR

1974 came to an end and I resolved to give up the pot, pull myself together, and return to school and complete my education. We moved to Clevedon Road in Muizenberg and Paula was fired once again. We were back where we started, my sunbeam, back in '75. The house in Clevedon Road was barely a block from the Sayers so I did visit occasionally, mainly to see Jill. We had only just moved in when Athena from three doors away came bearing a fat kitten in her hands, and asked me if I would like to have him. We had had cats all our lives, yet I have never been anything but mildly fond of some of them, yet William with his oversized head and large round eyes took me by storm, and became my cat. There were loads of girls who had to walk past our house to get home after school, and it became something of a custom for anything between two and eight of them to stop in and have a cup of coffee, which Stella would make. I sometimes did Tarot cards or read their palms. Generally I would tell them all that they would have long lives and happy marriages. That they would travel widely and have marvellous careers. Sometimes we would listen to the Moody Blues or Dark Side of the Moon and just gossip. Athena attached herself to me like a limpet, and I regularly had to boot her out of the house so I could do my own thing.

As it happened I fancied Gunnar's girlfriend Charmaine. One reckless Saturday night Gunnar and I were on the beach sharing a two litre bottle of cheap white wine, and he confessed to me that he was crazy about Athena. I told him I had a shine on Charmaine, and we agreed to try and instigate a swop. Gunnar did go out with Athena but I did not get Charmaine, instead Fiona kind of moved in to fill the gap left by Athena until I grew sick of her hanging about, and asked her to stop coming. That happened two and years ago, my sunbeam. It feels like it all happened in another lifetime, so very long ago.

'75 was a busy year. Our rugby team went on a tour to Johannesburg by train and we had a fabulous time. I got to see Jack again, but he was in a bit of a state as Noreen was in hospital having a colostomy. Our drama club performed two plays for the school, and I won a gold medal for experimental theatre at the Eisteddfod. I still occasionally went horse riding with Deneen. I swam in the sea all summer long, climbed the mountains, fished in the lake, read many books, wrote poor poetry, and played my guitar and flute. There was athletics and rugby, there were numerous parties and movies, I played music and sang with other guys, and we took part in an inter-school band competition, coming third. I took part in a few debates at the debating society. Yet all the time a conviction was growing in me that there was a disaster looming, humankind was in peril, we were going down the wrong road and courting Armageddon. I also became increasingly disillusioned with Christianity. I went to two church services, one in a Protestant church, and the other in a Catholic church. I found the services irritating and utterly uninspiring. There was no religious education, no thoughtful study of the scriptures. No wonder the churches were more than half empty, and the congregants generally averaging about ninety years of age. The services were more suited to an illiterate medieval audience. The only part I liked were the hymns; from them I learned something. I was searching for meaning, my sunbeam, searching for God. I was searching for it in books, in churches, in the synagogue, and from other people. Or was meaning searching for me? All the time the meaning lies within, in the depths of our own being. In us run the eternal healing waters, and the flame that cannot die. I am dying though, my sunbeam, I feel my end is coming.

They have come to take me for a shower, my dear friends Cadbury and Pug Nose. Pug Nose is beside himself with merriment at the sight of my knotted underpants. Cadbury just snorts and chortles at the gibes. I look down and keep my eyes almost shut to avoid the glare and see my pale white matchstick legs. The soap doesn't want to lather in the bitterly cold water, and I cut my face twice while shaving and bleed profusely. Cadbury has to give me some of his tissues to staunch the flow. I am taken directly from the shower to the captain and Brand, who waste little time in sentencing me to another seven days on spare rations. I am exhausted by the whole escapade and I am profoundly grateful to lie down again.

> *I am on a large beach watching the sea which is dark and turbulent; the water seems to be filled with bits of broken-off seaweed. There is a man fishing and he pulls a shark out of the water and throws it onto the beach to die. I am appalled when he catches another shark and does the same thing. I put both of the sharks on a child's pull cart, and take them back to the ocean and throw them in. The scene changes and I am at the back of the beach talking to a woman, she shows me some dilapidated broken-down chicken runs which remind me of Bryanston Farm. I see a few square metres of chicken wire lying in the sand and make a wheel from it. The scene changes and I am walking along the beach again, and in the distance I see a huge black tornado. It reaches up like a vast pillar of cloud to the very edge of space. This menacing mass is moving towards me and I stare at it in wonder and awe. As it comes closer I can see that it is spinning on its own axis with immense force, and from the dark cloud there are numerous flashes of lightning. It comes even closer,*

and I begin to feel great fear, but I am rooted to the spot. I know that there is no running away from this great pillar of cloud. Then I notice that in the stratosphere a colossal circular white cloud has gathered like a mushroom head around the top of the spinning black cloud. The white cloud is being sucked down the sides of the black cloud in gigantic cascades. As it falls to the bottom the white cloud wraps around the black pillar like a wedding dress. The ground is now shaking and the noise is deafening. I stand and wait for it to consume me. The scene changes and I am walking up the beach in the opposite direction, when I see a black man and a black woman making a barbecue on the beach. I look at him, and wonder if it is John, and decide that though he looks like John it is not. The black woman greets me and I give her the wheel made from chicken wire, before I continue walking up the beach drawing ever closer to the sea. There are some young girls playing on the beach who have gathered corals and shells and with these they have made a square sea garden which I admire for a while, and then a wave washes it into the sea. The girls are unperturbed and start doing it all over again. The wave had washed around my feet and it felt warm and inviting, so I take off my shirt and dive into the sea. Immediately I am struck by how unbelievably clear the water is. I can see hundreds of metres in every direction. I see fish swimming and crabs walking along the bottom. I am able to stay under the water for ages at a time without any effort. I am exhilarated, swimming out deeper and deeper, and when I surface to get my bearings I see a man swimming towards me from the deep. "I wonder why the water is so clear," I say to him. He says, "It is the sun. When the sun penetrates the waters it clears them." I carry on swimming, and go even further out where the water is over fifty metres in depth, and there I plunge down to the bottom. I look up and see two giant turtles swimming straight towards me from the deep, where the water is still dark. They swim right past me, one on either side. I am returning to shore when I see a giant man lying on the ocean floor with his legs up. I decide to let him be, and continue swimming until I reach the beach. I stand up in the shallows, and in the distance I can see the white and black cloud flashing with lightning. It is terribly beautiful.

The Divine is terrible and beautiful. It is yin and yang. Sun and moon. Black and white. The Divine is great and small, high and deep. Loving and cruel. Kind and grim. The Divine lies helpless in the psychic ocean, waiting for the light of consciousness to redeem it. When the sun of consciousness ventures into the depths, then the turbulent and chaotic ocean clears to reveal the true riches of life. The light and the dark, the male and the female, the rational and the non-rational can then unite in conjugal bliss.

I am in a great hall, filled with many finely dressed people and dignitaries who have gathered for a wedding. Only when the bride comes into the hall, carrying a posy of white myrtle flowers, do I realise with something of a shock that I am the bridegroom. She is very beautiful and approaches me smiling. Her hair is sprinkled with diamond dust which shines like stars. We embrace and kiss somewhat shyly, then taking hands we walk to the bridal chamber.

Midway through 1975 a very pretty girl called Charlene joined the school and caught my eye. By sheer chance my friend Shelley brought her around to my place. She sat on my bed and started pulling books out of my bookcase and thumbing through them without paying me any attention, which rather irritated me and we had a nasty spat. I can't even remember what we actually said, it was just an argument that arose from tension. A week later I went to have dinner with Shelley and her mom, and there was Charlene, and so it happened that we ended up going out together. She popped in one Saturday shortly after we met, and I took her through to meet Paula who was lying on her bed reading the papers, smoking, drinking, and listening to the radio.

"Mom, I would like you to meet Charlene."

Paula looked up from her newspaper and with a huge crocodile smile she said, "Hello my darling, it's a pleasure to meet you, you may call me Paula. By the way, are you a Jew?"

It had not even occurred to me that Charlene was a Jew, nor did it matter if she was. "What kind of fucking question is that, Mom? Or is it because of Ethel Cohen?"

Paula was stunned when I said this. "You know about Ethel? Did the old boy tell you?"

"She is still alive, you know. She owns bloody racehorses, for Christ's sake. We could have done with a relative like that! But you! You just loathe your whole family, you alienate them, and offend them, why?"

Charlene in the meantime was blushing crimson but she intervened. "Yes, I am a Jew. Is that a problem?"

"Oh no, my darling, my grandmother was a Jew," said Paula glibly, and then turning to me she said, "I suppose the bugger told you about Paul."

"I knew about Paul from the age of six. What I did not know was that he was older then Jack!"

Paula was in a real state of shock and wanted to pursue the conversation in spite of Charlene's presence, but I took Charlene by the hand and led her from the room. We did discuss Paul a lot after that. She told me that when she visited Jack in prison, which was naturally a very distressing time, Paul had been very kind to her and allowed her to break regulations by taking things to Jack that were verboten.

"Kind my ass, he was being seductive. He saw you coming, desperate for the father you never had!"

"Don't talk shit, Rod, you weren't there. I fell madly in love with him, you know. His wife was in a loony bin and she had been in and out of it for years. He was lonely and bringing up two kids on his own."

"With the help of some servants no doubt!"

"Anyway, you were conceived in love, I want you to know that. We even lived together for six months and unfortunately his wife recovered from her psychosis and came home. He loved that fruit cake and told us to leave."

Naturally I spoke to Charlene about my theological concerns and she invited me to the synagogue. The shul was held on a Saturday morning, and I met Charlene on the steps of the synagogue, where we chatted for a while, and then as I was entering, I was stopped by an elderly man and asked where my yarmulke was. One had to be found for me and meanwhile Charlene disappeared inside. When I finally went inside I could only see men. I looked up and saw that all the women were upstairs behind a grill. It was a sight of medieval patriarchy, and I was astounded by this segregation. A while later she took me to a Zionist meeting where there was equality of the sexes, and I was deeply moved by the impassioned argument for the right of Israel to exist. The Jews had wandered for nearly 2,000 years in foreign lands, always persecuted and reviled. Never able to root in and feel organically part of the land. They had endured pogroms that lasted hundreds of years, inquisitions, and genocides, and the speaker found me sympathetic to the cause. All the Jews wanted was this tiny dry patch of land in all of the massive Middle East. All my brief life I have been a wanderer, a nomad, a rolling stone, and a passer-by. Nowhere could I feel grounded or part of a community, but I have now discovered that part of me does not want to be part of any group. I am partly Scots, partly English, I am partly French, partly Dutch, and I am partly Jew. I am born in Africa but I am only loosely African. My ancestors transplanted from cold climate cultures to a place I have never really felt part of, though I love the land with all my heart. It will take a long time, if not ever, before the black people accept us Europeans, because we do not seem to accept them. I cannot put down deep roots in this fragmented country, so I know what it is to desire soil to root into.

In the latter half of '75, I was summoned to see the school psychologist. It happened while I was in the midst of a rather heated argument with Miss Agnew, our religious instruction teacher. She was a primly dressed spinster in her mid-fifties, who probably thought of sex as something disgusting, and I was a constant thorn in her flesh. She had started the lesson by saying something stupid about us Christians. "Excuse me, Miss Agnew. When you say us Christians, who are you referring to?" said I. She waved her hand to the class and to herself to indicate that she meant all of us in attendance, and this sent a hot flush of anger through me. "Miss Agnew, no pupil in this class is a Christian. Half of this class is engaged in premarital sex, the other half smoke, drink, steal, lie, and swear. None of us attends church regularly, and I am willing to bet that no one here prays to Jesus or to God. We are not Christians!"

Miss Agnew blushed and looked to the class appealingly, hoping that someone would contradict me, and her blush deepened to a raw crimson when no one did. Just then someone knocked on door, came into the classroom, and told Agnew I was wanted by the school psychologist.

Despite Muizenberg being a tiny school, it was one with a preponderance of troubled children and the state had allocated a shrink to effect some damage limitation. Mr. Stephen looked nuts, like many shrinks, with wild woolly black hair, an oversized forehead, a scruffy beard, and fierce blue eyes.

"Is there something you want to see me about?" I enquired.

His cheeks turned red and he said, "No, nothing specific, I chose your name at random from the form nine list. I try to see everyone if I can, you know, to touch base."

I did not believe him for a second, but I sat down to chat.

"Are you reading any books at the moment?" he asked.

An innocuous opening gambit, I thought. "I am reading a book called *The Varieties of Religious Experience* by William James," I replied. It turned out he had read the book, so we had a rollicking discussion about it, and I began to regard this gawky-looking character in a more respectful light.

"May I ask you to which psychological sect you belong?" I asked him at one point.

"What do you mean?" he asked.

"Well, there are widely different psychologies, are there not. Clinical, developmental, Freud, Skinner," said I.

"Well, I am an educational psychologist and we sort of take a bit from all of them I suppose. A sort of multi-faith system. Have you read any psychology?" he asked.

"Not much. I read an essay on Freud's idea of the Oedipus complex. And I read his book on dream interpretation which I think is mostly a load of rubbish," I replied.

"What do you think of the Oedipus complex?" he asked, blushing profusely.

"I think he was really onto something there," I replied.

So we became friends, and every week from then on till the end of the year I absented myself from so-called religious instruction with Agnew, and went to chat with Mr. Stephen. We talked religion, philosophy, poetry, politics, psychology, and rugby. I was sorry when he left at the end of the year.

One Saturday I popped into the Sayers, and I sat with Jill and we ate baked beans on toast with tea. I could see something was not quite right with her, expressed my concern, and she burst out with it. My jaw fell on the floor, and my heart broke into a thousand pieces for Jill. Ben was having an affair with Isabelle, and she had not even confronted them about it yet. Barely five minutes after this shocking revelation, the guilty parties arrived. They had apparently gone to Ben's factory in town to check on the weekend workers or some rubbish like that. Isabelle was gleefully showing us a new handbag which was given to her by a so-called boyfriend called Hank. Nobody except Ben had yet had the honour of meeting this mystery Hank, who was apparently too busy in Cape Town to come and visit, but smitten enough to bestow a stunning array of gifts. Isabelle was seventeen like me, and Ben was thirty-six like Paula, and I was so heartbroken and furious that I could not conceal it. "What's the matter Rods?" said Isabelle, and I just ignored her and walked out the house. Not long after that Ben and Isabelle moved out, leaving Jill who had never worked a day in her life with Bubsi and Patrick.

All the while the political situation in the country is becoming more volatile, sanctions are being imposed on the apartheid regime, and the country is feeling the squeeze. There is muted talk of civil war, some of the newspapers have reported gross human rights abuses against black political activists, and the government has clamped down on the press. There is a brain drain as the intelligentsia start to flee the sinking ship. The war in Angola is intensifying and military service has being extended. The body count of the war is kept under wraps, but talking to guys who came back from the border it sounds rather harrowing. Fidel Castro has sent 50,000 troops to Angola to help the liberation fighters. I began to seriously question the morality of fighting in such a war, especially with my own military service looming.

CHAPTER TWENTY FIVE

Then came 1976, the year we moved to the so-called pig farm in Philippi. The year we robbed the building society, and had our misadventure on the road. Then came '77 and Leo's nursery, the computer job, and the army. And then came '78 and this dark tomb, or is it a womb? It was a short life, there was some fun and more than enough adventure. There was plenty of anxiety, uncertainty, and fear. There were car crashes, four operations, broken bones, beatings, and hunger. I saw many beautiful things, and by and large I loved my short and brutish life. There is the long unwinding tragedy of Paula's and Dugald's debilitations. All of that lives in me, like a record that never stops playing, and I can now live with it, and in it, and from it. My memories are me, for they have added themselves to the eternal quintessence of my essential self.

I have had to drink my life to the dregs, and have found that it does have a purpose and a meaning. We have evolved that God may evolve. We have latent in us the diabolical Divine which seeks to be made manifest in us, that it may strive towards a place of rest. The Divine seeks healing in us, that it may find unity with itself through us. Only through sentient beings can the Divine become aware of itself, and it is only through us that the Divine can be made more conscious. This is sacred service, to become a vessel of divine consciousness, and I will that the Divine suffer with me and in me. There is no evolution without suffering. My former faith in God was a willing credulity, a deep desire for certainty in an uncertain and dangerous world. My former faith was a false shield to fend off the maternal void where God is incarnated in our very being. True faith comes with experience of the Divine, where one reaches the solid ground of being, where one can live with uncertainty. We long for salvation, but we are saved only when we have extended salvation to the divine in our selves. We are her divine vessels if only we let ourselves be. When we search for the Divine we find ourselves. "When people lose their awe they turn to religion," said Lao Tzu.

> *I am suspended above the sea looking down on to the valley at the foot of Table Mountain. The city has gone entirely and has become a beautiful patchwork of forest and fields. There is only one building, a magnificent white structure that looks futuristic. It has a tall central column that starts wide and becomes narrower towards the top, something like the Eiffel Tower. There are ten floors and each floor is round like a UFO, the biggest at the bottom, the smallest at the top. There is a gap between each of these floors so that the building stands at about twenty stories high, and on the top of the central column is a large round stone. It looks like a sort of wedding cake with spaces between the layers. The scene changes, and I am on the fourth floor of this building and apparently I live there. The phone rings. It is the woman on the tenth floor and she asks me if I would please come up. I take the lift up to the tenth floor, and she is there to greet me at the lift which leads directly into her apartment. She has long red hair, and she is wearing a gorgeous dove grey dress. She leads me through to the large sitting room, and her three black dogs follow us. She takes me to the south balcony which has a garden on it, and she shows me the view to the*

*south, which faces the mountain. It is a paradise with hippo
in the rivers and in the open grassland are herds of elephant,
giraffe, and zebra. After looking at this remarkable view for a
time I turn to find that she is lying propped up on a settee with a
writing pad on her lap and a pen in hand, apparently writing a
book. She reads me a sentence and asks my advice, "Should I use
the word beatify or beautify?" I suggest that beatify would be
the more appropriate word. She smiles and rising up she takes
me to the northern balcony which looks out over the ocean, and
I am a little worried her dogs may fall over the low wall but
they do not. She escorts me to the lift and I say, "Please send
down your writings any time, I would be glad to help." I push
the button for the fourth floor, but the lift goes all the way to
the ground floor, and when the doors open I see lots of children
playing and one shouts a greeting to me.*

God knows where Paula, Dugald, and Punch are now; there
is nothing I can do to help them, my sunbeam. At least I know
that the girls are safe, well–fed, and being educated at a good
school. They will have half a chance to be normalised to some
degree. They can sleep secure knowing they will not have to
move at half a moment's notice. At the end of the day it seems
I miss them far more that I could ever have imagined. I wish I
had been a better brother to them.

I have done seven more days on spare rations, and seven on
full rations, and they have come to take me for a shower and
trial. I walk like an old man with rickets. My legs feel like jelly,
and I seem to have developed a curved spine which will not
allow me to stand up straight like a homo religiosus. I have
never been this scared of a trial before and inside myself I am
repeating a mantra over and again, "Please Mother Father
give me strength." On the way to the captain we pass by van
Zyl, the block leader who would not let the prisoners beat me
again. "Hang in there, Mackenzie," he says, giving me a wink,
and the guards do not say a word. During the trial the date is

mentioned. It is the twenty-second of May, and I work out that I have been in the punishment cell for 117 days. I am exhausted by the whole escapade, and when they lock me up, I sob with a tremendous self-pity. I am in a dreadful pit of despair. I have to accept that for all my desire to serve the Divine, I cannot take any more of this. I am truly and completely spent. They have broken me and melted me down. I will do whatever they say; I will return to the army because I know that I cannot handle another trial. I blow my nose on the overall.

"And everything is gone, the body is gone completely under, gone, entirely gone. The upper darkness is heavy as the lower, between them the little ship is gone" (D. H. Lawrence, *The Ship of Death*).

I am so sorry Mother Father, I am so sorry my wife, my sister, my lover, my daughter. Everything is black now. I hang suspended in terrible pain, unbearable agony. I am torn apart, I am broken to tiny bits, gone way beyond the end of my tether. I let go and fall into eternity, into the blissful nothing. "It is the end, it is oblivion."

I am everywhere and nowhere, in the past, the present, and the future, I am nothing and everything, all things are clear. I know nothing but understand everything, cosmos and atom. This is the unnameable, it is the eternally real. It is the eternal void filled with infinite possibilities.

I awake from a long and profoundly deep sleep. They are coming, and I try to stand up but my legs will not obey; I am as weak as a newborn baby. I am feeling very ill, like I have been poisoned, and a cold sweat covers my body. I know that this is the end. I will put on the uniform. I will beg them not to put me back in this dark cell. The door is being unlocked and I make a desperate effort to stand up, but I fall over. The door is flung open and there stands an angel. About his head is a golden halo, and golden wings of light radiate from his shoulders. The angel stands looking at me for a while and then to my surprise says, "What the hell is going on in here! Get me the captain, and tell the office to call an ambulance!"

I am in the military hospital now, the very same one I was brought to when the army thought I had cholera, just five months ago, and it is simply heaven to lie in a proper bed with sheets. At first they bandaged my eyes, but from today I am wearing sunglasses. There is a drip in my arm, and I am being fed soft foods like a baby. I came to the prison weighing 150 pounds with no fat on my body and now I weigh ninety-six pounds. The ward is large with about sixty beds, and they are all filled with wounded soldiers from the border. It puts my little jaunt into perspective. Some of them will never see again.

I have written to Granny Stella, and to the girls. It is really great to see the nurses; each one looks like an angel to me. After lunch a military lawyer came to see me: a young lieutenant who can speak good English, though he is Afrikaans. He sat and took notes for over two hours. He wanted to know my military history in minute detail, about when and how I was arrested, and everything I could recall since being in the prison. At one point I asked him why he was doing this and he told me there was an investigation into the handling of my case. Yet he seemed most interested in the chap who committed suicide in the cell next to mine. Then the angel came to visit: I knew it was him as he walked into the ward. The gold braiding around his military cap shone like a halo, and the light glowed off his golden epaulets like wings. He was shown to my bed by the nurse and he came and stood next to me. His military bearing and manner reminded me of Jack.

"You do not know who I am," he said by way of introduction.

"I know who you are, sir, you are the angel that rescued me," I said, and he looked very taken aback by this statement.

"I am General Bob Rodgers, head of the Air Force."

"How is it. general, that you came to be in the detention barracks? What made you come to my cell?"

"It is strange you should ask that. I came because of a dream. I dreamt all night long that something was wrong at the detention centre. I told my wife about it the next morning and she said I had better pay attention and go pay a visit. You see as a general I can inspect any section of the armed forces, whenever I please, so I came. I walked right around the entire prison and only as I was leaving did I ask about those punishment cells. Anyway, are they looking after you well?"

"Yes thank you, general, they are treating me very well."

"I will be keeping an eye on you, young man."

"Thank you, general. Excuse me, general, your wife is a wise woman, sir. I am deeply grateful that you heeded her advice."

After I was discharged from the hospital, I was kept in normal solitary confinement for three months awaiting my trial. My new cell had a window, and the light was on till nine at night so it felt like a classy hotel. Finally I went before a military tribunal. The military police tried to make me march into the court, which I refused to do, and I was told to stand to attention, which I refused to do. There were three high-ranking officers sitting at an elevated bench surveying me sternly. After establishing my name, rank, and number, the charge was read out and I pleaded guilty. "You have been found guilty! You will serve three years in the military prison. You will do hard labour with no pay and no parole," said the officer in the middle. He banged his gavel and I was dismissed. My trial had lasted all of five minutes.

Altogether I spent three years and six months in prison in the blue overall of a conscientious objector. During my last year I was transferred to the military prison in Cape Town with fourteen other prisoners.

Stella and Laurie had finished school. They had both found good jobs and they lived in a little cottage at the foot of the hill overlooking Fishoek beach. Punch lived with Stella and Laurie, as Paula and Dugald were living temporarily in a cellar. They had to live like mice as their friend lived with his old mother, who knew nothing about their presence in the basement.

The day of my release eventually did come, and I was reunited with the clothes I had been arrested in, and my Timex watch which Jack gave me when I turned nine. Walking out of that prison gate was like being born fully conscious. I was both exhilarated and scared. Joyful for the freedom and wide open spaces, yet sad for my friends I left behind. I hitchhiked to Fishoek and there, lying on the balcony of my sister's cottage, was Punch. When I was about fifty paces away he stood up and looked at me, with his head to one side. I did not say a word but kept walking and as I drew nearer he realised that it was me and collapsed in a heap. When I reached him he just lay shivering and whimpering in a large puddle of wee.

I was so happy during those first few months of freedom that it sometimes terrified me. I knew that such bliss could not last forever. My years in a drab and cramped military prison had changed me profoundly. The idea of becoming an actor now seemed frivolous to me and I feared that if I did become one I would become a hedonist like my parents. I had become impressionable again and I saw the world afresh. It was of course more than wonderful to see women, and to hear music again. To walk and run for long distances, to see distant horizons, to climb mountains and walk on the beach. But the thing that struck me the most powerfully about the big wide world were the children. That came as a total surprise. I had not seen children or babies for over three and a half years and the sight of them was deeply moving, and thoroughly enchanting. I had not even realised for one moment of those long years that I missed them, yet nothing touched me so deeply as the sight of the little ones.

Laurie took me shopping for some clothes. Fashions had changed, gaudy Hawaiian garb had become all the rage, and everything I tried on looked ridiculous to me. I might just as well have put on the outfits of a clown, so ludicrous did I look to myself in the mirror. I ended up by just buying blue jeans and some blue shirts. It stuck me that I was having a bit of an identity crisis. Years of prison life had also left me with the unexpected difficulty of not being able to make simple decisions. I went to visit Jill and she said, "Would you like tea or coffee?" and this question had me dithering, for in truth I wanted both. Two months after my release I came home from work one evening and went down to the beach for a walk, as was my custom. I climbed the sand dunes and stood on top of one to survey the scenery. It was the most exquisite of evenings. The sun was setting over the Atlantic, and the high cirrus clouds were turning pink and orange. The golden full moon was rising up out of the Indian Ocean which was shot through with the reflected colours of the sky. Suddenly my body and being became lighter than a feather, and I was filled with a profound bliss, a peaceful ecstasy. She came as a phantom smiling, and we walked together down the beach. We sat for many hours on the catwalk, watching the silvery moon dance on the pulsing ocean. We did not need to speak because we are always together. Though my 118 days in a punishment cell were the most trying and difficult days of my short life, they have now become with the passage of time the greatest and most important event of my life. For it was during that dark night journey that I found my soul.

P.O. Box 76
Cape Town 8000
Tel 45 0531
23 May 1978

Brigadier Cyrus Smith
P.O. box 29512
Pretoria
0012

Dear Sir,

Re: My son, Roderick Mackenzie, in Detention Barracks in Voortrekkerhoogte.

It is with a mounting feeling of hopelessness that I write this to you, alleviated only by the reassurance of General Magnus Malan that no further harm will come to our sons if we lay complaints.

My son was arrested by MPs in January 1978 after having awolled for about four weeks. During this time on AWOL he had become a conscientious objector.

The army, rather understandably, did not believe this story.

He was then put into solitary confinement for nineteen weeks, not understandably at all, and I believe constitutionally illegal practice (for anyone to do solitary for more than an absolute maximum of six weeks).

When he came out of solitary, I have heard from men since released, he weighed eighty pounds and was in a very poor state of health.

When I had not heard from him for seven weeks, I went to Wynberg Military Barracks (his home base) to enquire as to his welfare.

They told me he was "not dead" or they would have heard (after consulting a roster). It's a great comfort, that.

I knew that if he was all right he would have got word to me somehow.

After twelve weeks of not hearing from him, Wynberg advised me to go to the Castle. I was in such a state of mental anguish by that time—I cannot even convey to you. One does not bring up a child for eighteen years and then find yourself able to discard him like a sock with a hole in it. (He is not an only child—by any means.)

At the Castle I was told to see one Lt Meyer, a welfare officer. This lady kept me waiting for over an hour outside her door, while she chatted on the phone (private calls, from what I overheard) and flirted with the various soldiery that went in and out of her office. I was obviously in a state of acute mental anxiety, and in a new job, and could not really afford to take time off.

When I finally managed to get through to her—there is a communication barrier because her English is not too wonderful (in fact I am wondering whether to have this translated into Afrikaans as I might have a better chance of success), she phoned Voortrekkerhoogte, where she had a long intimate conversation with someone in Detention Barracks.

She was at last able to tell me that my son "was getting on all right".

What does that mean?

At no time had anyone advised me that my son was in solitary and so unable to receive or send letters.

The second encounter with this lady, Lt Meyer, in which I produced medical evidence to prove that I have cancer and that my life expectation is not very good—in order to ask if my son could be transferred to Wynberg where I would have the opportunity of seeing him once a month, this lady sent off a strange Afrikaans telex to Pretoria, recommending that he should not be sent back to Wynberg, and yakking on about her dog.

Brigadier Smith, this lady is not the right person for the job.

The purpose of this letter is to try once again to have my son transferred to Wynberg.

Oh, incidentally, during our last encounter, this lady, Lt Meyer, mistook me for someone who had twins on the border, so the confusion was ghastly for quite some while.

I did not just "have a feeling" but knew for a copper-bottomed fact, that as an English speaking South

African, I did not have a ghost's hope in hell. I was perhaps foolishly reassured by the news media.

It seems incredible that this petticoat Hitler is solely responsible for the decision NOT to send my son to Wynberg. Why not? On what grounds? Perhaps my legal training unfits me for understanding the army juggernaut.

On rereading, this letter looks like a personal vendetta against Lt Meyer.

It is not.

It is really an honest attempt to ask you to reconsider having my son transferred to Wynberg Military Barracks. It would be greatly appreciated if you could look at it in this light.

However, under no circumstances will I consider another interview with Lt Meyer. Please do not refer me to her. On the next occasion I may not be able to control myself.

In the last interview she asked me some personal questions, which I will answer now.

Roderick is the illegitimate son of one Harry Paul Cluer. He was born in Salisbury, Rhodesia on the 11th of July 1957. His father's wife was in an insane asylum, so we were unable to get married. His grandfather was a Judge President of the Cape.

He has since been adopted by my present husband (of twenty years) which is why his name is Mackenzie.

Yours sincerely,
P. M.

ABOUT THE AUTHOR

Roderick Mackenzie was born in Zimbabwe in 1957 but was raised in South Africa. He spent his early career as a garden designer, a columnist, and he hosted a radio gardening programme. He also wrote and published a book on garden design. He emigrated to Britain in 2001, and took a Masters degree in Jungian and Post Jungian studies with Essex University. He lives in the county of Buckinghamshire with his wife, and practises as a Dream Analyst.